"Here's the thing—you're probably going to notice that I'm preoccupied today, and I don't want you to think it's because of you."

"That would be bigheaded of me," he agreed solemnly.

"Given yesterday's finale, no. It wouldn't be." She crossed her arms over her chest. "I'm fighting on too many fronts, Travis. It's taking a toll." The honesty of the unguarded words ignited that same gut-level protectiveness he'd felt when she'd faced off with Ray Quentin.

Cassie glanced up at him when he didn't answer and the sunlight slanting in through the open door spilled across her face, illuminating shadows beneath her eyes. Shadows that had not been there yesterday.

He reached up to lightly touch her face, but his hand froze before he made contact. He slowly lowered it as heat started traveling up from his collar. What had he been thinking?

Dear Reader,

Welcome to the final book of my Sweet Home, Montana series!

When I was a kid, I had a small problem with impulse control—if someone dropped a challenge, I was all over it. My motto was to act first, think later, and, as you might imagine, it got me into a situation or two. As I grew older, I learned to control my impulses and may have gone too far the other way—thinking too much before I acted. I think I've found a happy balance now, and I tapped into my journey as I wrote Cassie, the heroine of this story.

Another aspect of the story that spoke to my past was the wedding barn. I grew up exploring barns, old and new, swinging from ropes (I'll never forget the time the rope broke with three of us on it, and I was on the bottom when we landed...ouch) and marveling at the sheer amount of old stuff that could be crammed into a barn "just in case" it was needed later.

If you enjoy this story, please consider following me on my Facebook page, Facebook.com/jeannie.watt.1, or visit my website, jeanniewatt.com. I love hearing from readers and you can contact me at jeanniewrites@gmail.com.

Best wishes and happy reading,

Jeannie Watt

HEARTWARMING

Montana Homecoming

———

Jeannie Watt

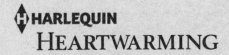

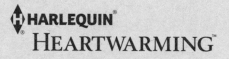

ISBN-13: 978-1-335-88979-9

Recycling programs
for this product may
not exist in your area.

Montana Homecoming

Copyright © 2020 by Jeannie Steinman

All rights reserved. No part of this book may be used or reproduced in any manner whatsoever without written permission except in the case of brief quotations embodied in critical articles and reviews.

This is a work of fiction. Names, characters, places and incidents are either the product of the author's imagination or are used fictitiously. Any resemblance to actual persons, living or dead, businesses, companies, events or locales is entirely coincidental.

This edition published by arrangement with Harlequin Books S.A.

For questions and comments about the quality of this book, please contact us at CustomerService@Harlequin.com.

Harlequin Enterprises ULC
22 Adelaide St. West, 40th Floor
Toronto, Ontario M5H 4E3, Canada
www.Harlequin.com

Printed in U.S.A.

Jeannie Watt lives on a small cattle ranch and hay farm in southwest Montana with her husband, her ridiculously energetic parents and the usual ranch menagerie. She spends her mornings writing, except during calving season, and during the remainder of the day enjoys sewing, doing glass mosaics and fixing fence. If you'd like more information about Jeannie and her books, please visit her website at jeanniewatt.com, where you can also sign up for her newsletter.

Books by Jeannie Watt

Harlequin Heartwarming

Sweet Home, Montana

Montana Dad
A Ranch Between Them

Her Montana Cowboy

Harlequin Western Romance

Montana Bull Riders

The Bull Rider Meets His Match
The Bull Rider's Homecoming
A Bull Rider to Depend On
The Bull Rider's Plan

Visit the Author Profile page
at Harlequin.com for more titles.

CHAPTER ONE

NEVER GIVE THE opening bid.

Cassie Callahan gripped her auction paddle, determined to keep it on her lap until the proper moment. She was, after all, the queen of self-control. The embodiment of coolness under fire. As an assistant school district superintendent, she dealt with unpredictable school boards, principals, teachers and students by calmly addressing facts, laying out pros and cons, refusing to budge unless a decent compromise presented itself. And then she became a master negotiator. She loved it—or at least she used to love it. Lately she'd had the nagging feeling that she was putting more into her job than she was getting out of it.

Burnout, pure and simple, so it made sense that if she had something to occupy her time when she wasn't on the job, she'd once again feel the thrill of battle as she headed out to work each morning. Thus, the auction paddle.

"Sold!" the auctioneer bawled as a nice palomino gelding was led out of the auction ring, and Cassie shifted in her seat. Showtime.

The palomino had sold for a lower price than Cassie had expected, as had the two horses before. Maybe she'd be able to buy McHenry's Gold for a reasonable price; maybe the people attending the semiannual Gavin, Montana, horse auction didn't understand the bloodlines the mare represented. Or perhaps they didn't care.

Unlikely. McHenry horses were legendary, but that wasn't why Cassie was bidding. This particular McHenry mare was a daughter of the mare that had seen her through her turbulent teen years. The last daughter. The mother, McHenry's Rebel, had died the previous year.

"The next mare up is something of a gem, folks."

No. Don't make her look good. Just start the bidding.

Cassie clenched her teeth together, then instantly relaxed her jaw. No more of that. She'd promised her dentist.

The auctioneer continued singing the praises of McHenry's Gold and Cassie had to fight to not stand up and tell him to just shut up and get on with the bidding.

Of course, she didn't, because that was what old Cassie would have done, back before she'd had a couple thousand classes in management and psychology. Back before she realized that direct confrontation didn't always work.

"We'll open the bidding at ten thousand. Do I hear ten? Ten? Ten?"

Ten? The last horse had opened at three.

The ring steward led the mare in a circle. She had excellent conformation but wasn't flashy otherwise. A bay with a broad white blaze and one white hind foot—a carbon copy of her mother, and Cassie wanted her. She practically had to sit on her paddle.

The auctioneer continued his patter. The guy in front of Cassie leaned forward as if to get a better view of the mare. His paddle hand twitched when the auctioneer lowered the opening bid to five thousand dollars and suddenly Cassie's paddle was in the air.

The spotter pointed at her. "I have five," the auctioneer announced. "Do I hear six? Six?"

No six. No six.

"Five and a half? Five and a— I have five and a half."

Cassie leaned forward as she searched the crowd on the opposite side of the sale ring to see who had the temerity to bid against her. She couldn't see who'd bid in the sea of cowboy hats. Well, she'd spot him next time if he dared do it again. She raised her paddle for a bid of six thousand, then narrowed her eyes as she spotted the man who bid six and a half.

No.

Really?

Her dentist would have hated what she did to her teeth when Travis McGuire met her gaze across the distance that separated them, looking very much the smug know-it-all she knew him to be.

She was in trouble, because when Travis wore that expression, it meant game on. She searched her memory, trying to remember who had won their last confrontation years ago.

Maybe it had been a draw.

This one would not be a draw. Or a loss.

No one appeared interested in bidding higher than six thousand five hundred. The auctioneer worked the crowd, then began intoning, "Seven? Seven? Six and three-quarters... No? Going... going..."

Cassie thrust her paddle in the air just after the second *going*. She didn't look at Travis, because she told herself she was beyond their old rivalry. She'd thought he would be, too. They were never going to be friends, but after so many years, surely they could be civil?

"I have a bid of six and three-quarters," the auctioneer announced.

Cassie could go to seven. That was her limit.

But when Travis raised his paddle at seven thousand, she knew that she was going over budget. She wanted that horse.

"Seven and a half? Anyone? Sev—"

Up went her paddle.

"Eight?" He pointed at Travis, who sat motionless, giving Cassie a flicker of hope. "Seven and three quarters?"

Travis nodded and Cassie's stomach fell.

The auctioneer pointed at Cassie. "Eight?"

She hesitated, then lifted the paddle. After that things became a blur as Travis continued to meet every bid and her blood pressure continued to rise. The seesaw continued until the auctioneer reached ten thousand five hundred. He pointed at Travis, who grimly shook his head. Cassie's chest swelled. Unless someone had been waiting in the wings for just this moment…

"Sold to number 325."

Only then, when the heat of battle began to ebb, did she fully process what she'd just done. Ten thousand five hundred dollars. Three thousand five hundred more than she'd allotted. She never got carried away like that. Her gaze strayed across the auction ring to where Travis sat with his forearms resting on his thighs, staring at the ground between his boots. She hadn't seen the man in over five years, and he still had the power to bring out the worst in her.

But she couldn't let this horse slip through her fingers. With this mare, she'd have something to focus on other than the job. A way to relieve pressure and maybe relive a little of her past. She and Rebel had spent hours roaming the mountains behind the ranch. She'd made plans, set goals, sometimes discussed guys she liked with the mare, who never made fun of her for wanting to date out of her league. Cassie was the kind who kept both feet on the ground, so it was safer to engage in a soliloquy while riding Rebel than to talk about guys with her younger sister Katie, who'd hero-worshipped her at the time.

She picked up her purse and eased her way down the aisle of folding chairs. Never in her life had she thought she'd charge a horse on her credit card, but here she was.

She just had to be careful about one impulsive act leading to another. She'd left that side of herself behind years ago, having found it detrimental to career building, but if anyone could bring it out again, it would be Travis.

TALK ABOUT BEING BLINDSIDED. Travis McGuire faked a smile at the lady who had to move her chair so he could escape the auction bidding area, then, once he was free, he allowed himself the grim expression that felt so much more satisfying and genuine.

What was Cassie Callahan doing back in Montana, and why on earth had she bought the very horse that had brought him to the auction?

Actually, he could guess why she'd bought the horse—she'd owned the mother. But he still had no idea what she was doing in Montana. Had the high-powered job that had kept her from coming home, even for holidays, eased up? Had it ended?

If so, why hadn't his grandfather, who was dating Cassie's grandmother—a circumstance that still blew him away—given him a heads-up?

Travis dropped his auction catalog into the trash as he headed toward the portable stalls where the sale horses were housed. Sometimes it was best not to court trouble, especially where Cassie was involved, but he wanted answers. More than that, he'd wanted the mare and it stung that he hadn't been able to buy her. He had two McHenry mares with which to start his breeding program and he wanted a third. McHenry's Gold was young and green broke, and because this particular auction was geared toward the sale of seasoned working horses, he'd thought there was a chance she'd sell within his price range.

She probably would have if it hadn't been for

Cassie. He'd gone above his price range by a couple thousand dollars, and then, when Cassie showed no indication of having any kind of budgetary limit, he'd had to stop. He didn't have a high-paying job in a faraway city. He was a ranch guy making ends meet during a good year.

He walked around a long aluminum trailer he recognized as belonging to the Callahan ranch, then slowed when he spotted Cassie standing next to an open stall, talking to the mare she'd just bought.

Unlike the rest of her dark-haired family, Cassie was a blonde. Her hair, which had been waist-length back when they'd competed against each other in just about everything, grazed her shoulders in a smooth, professional-looking cut, and swung like a curtain when she moved. He missed the wild waves, but people changed, and Cassie appeared to be a whole lot more buttoned-up than she'd been back in the day.

But despite looking sleek and professional, the old Cassie was still there. He'd seen the fire in her eye, even at a goodly distance, when she'd thought he was purposely bidding her up—and there was not a doubt in his mind that was what she thought was happening.

Her back straightened when his boots hit

gravel and she turned, her automatic smile fading when she recognized him.

"I didn't know you were back," he said by way of greeting.

"It's been less than a day. I came home early specifically for this sale."

So she'd also come for the horse.

She tilted her chin and he saw her jaw muscles tighten—an old tell—as they silently regarded each other, old nemeses meeting in an unexpected setting. Except Travis wasn't all that into it anymore.

Myriad emotions played across what she probably thought was her poker face. Travis had known her for too long, had been in heated combat with her too many times, not to be able to read her like a book—smugness at her hardwon victory, determination to win if he dared challenge her again and…something else.

Was she reading him the way he was reading her?

If so, what did she see?

He shook off the question. "I wasn't bidding you up."

There. That was out of the way.

"You wanted the mare?" She seemed surprised, but he wasn't sure why.

"I did. I'm starting a breeding program and

the McHenry lineage has the characteristics I'm looking for."

"Ah." She patted the bay's neck in a possessive way and Travis wondered if the action had been unconscious or deliberate. Was she rubbing it in?

He decided no. "You said you came back early."

Cassie gave him a cool look and suddenly he couldn't read her. "Yes. I've decided to take a sabbatical. I'd like to get to know my little nieces before they grow up."

"How long are you staying?"

"Close to a month."

"I thought sabbaticals lasted longer than that."

"A month on the ranch, then a few months taking classes at the University of Wisconsin. I'll go back to work in January."

"Working on your doctorate?"

"I will be." Her chin lifted as she looked past him. "I think the guy's coming to check me out."

Travis looked over his shoulder and saw Jim Newton heading toward them from the sale office. "What are you going to do with this mare?" he asked as he brought his attention back to Cassie.

Her eyebrows lifted. "Take her to Wisconsin. I plan to start riding again."

"Ah."

"Sorry about this, Travis, but I want Rebel's daughter."

"She may not be the same horse her mother was."

"But then again she may, and I'm banking on that." She shifted her weight. "I always regretted selling Rebel when I headed off to college, even though she had a good home and kids to ride her."

Travis nodded. It wasn't unusual to sell good horses to families who would use and love them at certain transition points in life. And it wasn't unusual to regret the sale, no matter how good of a home the horse got.

He held Cassie's gaze as Jim approached, clipboard in hand. There was still a glimmer of challenge in her eyes, as if she thought he was trying to lull her into a false sense of security. He might have done that a time or two in the past, like when he pretended he wasn't going to run against her for senior-class president, only to sign up in the eleventh hour, and then win by a slim margin. It'd driven her crazy and he'd enjoyed the payback for the other things she'd bested him in.

What a jerk he'd been.

"Maybe I'll see you before you leave." It

seemed likely that in two months their paths might cross again.

Cassie gave him a startled look that clearly said, *Why would you think that?*

"Yes, maybe," she said in the voice he imagined she used in her job as a school district administrator.

Jim Newton came to a stop near the back of the trailer, and his gaze bounced between Cassie and Travis as if searching for visible wounds. "Long time, Cassie. Good to see you, Travis." He sounded like he meant to say, *Good to see you in one piece.*

"Jim." Travis touched the brim of his hat, then nodded at Cassie. "I gotta get going."

With that he turned and headed for his truck, feeling like he'd escaped something, but he wasn't sure what.

His truck was in the graveled lot on the far side of the fairgrounds and it took some time to get to it, so when he drove past the Callahan ranch trailer, Cassie's horse should have been loaded. Instead she stood just outside the open door, her head up, her body shaking.

Travis slowed to a stop and rolled down the window. "Need help?"

He expected Cassie to turn him down flat. After all, Jim was still there helping her try to battle the horse into the trailer. Instead she said, "Yes."

Well, he did offer. Travis pulled the truck up beside the trailer and got out.

"Jim has to head back to the sale office," she said in a low voice.

"In other words, you need me." He had no idea what possessed him to say those words. Maybe because of all the times she'd left him in the dust or refused help from anyone and got a difficult job done on her own.

She met his gaze with a "really?" expression. "Are you going to make me say the words?"

"Nope," he said lightly, reaching for the lead rope. She hesitated, then put it into his hands, her fingers brushing his during the transfer.

"Thanks," Jim said as he picked up his clipboard off the trailer fender.

"No problem."

Jim gave him one last look—a funny look, really—and then headed back to the sale office where a small line of people waited to pay for and claim their purchases. Well, it *was* kind of funny for him to come to Cassie's rescue, but time had passed. Things had changed. Despite the bidding war, the result of an odd coincidence, they had no reason to be at each other's throats.

The one thing that had remained the same, however, was the fact that Travis suspected that somewhere along the line, he'd fallen in love with his nemesis.

CHAPTER TWO

TRAVIS HAD MCHENRY'S GOLD loaded in less than ten minutes, using a method that Cassie recognized, but had never used herself because she'd never owned a horse that refused to walk into a stock trailer. Travis seemed quite practiced at the technique of leading the horse as close to the trailer as he could without her balking, letting her relax, then leading her away and starting over. Eventually she stood with her head in the trailer, then her front feet and finally all four feet. Then, instead of slamming the door shut so that Cassie could drive away, he calmly led the mare out of the trailer and then back in again. He did it three times. On the final go, he tied her and then closed the divider panel.

"She should be fine now," he said as he stepped out of the trailer and swung the door shut. "If she isn't, then just do what I did."

Cassie folded her arms and stared at the closed door, her dreams of trailering Rebel's daughter to training arenas and trailheads shaken by the episode. "My new mare has issues."

"It happens. All it takes is someone who doesn't know how to handle a small issue and, boom, a big issue is born."

"I hope this is her only trouble," Cassie said before meeting Travis's gaze. What was she doing unloading on Travis anyway?

"It might well be."

"Thank you." She hadn't expected this kind of help from the man she'd bested at the auction, and in some other life arenas, but he'd given it. She automatically put her hand out, as she did when she finished a one-on-one meeting.

Travis held her gaze as he took her hand, as if expecting her to draw it away at the last moment, then his calloused fingers gripped hers and she had the stunning realization that, even though they'd known each other since they were ten or eleven, this was the first time they'd actually touched on purpose. Unless one counted a tackle. But there were extenuating circumstances there. No one had ever said, "Shake hands and be friends," and maybe it was because of the years of thinking of him as her rival that the feel of his palm against hers ignited a small spark of warmth that curled through her.

She slowly withdrew her fingers from his and dropped her hand to her side. "Thanks, again." She smiled her this-meeting-is-now-at-an-end smile.

"I assume there's someone at the ranch who can help unload if there's an issue?"

"Yes. If Nick isn't home, Katie will be." Actually, she could unload the horse herself without either of her siblings' help now that she knew what she was up against. She hadn't expected the mare to balk at the trailer, and Jim taking hold of the rope and attempting to manually pull her in didn't help matters. The mare panicked and she never should have allowed that to happen.

But it had, followed by Travis coming to the rescue.

Travis, whom she'd watched grow from a wiry ten-year-old to the rather impressive guy standing in front of her.

She hadn't come home to be impressed by Travis. She'd come home to have a much-needed breather from a stressful occupation followed by a round of coursework that would allow her to dive back into the fray with a larger skill set.

Travis sensed his dismissal and, surprisingly, accepted. He touched his hat, just as he'd done with Jim, then turned and headed back to his idling truck. Rather than watch him go, because part of her wanted to watch him go, Cassie double-checked the doors on the trailer, then got into her own truck—or rather her brother's truck—and started the engine.

She eased out of its parking spot, watching the mirrors as she made the turn from the parking lot. In the distance she saw Travis's truck pull onto the highway leading to their respective ranches, which were separated by the Ambrose River.

But even though their ranches were not that far apart, the McGuires and the Callahans hadn't really socialized, except for at community and school activities, brandings, cattle gatherings and the like. The families were neighbors and friendly acquaintances…with the exception of her and Travis…but not particularly tight.

That part of her life—the part where she was in full-time competition with Travis—was over, and maybe it was a good thing that McHenry's Gold had brought them together. She had no intention of seeing Travis again, and now they had a measure of closure.

TRAVIS PULLED INTO the ranch with his empty trailer and backed it into the spot between the long cattle trailer and the now-vintage trailer with the living quarters that he'd used while rodeoing during high school and college. He'd never had any intention of going pro, like his neighbor Brady O'Neil had done, but had still put everything he had into the sport which offered him an outlet for his competitive nature.

It was the one sport in which Cassie hadn't tried to best him after they started high school—but he had a feeling that was only because women's bronc riding wasn't sanctioned by the National High School Rodeo Association.

Well, she bested you today.

She had the horse he wanted. The horse he might still get if the mare turned out to be trouble. A horse that wouldn't load still made a fine broodmare, but there was no way he was paying what Cassie had paid for her. Her last bid had been a godsend, saving him from digging deeper into his savings than he wanted to.

After uncoupling the trailer, he parked the truck, then went through his mental checklist for the remainder of the day, which was identical to yesterday's checklist. Feeding, fences, weeds. He'd check his mares, admire his foals, then wake up the next morning and do it all over again.

"Reynaldo called."

Travis turned to see his grandfather Will McGuire come out of the machine shop, wiping grease off his hands with a shop rag.

"Couldn't get you on your cell," Will added as he came to a stop next to the empty trailer.

"I ran out of juice. Forgot to charge it last night."

"The guy is persistent."

The "guy" was his former college roommate and fellow agribusiness grad trying to recruit him for the same job he'd turned down to return home and take over his dad's position on the ranch years ago. He called every six months or so, and by some quirk of fate, his grandfather always seemed to be present when the calls came in. Not that they worried him. He was supremely confident in Travis's desire to stay on the ranch where he was raised. Probably a good thing he didn't know that the calls always touched a nerve in his grandson. He also didn't know that Travis jokingly offered Rey a job every time he called.

"Where's the horse?" Will gestured at the empty holding pen where they kept new animals as they acclimated to the place.

"No horse today."

"Huh. I thought you had a shot at it."

"Cassie Callahan bought the mare."

"Huh." Will concentrated on wiping grease off his wristwatch. "She's back early."

For a moment all Travis could do was stare.

"You knew she was coming back?"

"Yeah. Rosalie told me a couple of weeks ago."

Rosalie, Cassie's grandmother, and Will had been spending a lot of time together lately. The change in Will since he'd hooked up with Rosalie was profound. Gone was the lonely man who'd thrown himself into his work with a vengeance as if trying to keep his mind busy enough to make it through another day. In his place was a man who seemed at least a decade younger on the mental front.

"You might have passed that information along."

"Why?" Will asked reasonably. "It isn't like you were going to rush over to the Callahan ranch to see her...although—" he made a resigned face as he wadded up the rag in one hand "—you will be."

"What does that mean?" Travis asked suspiciously.

Will smiled the goofiest smile Travis had ever seen on the old man's face. "Rosalie has done me the honor of agreeing to be my bride. We're getting married before Cassie goes back to Wisconsin." Will continued to beam. "And I'd like you to be my best man."

"No." CASSIE'S MOUTH literally dropped open before Rosalie Callahan finished dropping her bomb.

"Yes. It's true. I'm about to be a bride again." Rosalie was not surprised at her oldest granddaughter's reaction to the news that she was about to marry the grandfather of the man who'd driven her nuts while she was growing up.

Katie, the youngest of her grandchildren, laughed. "This is wonderful, Grandma. And you timed it perfectly."

Indeed, she had. Rosalie didn't believe that Cassie would purposely miss the wedding, but she'd come up with a work-related excuse to miss every family holiday for the past two years. It was no wonder that she'd burned out. Not that Cassie would admit it. No…according to her, she was on the ranch for family time before heading off to take classes for her doctorate in school administration. She didn't realize that she wasn't as good at hiding her stress as she thought she was.

"Have you told Nick?" Katie asked.

Nick—her widowed grandson, who'd moved back to the ranch with his young daughters, Kendra and Bailey, a little over a year ago— was stretching himself thin between contracting jobs, ranch maintenance and keeping his girlfriend's house repaired. But he always made it home by dinnertime and spent his evenings with his girls.

"I'll see him this afternoon and share the good news." She smiled.

"Will it be a full-on wedding, or a visit to the courthouse?"

"Kind of a compromise. We'll have a ceremony with a judge followed by a big party on Will's ranch."

The interesting thing about getting older was that despite the rumors that one became more stubborn and set in their ways, Rosalie had found it was much easier to compromise than it'd once been—possibly because she had a stronger sense of what mattered and what didn't.

Will was a rancher. He'd always been, and would always be, a rancher. Rosalie wasn't a fan of rural life, but she'd been happy living on the Callahan ranch, raising her children and grandchildren, working shoulder to shoulder with her beloved husband. But after Carl died, she'd fulfilled her dream of starting a gift-and-garden shop with her best friend, Gloria Gable, and she had no intention of giving that up and moving to another ranch. Will, bless him, understood that. So, he'd bought a house in town, just down the street from the Victorian mansion that housed Rosalie's gift shop, The Daisy Petal. The new house had been his engagement present to her.

He would still work the ranch, he'd told her. And there would be nights when he wouldn't make it back into town, but he'd be there every night he could. Rosalie, in turn, had agreed that there would be nights when she would stay on his ranch with him, even if she didn't want to make it her permanent home. *Cooperation* and *compromise* were her new key words.

"That's a lovely idea, Grandma." Cassie worked up a smile, even though she still looked a little shell-shocked.

Rosalie held her teacup between her hands, smiling over the top of it. "I may never again be a full-fledged ranch gal, but I'm happy sharing my husband's life."

Her husband.

Having a new husband was still a concept that was difficult to fully grasp. Rosalie had had a husband for fifty years and had never anticipated having another. But then Will came along, all gruff and ready to do battle for her. The fact that he didn't do battle after she'd asked him not to was the deciding factor for her. He was protective by nature, and a man who was used to fighting for what he got. The fact that he was able to back off and allow her to fight her own battles—most of which involved her troublesome next-door neighbor, Vince Taylor—was huge.

"I love the idea of having it on Will's ranch, Grandma. That would give us more time to decorate and we'd have refrigeration for the food, so we could prepare it in advance." Katie shot her a look. "Unless you're having it catered, of course."

"I was thinking a little of both."

"Good. When are you planning to get married?"

Cassie's gaze moved from Katie to Rosalie and back again, then held on Rosalie as she said, "Before Cassie leaves." She tilted her head at Cassie. "Before you leave. That's August…"

"Twenty-second. Classes start a week after that, so I'll have time to settle into the room I'm renting."

Rosalie consulted the farm-store calendar that hung next to the refrigerator. "Then I believe Will and I will get married on August 15." He'd given her carte blanche as far as dates went. All he said was the sooner, the better. He'd been lonely for too long to have a lengthy engagement.

"I can't wait to start planning," Katie said. She gave her grandmother a sassy smile. "I can't believe you're getting married before Brady and I tie the knot."

"We're not young," Rosalie said pertly. "We can't afford to dillydally around like you two."

Katie wanted a Christmas wedding, but had yet to pick a venue. At the rate she was going, she'd get married not this Christmas but the following one. That said, she and Brady didn't seem one bit concerned about the time factor. They'd found each other and that was enough.

"Guess she told you," Cassie said to her sister with a wink.

Katie laughed, making Rosalie realize just how much she loved having all her grandkids back on the ranch. Yes, the house was a little crowded with Katie, Nick, Cassie and two young girls sharing a space, but no more crowded than it had been when her son moved home with his three motherless children almost thirty years ago. Since Rosalie spent most of her nights at her house in town, it was actually less crowded. And, unfortunately, Cassie would be gone all too soon.

As if sensing the direction of her thoughts, Cassie moved in to give her a one-armed hug. "Congratulations."

"Thank you. Will is going to ask Nick to stand up for him, and I'd love it if you and Katie would stand up with me…and help me plan."

"Yes to both. This is going to be fun." Katie was practically rubbing her hands together.

"I'd love to stand up with you." Cassie gave her another squeeze before stepping away, but Rosalie had a suspicion that she was working over the idea of her and Travis finding new footing in a world where they would see each other more frequently. Unless, of course, Cassie's job once again got in the way of her family time.

It could happen, but Rosalie hoped it didn't.

Cassie looked tired. Weary, really. Like she'd been trying to hold too many corks under water at the same time and was *this* close to giving up.

Because she'd done what she'd always done and put achievement ahead of self-care.

She's come home, her little voice whispered. *Maybe she'll decide to stay.*

Rosalie told her little voice not to get too stuck on the notion, but…there was always a chance.

"I'M GONNA WEAR a big white dress," Cassie's four-year-old niece, Bailey, announced after hearing the good news about her great-grandmother. "And a veal."

"Veil," Kendra, her older sister, corrected. As an almost official first grader, Kendra did a lot of correcting. She reminded Cassie a little of herself.

No. Kendra reminded Cassie a lot of herself.

"I think that's what the bride wears, honey." Cassie knelt down to help Bailey zip her jacket. "You'll be a flower girl, so you'll wear a pretty wreath in your hair, with ribbons that hang down your back."

"Like a princess," Bailey said.

"Exactly." Cassie straightened the shoulders of her little niece's jacket and decided not to take advantage of the moment to point out that there were many kinds of princesses, including warrior princesses. "Now, let's go see those flower seeds you guys planted."

The girls loved helping their aunt Katie in the greenhouse and welcomed any excuse to show off their fledgling green thumbs.

Cassie had to admit to feeling wary about Katie's decision to abandon her career as a human resources manager in order to live on the ranch and grow herbs, but her fears had been groundless. Katie not only had a green thumb, she had a great rapport with her clients. One greenhouse had already become two with plans for a third after Nick and Brady, Katie's fiancé, dismantled an old shed to make room.

"You know," Cassie said conversationally, "you and Brady should probably pick a date."

Katie shot her a sidelong look. "I'm just waiting for him to get home for good in a few weeks. He'll be done with his final welding course in time for haying and then I'll never see him because he'll be on a swather in the field."

Cassie laughed, partly because what Katie said was so true. Haying waited for no man.

"And he already has a job offer."

Cassie offered her palm for a high-five. "Congrats."

"Yep," Katie said. "Between Nick and Brady and I, someone will be free to handle the ranch work and it's so nice to have an outside income that isn't reliant on cow or hay prices."

"*I'm* growing herbs," Kendra piped up. "Aunt Katie will sell them for me."

"Great," Cassie said. "Then you can save the money for college."

"Half to savings, half for fun," Kendra informed her. "Daddy said."

"Well, we won't cross Dad," Cassie replied with a smiling glance at her sister. Katie smiled back, but it didn't quite reach her eyes and once again Cassie had the feeling that her sister was on the verge of saying something, but wasn't sure how to go about it, and she'd gotten the same feeling from her brother, Nick, while they'd been playing Sorry! with the girls the night before.

Okay, she hadn't been home in a while, and that wasn't good. She'd managed to get home for two days the previous Christmas, before having to fly back to Wisconsin to tackle a serious personnel issue. At least she'd connected with her father, who'd flown in from Australia with her stepmother, for twelve whole hours. It would have been very disappointing to have not seen him, even if he'd joked that his flight was longer than their visit.

But life wasn't always easy. She had a demanding job as assistant district superintendent.

When fires needed putting out, she needed to be there. Her job was not one that fell within the boundaries of nine to five on weekdays only. If a school was vandalized over the weekend, she was the one called. If something happened to a student which would impact the school they attended, Cassie was called. Parental problems— Cassie. If a teacher was fired over the Christmas holidays, she was the one who ended up teaching English for two weeks while the district searched for a replacement.

The only reason she was able to take this sabbatical was because the district had lost student population. The administrative office had been top-heavy with a superintendent and two assistant superintendents. One position had to be cut at the beginning of the current budget cycle which had commenced in July, so to help the other assistant superintendent get the necessary years for a full retirement, Cassie had agreed to step back, take an unpaid sabbatical and work on her doctorate. Next summer, Rhonda Olson would retire and Cassie would be stepping back into the fray as the one and only assistant superintendent, with her eye on the prize of becoming the Grand Pooh-Bah. *The* superintendent. Yes, she was young, but she was driven, and she had already shown that she had the skill set to do the job and do it right. She'd even demonstrated that she could successfully substitute teach in a pinch.

"Wear this coat, Aunt Cassie." Bailey appeared from inside the hall closet with the fluffy fake-fur jacket she must have tugged from the hanger.

"I haven't worn that jacket since high school, sweetie. I don't know if I can fit into it."

Sure enough, it was snug when she got it up over her shoulders, but Bailey beamed and Kendra told her it looked nice, so she wore it as she headed out the door holding her nieces' hands. Katie shut the door, then caught up with them on the front walk. She stroked the coat like she was petting an animal and Cassie gave her a look.

"Tastes change over the decades." And she had no idea what she'd been thinking when she'd bought a fuzzy bubble gum–pink coat. She certainly hadn't expected it to be waiting for her in the hall closet when she returned to the ranch.

"I think Grandma hung on to some other bits and pieces of our pasts if you want to split a bottle of vino and take a trip down memory lane," Katie said.

"What's vino?" Kendra asked.

"Wine," Cassie replied matter-of-factly. She wasn't a big one for using secret talk around kids, whom she found were often underestimated.

"I don't like it," Kendra said, screwing up her face. "We had sips at Christmas. Yuk."

Bailey made a choking sound to indicate her dislike of the fruit of the vine, and Cassie laughed.

"About time," Katie muttered.

She shot her sister another look. "What?"

Katie shook her head, but as soon as the girls raced ahead to open the greenhouse and made a show of how hot it was inside by pretending to wilt, she said, "It's about time you loosened up and laughed. You're so tightly wound that I expect you to snap at any minute."

"I am not," Cassie said, insulted. She was a master at keeping her cool…except for the recent incident with Travis. But that was instinct kicking in. Eventually she'd found the override switch and gotten control of herself.

"You are. You just don't know it. Probably because it was a slow process." She gave Cassie a hard look. "You know, the frog in boiling water and all that."

Cassie just shook her head and followed her nieces into the greenhouse with its neat benches of herbs in different stages of growth. There might be a grain of truth in Katie's words. Before school ended in May, she'd been visiting an elementary school and overheard one of the kids calling her *the scary lady*. It had stung more than it should have. Kids used to love her, but now they gave her wide berth. And were shoulders supposed to ache all the time? She'd assumed it was an aftereffect of her workouts, but…

Kendra took her by the hand, reminding her that some kids still liked her, and led her forward, naming each herb as they passed. "I grew those violets," she said, pointing to the last bench, which held flats of flowers. "Did you know you can eat flowers? We're going to sell 'em to a restaurant to put on desserts to make them pretty."

"Excellent," Cassie said. "What did you plant, Bailey?"

"Violets and catnip for Tigger. He gets all funny when we bring it into the house."

"I bet he does," Cassie said, laughing again. If she kept laughing, then maybe Katie would see that she wasn't really that uptight. She was just… What?

A woman with a demanding job, which required her to hide her emotions in the name of professionalism. She may want to lean across her desk and throttle the whining board member on the other side, but, hey…that didn't get you funding where you needed it.

Actually, she was glad to take some time off, even if she was a bit nervous about being out of the loop for almost a year. Time off would help her get perspective and perform better. Nothing wrong with that, or with taking the time off so that Rhonda could retire without penalty. She'd go back to the school district feeling fresh and would bring with her new ideas gleaned from the classes she'd be taking. She'd be back in the loop.

A win-win.

So why did she feel so edgy about the situation?

CHAPTER THREE

TRAVIS LEANED ON the rail fence and smiled to himself as he watched the new foal nurse. His third and last McHenry baby, the first filly, was the spit of her mama, and in all probability, he'd keep her. Grow his herd.

And he couldn't help but wonder how Cassie was getting along with her recent purchase. Her grandfather Carl had only purchased well-trained animals for his grandkids, so although they'd ridden some rank mounts owned by other people, neither she nor her brother, Nick, had the joy of rehabilitating a horse with bad habits, while Travis had been up to his ears in such animals—by choice. He'd enjoyed the challenge, and being a bronc rider, it was the rare horse who could put him on the ground, especially when he could use both hands.

He had a knack with horses who were slow to trust. He knew when to proceed. When to stop, and when a horse was too far gone to help.

Funny how he didn't have that same knack with Cassie.

Nothing saying you can't develop one.

True.

He pushed off the fence and headed to the house to grab his wallet and phone before driving to town.

He could honestly say there was a time in his life when he hated Cassie Callahan. When just seeing her strut into an event was enough to make smoke start rolling out of his ears. She'd not only bested him more times than he wanted to think about before he'd reached the age of twelve, she was vocal about it. Rubbed it in.

A fourth-grade footrace shortly after she'd moved onto the Callahan ranch had started it all, but matters had snowballed thanks to laughing friends and fourth-grade pride, and it wasn't long before they were sworn enemies. One-upmanship ensued and as the legend of their rivalry grew, so did the ferocity of their competition. She was just such a know-it-all.

As they continued through school, their competition became quieter—less direct confrontations, because frankly that was exhausting—but retained myth-like status. Cassie was a worthy adversary, so he gave back as good as he got until the day they'd graduated high school. He'd been valedictorian, while she'd held the runner-up spot, thanks to the fact that he'd gotten a slightly higher grade in AP government. And on that day, something odd happened. Cassie had tripped on her way to the stage. Seeing her down was nothing new. Travis had seen her get knocked end over teakettle by calves and rampant goats she'd been trying to tie during rodeo practice. He'd seen her get bucked off horses she shouldn't have gotten on, and he'd seen her trip and fall in a mud puddle with an ice-cream cone in each hand at the county fair. All of those instances were different than seeing her hit the ground in front of a crowd, then struggle to her feet, her face bright red with embarrassment. He'd unconsciously started toward her to offer his hand when the principal beat him to it, and he had then retreated to his seat again.

Cassie had headed to the mic and made a laughing comment about the dangers of graduation robes and then took her place on a chair on the opposite side of the podium from him. The ceremony continued, followed by the graduation after-party, and even though he'd only seen her a couple of times during the events that followed, he couldn't stop thinking about her. Thinking about how vulnerable she'd seemed during those few seconds. *Vulnerability* and *Cassie* were two words that he'd never in his life connected, but once connected, they stuck with him.

He didn't get a chance to see her again that

summer. She'd taken off almost immediately to a summer internship in Seattle, while he'd continued working on the ranch until his first semester at Montana State started in September, pinch-hitting for his dad, who was having increasing difficulties with his mobility due to rheumatoid arthritis. His parents relocated to Arizona during his senior year in college, thus sealing Travis's fate. His grandfather needed his help on the ranch. He couldn't find a manager he could work with, and more than that, he'd believed that Travis's dream was to return home and take over the ranch. Travis had never dissuaded him of the notion.

He'd come home willingly. He'd always planned to return to the ranch at some point in the distant future, so why not start fresh from the gate? His grandfather needed him—for company, as much as for management. He didn't get to spend his twenties seeing new countries and experiencing new ideas and perspectives, but he did get to carry on the family legacy. He knew a lot of people who would have given their right arm to do just that.

But that didn't stop Reynaldo from calling and asking when he was ready to go to work. Travis gave him a firm no every time, but his charmingly persistent friend refused to be dissuaded. He kind of reminded Travis of Cassie in that regard.

Travis made Hardwick's Grocery and Hardware his first stop, since the cupboards were bare. His grandfather rarely spent time on the ranch after he started keeping company with Rosalie Callahan, and now that his grandfather had bought a house in town, Travis assumed that he pretty much had the ranch to himself, with the exception of the two day hands he was in the process of hiring.

Travis filled his basket as he walked up and down the aisles, tossing in anything that looked easy. Long days didn't lend themselves to cooking gourmet meals. Or cooking, period. He spent a lot of time in the microwave and frozen-food sections.

After checking out, he was in the process of dumping a bag of ice over his frozen food in the insulated cooler when someone behind him said his name. He turned to see Mrs. Gable, his former high school English teacher and Rosalie's business partner, hailing him.

"Isn't it exciting?" she asked as she stopped next to his empty cart.

"I assume you mean the upcoming wedding?" he asked with a smile.

"I've never seen your grandfather so…approachable," she said with a wink. Mrs. Gable had a way about her, and she still dressed in bright tunics and dark leggings, just as she had when she was teaching.

"I wouldn't know," he teased back. "I never see him."

"You'll probably be seeing more of him soon. After all, there'll be a lot of work to do on the ranch before the wedding, and he'll want to help."

"Which ranch?" Travis asked slowly.

"Your ranch, of course. Didn't you know?"

Travis shook his head. "I didn't."

Mrs. Gable made a dismissive gesture. "They decided for certain when Nick made sushi for everyone last night."

"Wait a minute… Grandpa and sushi?"

"California rolls. Nothing raw."

Even so, Travis had a hard time imagining (a) Nick Callahan making sushi, even if he had lived in California for almost a decade, and (b) his grandfather partaking. After all, there was seaweed involved.

Who was this man who'd taken over his curmudgeonly grandfather's body?

"I don't suppose they set a date?"

Mrs. Gable frowned at him. "I'm sure that Will wants to tell you himself."

"I won't let on I know. It'll help me with the ranch calendar."

Mrs. Gable's gaze shifted, then she said, "A week before Cassie leaves for her classes."

"I'm sure he plans to tell me next time he sees me."

"Of course he does." Mrs. Gable beamed and patted his cart. "May I take this off your hands?"

"You may. Have a good one, Mrs. Gable."

"Gloria," she said firmly.

"Right. Gloria. Thanks."

Thanks for the permission to use her first name and thanks for the information he didn't have. There would be a wedding on the ranch in a few weeks' time.

Travis blew out a breath as he closed the cooler. Should make for interesting times.

McHENRY'S GOLD LOOKED just like her mother, but her temperament wasn't anywhere near the same. Instead of a soft eye, she had a watchful eye, as if expecting something bad to happen at any given moment. Like, say, now, while Cassie brushed her way around the horse's back quarters.

Cassie let out a sigh and continued to brush, noting that the mare's muscles didn't give as she stroked. She had work ahead of her. Well, she was no stranger to work, but in this case, she also had research to do.

Or you could reach out to Travis.

Cassie continued to brush as she played with the idea. When Travis had bid against her at the auction, she'd instantly assumed that, even though they hadn't seen each other since she graduated college, he was out to get the better of her. Again.

That had been a big jump, and honestly, one she shouldn't have made. She'd allowed past experience to dictate her responses rather than discovering what the actual circumstances were, and that was unacceptable. She stopped brushing and settled a hand on the crest of the mare's neck. It was time to move past knee-jerk reactions. She'd promised herself that she would come home for the holidays from here on out, no matter what, which meant that she'd see Travis when she came home. She needed to make peace with the man. And with herself.

Ten-year-old Cassie would be so angry with her.

Ten-year-old Cassie had her day. Now it was time for something different.

Now the big question was, how to make peace? It seemed rude to ask him for help with the mare she'd bought out from under him, so it had to be in another way.

Cassie was a fan of the direct approach, so after she'd put the mare back in the small pen to keep her away from the other horses while she acclimated to new surroundings, she went into the house and asked Katie if she had Travis's cell number.

"Plotting an ambush?" Katie asked mildly, not bothering to look up from the cookbook she was perusing.

"I'm going to make peaceful overtures."

"Good." Katie pulled out her phone, unlocked it and handed it over. Cassie found the number in Katie's contacts and put it into her own phone. Now the big question was, would he answer an unknown number?

"Call from my phone. He'll answer," Katie said, making Cassie wonder for a split second if she'd asked the question aloud.

"Thanks." She hit the number, and, sure enough, Travis answered on the second ring.

"Hey, Katie."

"It's Cassie."

Stone-cold silence, and then… "Having trouble with the horse?"

Cassie's hackles started to rise at the inference that she couldn't handle the horse on her own, but she told herself that it was a legitimate question, given the situation the last time she saw him. Maybe he thought she was ready to sell the mare to him for the bid price. "I don't know yet," she said honestly. "But that's not why I'm calling."

Her statement was met with another silence, so, speaking more quickly than she'd intended in order to fill the void, she said, "I'm calling because I think we need to iron out some issues."

"What do you suggest?"

"I…" Should have figured that out before she'd called. The fact that she hadn't was out of character, which perhaps spoke to the fact that she was a little burned-out. Weary of fighting the good fight and in need of rest in order to get back into top form.

"Why don't we discuss this face-to-face?" Travis asked.

"Great plan." That would give her time to figure out exactly what she wanted to discuss. If all else failed, they could discuss the horse.

"My place or yours?"

"Neutral ground."

"Maybe we could meet in the middle of that new bridge leading to your ranch. You know, like in the movies?"

"Or we could do something logical," Cassie said coolly. She didn't let angry parents get her goat and she wouldn't let Travis do it either— even though he had a lot of practice and was good at it.

"Yeah."

She heard a smile in his voice and wished she could sound as relaxed as he did. She was about to suggest that they meet at the county library, when he said, "Why don't we go out to dinner?"

"Like on a date?" The words blurted out of her mouth. She instantly regretted them. A date with Travis. Right.

"If you want to call it that."

Cassie's cheeks began to warm as he expertly bounced the ball back into her court. "It doesn't matter what we call it," she said, taking care to keep her voice neutral and even. "We'll meet, settle a few matters, set the tone for the future. If you want to eat dinner while we do that, fine."

"I want to eat dinner."

It was an odd feeling, scrambling to keep up. Usually she was the person causing others to scramble, which meant she was going to have to rehone her Travis skills. "Fine. We'll meet at a dinner place."

"When and where?"

"Six o'clock tomorrow at the Cedar Creek Inn." At least she'd get a nice steak out of the meeting.

"Which has been closed for two years. We should have the entire place to ourselves."

Cassie bit back a curse word. She really had

been gone for too long. Katie looked up from her cookbook, frowned, then mouthed, "Tremaine's."

Cassie blinked at her. That was the worst place in town the last time she'd been home for any length of time. Katie gave her a trust-me nod, so Cassie said, "How about Tremaine's Diner? Six o'clock."

"Tremaine's it is."

He didn't seem one bit taken aback at the idea, as she would have been had he suggested the place.

"See you there." She hung up the phone before he could say anything that would make her have to say something back.

"Tremaine's Diner? Really?" she said as she handed Katie her phone. The place had been notorious for being periodically closed down for health-and-safety violations since she'd been a kid.

"New owner. Actually, a whole new place. The interior was gutted by a grease fire three years ago. They renovated and all's good, including the food."

Cassie poured a cup of coffee and joined her sister at the table. "I guess some things do change."

"Yes, they do." Katie gave her another one of those questioning looks, and Cassie decided it was time for her sister to speak freely.

"Something on your mind?"

Katie gave an innocent shrug. "I'm glad you're home."

"And…" Cassie tilted her head, but waited rather than speaking, since it appeared that Katie was gathering her thoughts.

"You're different."

Cassie almost said she wasn't, but stopped herself. "How so?"

"That's what I'm trying to nail down. It's like you're here, but you're not."

"I'm here." And she was glad to be there. It had taken her some time to get used to the idea of not picking up the phone and asking for a status report on various situations, but she was doing better.

"You're also somewhere else." Katie leaned back in her chair. "It's like you're plotting strategy for future battles."

"You could be right," Cassie said, figuring it was best to be truthful rather than to stonewall. Katie had worked in HR. She was shrewd and she could be relentless once she decided to wiggle the truth out of someone. And she was equally driven when she decided to rescue something or someone. Cassie had to convince her that she didn't need rescuing. "I spent the past three years not only being on top of everything, but also staying one jump ahead. Anticipation has become a habit."

"Do you like your job?"

"I love it."

"How many hours do you work a week?"

Cassie waved a hand. "It depends on the week."

"Your shortest week."

Cassie let out a sigh. "I'm single. I have no pets. I don't log my hours, because I'm doing something I love."

"And you're burned-out."

"Yes. I am." Confession was good for the soul, but this confession didn't feel so good. She was burned-out and had become the scary lady.

"How are you going to fix that?" Katie asked.

"I took the sabbatical to figure *that* out." She lifted her coffee cup as if to make a toast. "I bought a horse. I plan to ride to relax."

"Oh. You mean the horse that almost took the trailer apart before you got her unloaded?"

"Yep. That's the one." Cassie met her sister's gaze, careful to keep her expression open.

"I'm sure that'll take your mind off work."

Cassie let out a sigh and leaned her forearms on the table. "What exactly do *you* think I should do?"

"Connect with some friends while you're here?"

"Funny you should mention that, because Darby is driving up from Salt Lake City for a family visit next week and we're getting together." There. One box on the Katie list of things to do better checked off.

"That's a start," Katie admitted, "but not enough. You need to find a balance." She held up a finger as Cassie's mouth automatically opened. "I know that *you* already know that, and you're working out a plan, but I'm worried that you won't follow through. Some emergency will crop up, just as it did last Christmas, and you'll think you're the only person who can solve it. And that will keep happening until your head explodes."

"That was a real emergency." They'd had to fire a teacher for unprofessional conduct, which involved lawyer meetings and developing a contingency plan for covering her classes until a replacement could be hired. Cassie cocked her head at her sister. "Do I really come off as being that stressed?"

"Yes," Katie said simply. "You do. And that means you are."

"Let me get this straight…you're taking out Cassie Callahan." Will gave Travis the look he always gave when trying to shake the truth out of him. It still worked pretty well.

Travis took a seat across from his grandfather at the kitchen table, setting his longneck on the worn oak. "I am." Kind of.

Will tipped back his beer, as if needing fortification before continuing the conversation. After wiping away the foam with his forefinger, he gave Travis another quelling look. "Well, for criminy's sake, don't do anything to tick her off."

"That'd be a neat trick."

"Seriously," Will said.

"We are going out in order to settle a few things between us, because now we're probably going to be seeing more of one another."

"That's real possible," Will agreed. "Rosalie says that Cassie has agreed to come home for the holidays from here on out, and since you spend the holidays with me..."

Yeah. He'd already figured all that out. But Travis sipped his beer and listened as his grandfather continued to explain why he'd see Cassie a whole lot more often than he had in the past.

"I don't want you guys at each other's throats," Will concluded.

"Those days are gone," Travis said simply.

"Good." Will leaned back in his chair, his hand still on his beer. "Rosalie sent us a casserole. All we have to do is take it out of the fridge and put it in the oven for half an hour."

Travis smiled. "She takes good care of you."

"She does."

"Why?"

Will made a face at him. "Darned if I know, but she does."

Which made Will happy, and that in turn made Travis happy. His grandfather had been alone for a long time. Travis didn't know his grandmother, who'd left after two years of marriage and one baby—Travis's father. Travis's parents were doing well in Arizona, where the warm, dry climate helped his father deal with the symptoms of RA, but despite constant contact by phone and email, Will missed having his son around. Another reason Travis had felt compelled to stay on the ranch.

"I imagine that taking-care thing goes two ways," Travis said.

Will nodded. "I'm lucky."

"Yeah." Travis tilted his bottle toward his grandfather. "You are."

"So don't go screwing things up with Cassie," Will said seriously. "It'll upset Rosalie."

"I won't."

"You two have a lot of baggage to sort through."

Travis gave his grandfather a wry half smile before raising his beer. "You're right. Maybe we'll have to have two dates."

"Heaven help us," Will muttered. "I'm just hoping you guys make it through the first one." He fell into silence, one hand on his beer as he stared at the table in front of him. Was he picturing scenarios of mayhem?

Travis decided to probe. No sense having his grandfather worry about stuff that wasn't going to happen. "Anything else weighing on you?"

Will continued to study the table as if debating whether or not to discuss what was on his mind. Then he looked up and blurted, "I don't have anything to wear to my wedding, *and*, looking at the long-term weather forecast, it's probably going to rain anyway."

"Hey, that is good news," Travis said. "You won't have to worry about what to wear as long as you have a raincoat covering everything."

"Ha ha." Will's jawline tensed. "I have to go shopping, blast it, because I'm not wearing no darned raincoat to my wedding."

"I'm not going."

"Guess again."

Will looked so beleaguered that Travis almost laughed. The guy who'd faced off with a cougar that was threatening his favorite dog looked terrified at the prospect of shopping.

"Won't Rosalie help?"

"Of course she will, but I'm not going to do that to her."

"Have you considered the possibility that she might like shopping more than you do?"

"I'm taking care of myself—with your help."

Travis blew out a breath. "Okay. Shopping it is. Anything else?"

"Yeah." Will stared at his beer. "We need to clear out the barn so we can have the festivities inside if it does rain."

Clean out the barn. Right. The labors of Hercules came to mind. The barn acted as storage central and, as such, was packed with equipment, old and new, things that didn't have any better place to be—hay, straw, grain. And everything had a layer of dust at least a quarter-inch thick. "That'll be a job."

"It'll take some doing. I'm going to hire a crew. It's time we sorted through all that junk anyway. It isn't like it's going to just disappear on its own."

Travis let out a silent breath of relief. "I'm going to be honest with you, Grandpa. I won't fight you on that front." Not the crew, nor the sorting.

"I figured that on top of everything else, we just don't have the time. *We* meaning you, of course."

"You're retired." He wanted his grandfather to enjoy his retirement and it wasn't much of a retirement if he spent all of his time at the ranch.

Will nodded and went silent again.

Travis was about to find out what else was on his mind when his grandfather raised his gaze, meeting Travis's eyes with the very same expression he'd worn when he'd laid down the law about driving his "good" truck when Travis was sixteen. "And for Pete's sake, don't go drawing any lines in the sand with Cassie when you go on this date or whatever it is. Just…make peace."

"That's why we're going out. To address the past and set a path for future interactions."

"That's why you mean to go out, but when she tells you she can do something better than you, what are you going to do?"

"We're not ten."

"You were still doing that when you were twenty."

"Okay. We're not twenty. We'll work things out. I promise."

CHAPTER FOUR

TREMAINE'S DINER HAD CHANGED.

Cassie arrived early, but couldn't find a parking place in the lot behind the once notorious eatery. She'd frequented the place as a teen, because the food was cheap, and it was never crowded. Being more interested in socializing than in pleasing their palates, she and her friends had spent many an afternoon or evening in "Ptomaine's," laughing, gossiping, plotting and planning.

Cassie's dark secret was that, even though she'd complained along with her friends, she'd secretly loved the frozen pizza they'd tried to pass off as homemade. Her freezer was currently stocked with the same brand, but while she might still eat the pizza, she hadn't laughed or gossiped in a long time.

She missed having close friends, but the circumstances of her job made that difficult. Healthy dinners had turned into frozen pizzas, and weekends with friends had turned into marathon cleaning/laundry/finishing work from the office sessions as she rose through the ranks and strove to prove herself while simultaneously taking classes for an advanced degree.

While she'd been busy furthering her career, many of the friends she'd made while teaching had moved on, taking jobs in districts that offered more pay, or following spouses to other areas of the country. The same had happened in Gavin. Even Darby and Shelby—her two high school friends who had laughingly called themselves the Busy Bees—had settled elsewhere despite their resolve to stay in Gavin forever.

So here she was in a lonely, pizza-overloaded phase of her life. It was time to regroup, learn how to take better care of herself. Perhaps it was a good thing that she'd eased into a sabbatical she wouldn't have taken otherwise. Silver linings abounded.

After finding a parking spot on the street, Cassie got out of her car and smoothed her tiered skirt, then started down the sidewalk, only to stop when she heard her name. A little jolt went through her at the sound of Travis's voice.

Enough of that.

There would be no knee-jerk reactions tonight. She and Travis were adults, and she hadn't acted like an adult at the auction. She'd acted like her teenage self, facing a line in the sand that Travis had drawn. Only he hadn't.

Not her proudest moment.

After all the personnel management classes she'd taken, she should be able to handle a night out with her former nemesis. They'd both grown and changed and now they needed to get to a place of understanding so that old habits could be pushed aside. But if that didn't work, she'd pretend that he was a difficult parent. An unknown entity that she needed to find common ground with, and in many ways, Travis was an unknown entity. Yes, she'd known him back in the day, but only on a competitive level. For obvious reasons they'd never let down their guards and really talked.

As she turned toward him, she curved her mouth into her professional smile. The one that didn't make it to her eyes but gave an indication that she was willing to listen and search for solutions in a cooperative manner. One of her colleagues once told her that her professional smile kind of scared him. She'd taken it as a compliment at the time. She didn't want to frighten children, but adults with an ax to grind—that was a different story.

"You're early," Travis commented as he caught up with her. Everything about him seemed relaxed, from his easy smile to his loose gait as they fell into step. Cassie wondered if he was really relaxed or faking it. She was faking it. She, who met with angry individuals on a regular basis and had spoken in front of the state legislature, was far from relaxed.

"You appear to be even earlier." He hadn't driven onto the street, so he must have been already parked and waiting.

"Yeah. Grandpa needs me to look at plumbing in his town house, so I left the ranch early, but not early enough. I'll have to see to it later."

"He bought a town house?" Cassie asked in surprise. The town houses in Gavin were few and far between, but there was a row near the community college.

"No. That's what he calls his house in town, and I'm not going to try to change his mind."

"I can't fault you there."

Will was notoriously stubborn, although her grandmother seemed to have made progress on several fronts. According to Katie, Rosalie had told Will in no uncertain terms not to rescue her while she was doing battle with her bull-headed neighbor, Vince Taylor, or the county commission, who'd thrown up roadblocks when the family had tried to replace a washed-out bridge the previous summer.

"You look nice," he said, glancing down at her swirly chiffon skirt—her go-to outfit for anything that didn't require jeans or a business suit. Skirts were comfortable and covering. She loved them.

She cast an eye over Travis before saying, "Thank you. So do you." And not only because of his pressed white shirt, well-fitting jeans, polished boots and the trophy buckle she recognized as the one he'd won for being the Montana High School Rodeo saddle bronc champion.

He'd still been somewhat boyish at twenty-five, the last time she'd seen him, but there was nothing boyish about him now. His dark brown hair was more closely cropped and those blue eyes of his seemed a touch more world-weary. She suspected that her eyes were kind of the same.

He was taller than she remembered, his shoulders broader, and his face had hollowed out in all the right places, giving him cheekbones to die for. Cassie absently touched her own more rounded cheeks, then dropped her hand.

So, he was good-looking. Big deal. She knew a lot of good-looking guys. She was on a peace-keeping mission. Nothing more, nothing less. Therefore, when they reached for the door at the same time and ended up practically holding hands as they vied for control of the handle, she should not have felt that plume of warmth flow through her. Embarrassment? Or something else?

Embarrassment. Travis's hands might be warm and strong, but they were also off-limits.

A small dust devil whirled by, billowing Cassie's chiffon skirt and tipping the balance of power. She instantly relinquished her hold on the metal handle to push the fabric into place, and Travis took advantage, opening the door.

"Well played," she murmured as she walked past him into the foyer, accepting his nano-victory in good grace. She stopped just inside the door, and Travis had to sidestep to keep from bumping into the back of her. "Wow."

"It's changed," Travis agreed.

It had indeed. Gone were the former pizzeria's red vinyl booths with the duct-taped seats, the sagging red gingham curtains and the worn tile floor. In their place were booths made of dark wood with cream-colored padded cushions. The lighting was low, unlike the glaring zillion-watt bulbs that once lit the place. Cassie hadn't been prepared for a charmingly intimate pricey steak house atmosphere, which made her not-a-date feel like more than it was. What had Katie been thinking, telling her to come here?

"Ptomaine's is no more," she murmured. Travis was close enough that she felt his low laugh more than she heard it and another warm ripple traveled through her.

"Travis." A stunning dark-haired woman stepped from behind the host's station, holding menus and a wine list against her chest. "It's good to see you again."

"Good to see you, too, Brenna. This is Cassie. Nick Callahan's sister."

The woman gave Cassie a bright smile, which closely resembled the smile Cassie gave difficult parents and whining administrators, before guiding them to a table in the corner. Cassie sensed an air of possessiveness, but years of training kept her from saying, *Honey, he's all yours.*

Brenna presented Travis the beverage menu after they were seated. "Andie will be here in a few minutes to take your drink orders."

Travis murmured a thank-you and the dark-haired beauty drifted back to her station.

"There are a lot of people here," Cassie said as she surveyed the room. There was only one other empty table and it was barely six o'clock.

"Popular place."

"But maybe not the best place to discuss business." Really, it wasn't. "Why are we here?"

"You suggested it," he said innocently.

"No," Cassie said as she picked up the drink

menu. "My sister suggested it." A matter they were going to discuss when she got home.

Travis gave a casual shrug. "We can discuss business elsewhere after we eat."

Prolong the evening? Fat chance of that happening. Not when she was dealing with the unfamiliar sensations of finding Travis attractive. As it was, dinner was starting to feel like a mistake. She hated that he had this effect on her, because she didn't know how to counter it other than pretending it wasn't happening.

"I think we can manage to conduct our business here," Cassie replied coolly. "Make it an early night." As opposed to dragging things on.

"Do you need to get home?"

"Yes. I… Yes." Cassie gave a firm nod. Of course, she needed to get home.

She glanced up as the server approached the table, then blinked. Had Brenna changed clothes? Because a moment ago she'd been wearing a black sweater and camel skirt with boots, and now she was wearing dark pants and a white shirt.

Travis laughed at her stunned expression, but not in an unkind way. "Andie. Hi. I'm going to have Jameson. Neat."

Andie. Not Brenna. They had a twin situation going on.

"Hi," Cassie said. "I'll have a gin and tonic. Sapphire."

After Andie left, Travis adjusted his chair and leaned his elbows on the table. "I assume we're not here to spend the evening battling over the door handle."

"I hope not. Nice metaphor, by the way." Cassie murmured.

"Thank you." He cocked an eyebrow at her. "I was valedictorian, you know."

"Yet you ended up working on a ranch."

A shadow crossed his face, and Cassie was instantly ashamed of herself. "I told myself I wasn't going to jab at you. I apologize."

"I told myself the same thing, yet here we are, two jabs in and the score is tied."

She refrained from reminding him that he'd won the door-handle skirmish. "That's why we're here—to work through this."

His eyes crinkled attractively at the corners. "Do you think we can?"

Cassie forced herself to stop admiring his eyes, but there was something about the way he was regarding her that made her breathing go shallow. "I think we have to. We're going to see each other more often than before what with Grandma and Will getting married."

"So, you plan to come home every now and then?"

He spoke lightly, but the congenial attitude they'd shared for almost twenty seconds evaporated. Cassie's jaw muscles began to tighten even as she tried to convince herself that not every word that came out of his mouth was a dig.

"Yes," she said simply, having learned early in her career that the more one spoke, the more possibilities there were for someone to grab on to something to bolster their argument.

"That will make Rosalie happy."

Meaning, of course, that her absence was making Rosalie unhappy. Unfortunately, that was true. Cassie could have come forth with her justifications for missing holidays with the family, or for cutting them short, but she wasn't here to convince Travis that her career and family decisions had been correct.

"That was a statement of fact, not a jab," Travis said, easily reading her.

Before she could answer, Andie approached with the drinks.

"Thank you," Cassie murmured, glad that she ordered something alcoholic to help calm her ridiculously jumpy nerves. Andie smiled back at her, then set the whiskey in front of Travis.

"Anything else?" she asked brightly.

"I think we're good," Travis said before lifting his glass in a silent salute at Cassie.

"Are we?" Cassie asked, reaching for her drink as Andie headed off to another table.

"For now."

The gin was sharp on her tongue, but she rather liked the effect. It matched her mood. "So that honestly wasn't a jab about never coming home?" Because it had felt like one.

"I understand that you have a time-consuming job."

"More like all-consuming."

"Do you like it that way?" he asked with a faint frown, as if ranching wasn't also an all-consuming job.

"I accept it," she said matter-of-factly. "Because I like my job."

A silence fell, but Cassie was in no hurry to break it. Instead she gently swirled the ice in her drink as she waited for Travis to make the next move.

Travis leaned his forearms on the table and said, "Here's how I see our situation. We've spent so many years in competition that we've developed something of a Pavlovian response between us. Time has not softened it."

"Apparently not."

"Because we're working from old data. We don't know each other—not the adults we've become."

"Good point. What do you suggest?"

One corner of his mouth curved up in an expression close to the smirk she was so familiar with, but this wasn't a smirk. It was more of a dangerous smile, but dangerous how? Something low in the pit of her belly told her it was dangerous in a way she'd never considered him dangerous before and it had to do with the tug of attraction. "We either pretend we don't rub one another the wrong way while we're around family, or we do something about it."

"Neither of us seems to be very good at pretending," Cassie pointed out wryly as she smoothed her fingers over the stem of her glass. Which was odd, because she had no issue keeping her emotions in check in the course of her job.

"We need to spend time together. The setting doesn't matter."

"It'd probably be best if there were no witnesses, right?" She wasn't being facetious.

His eyes narrowed thoughtfully as he considered her comment. "Not in the beginning."

"That way we can duke it out, test our limits? Find out what works?"

"Pretty much." He held her gaze and Cassie had to remind herself to breathe. Why was he having this effect on her?

"Are we ready to order?"

Cassie jumped. She had been so focused on

Travis that she hadn't noticed the server approaching. She also had yet to crack the menu. "I'll have what he's having," she said politely, noting that the server wasn't a clone of Andie and Brenna. No triplet.

"I'm going to have a cheeseburger."

"Perfect," Cassie murmured. He could have said he was having a sandpaper sandwich and she would have agreed just to get the ordering over with.

"No steak?"

Cassie wondered if he knew that she loved a good steak, or if he'd made the suggestion because they were in a steak house. "A cheeseburger."

Travis set his menu on top of Cassie's. "Two cheeseburgers. The works."

"Excellent choice," the server said without a hint of irony as she gathered up the menus.

"Cheeseburgers *are* faster than steaks," Travis commented as the server walked away. "Easier to make it an early night."

So true.

"I'm not trying to escape." Cassie delivered the half-truth with a straight face. "This was my idea, after all. I made first contact."

He planted his elbows on the table. "Then we best get to it. What's the next step?" He gave her a look that said the ball was now in her court.

"You're expecting me to ask you for help with my mare." It seemed obvious, since it was the one thing that could bring them together.

"And you'd prefer to do it yourself."

"No. Not at all." She spread her palms in an I'm-game-for-anything gesture. "I'd be foolish not to take advantage of an expert."

His eyes narrowed as if he suspected a trap. "Uh-huh."

She shrugged. "I've changed…in some ways," she added, since it was obvious that she hadn't changed when it came to sparring with him.

"I noticed."

Maybe it was the gin—no, it was definitely the gin—but Cassie felt a calm come over her. "How so?"

"Well, for one thing, you used to swagger."

"What?" Cassie thought about the way she walked, and she did not swagger.

"It was your attitude," he explained. "You were good, and you knew it." A faint smile curved his lips. "You had to be good to beat me."

She made a face at him. The gin again. "And now?"

"Now you're more…"

"Composed?"

"Stiff."

Her eyebrows lifted. She was not stiff. She was professional.

Her eyes narrowed as she fought with herself, and then she gave in to temptation. "Okay. I may have developed…stiffness…but your cocky attitude seems to have stood the test of time." Even as she used the word, she knew it wasn't accurate. Travis wasn't so much cocky as confident.

His lips curved in a way that made a crazy tremor go through her. "Guilty."

Cassie sighed and leaned back into her chair, then gave him a small salute before draining the contents of her glass. "I'd like help with my mare." She set the glass back on the table as if to seal the deal.

"I will give you that help."

"When do we start?"

"Tomorrow. Before the wedding prep gets in the way. Say ten o'clock?"

Cassie gave a slow nod, then met his gaze. "Very well. Thank you."

"You might not want to thank me until we find out whether we can work together."

"I'll just retreat behind my stiffness and we'll be fine."

"Can you do that?" His lips curved into a smile that made her want to keep staring at his mouth. She tore her gaze away.

"Can you tone down the attitude?"

"I'll give it a shot."

They both looked up as the server approached the table and set two plates containing huge cheeseburgers, each with a heap of golden fries, in front of them.

"Anything else?" she asked brightly.

Travis glanced at Cassie, who shook her head, then said, "I think we're good."

"Better, anyway," Cassie said in a low voice as the server started checking the nearby tables.

Travis caught her meaning and smiled before placing the bun on top of the burger, lifting it and taking a huge bite.

After he put the burger back on his plate and wiped his mouth, Cassie said, "How's your dad doing?"

"Okay," he said. "I mean life is never going to be a picnic with RA, but Arizona agrees with him. He and Mom have a community of friends…and yeah. He's doing well." He picked up his burger. "How are your folks?"

"If things go according to plan, they'll start easing their way out of the clinic and then make the big move back to the States."

"Your stepmom is okay with that?"

Cassie gave a small shrug before taking a bite of the best burger she'd had in forever. She set the thing down to deal with the juice that had dribbled down her chin. "Messy, but excellent. And yes, as far as I know, Frances is fine with emigrating." The deal was that she and Pete, Cassie's dad, would live in Australia until she retired from the veterinary clinic she'd established there, then they would sell and move to the States to be closer to Pete's family, since Frances had no family of her own.

A silence settled in as they dealt once again with their ginormous burgers, then Travis said, "Hear anything from Shelby or Darby lately?"

"I plan to see Darby next week. She's driving up from Salt Lake."

"Ah."

Another silence. Cassie dabbed at her chin again. "How are Amanda and the kids?" Travis's sister had moved out of state a few years ago.

"Good. Good."

It was the first polite conversation they'd engaged in probably forever, and it stretched on between bites—the weather, the new bridge her family had recently put in, Rosalie's store. Superficial topics to which they could give superficial answers.

It was polite. And boring.

Cassie played along, but she was itching to dig deeper, to ask Travis more personal questions, like was he glad he came back to the ranch? From the way he reacted when she'd brought up the ranch, she wondered. But she wasn't going to be the one who broke protocol, although she began to suspect that something else was going on as the topics became more mundane.

"You're trying to out-polite me," she said after he brought up the expansion of the public library.

"Not everything is a competition, Cassie."

"This is. It's like the blinking game. If you bring up enough boring topics, I'll have to choose between firing off a zinger or having my head explode."

"You're right." Travis smiled as he spoke, sending the crazy tremor back into action, but Cassie was ready for it and firmly told herself to get a grip. "We'll delve into deeper topics when we're alone."

"Something to look forward to," Cassie said as she folded her napkin. Oddly, that was true, but only because she wanted to practice not triggering.

They split the check, then made their way to the exit. In the name of peaceful relations, Cassie stood back as Travis opened the door.

"Nice restraint," he said when she didn't make her own grab for the handle.

"Thanks. I'll get the next one." Despite the show of cooperation and camaraderie, she felt unsettled. This had been too easy, and there was something else at play here. Something she didn't quite understand, just like she didn't understand her reaction when Travis's hand casually grazed the small of her back as they stepped out into the sunlight. It was nothing really. Just a small brush of the fingertips, probably an accident, but it sent every one of her nerves into high alert. Yes, he was an attractive guy, but her reaction was over-the-top.

He walked her to her car, stopping next to her door. When he stayed put longer than necessary, she sensed something was up.

"Do you want to get a drink?" he said at last. "Practice some more? Dig into deeper topics with less of an audience?"

Cassie was shaking her head before the last word left his lips. They could spend time together tomorrow after she had time to dissect the reaction she was having to him. Doing so tonight, when she hadn't had time to develop a game plan that involved these new facets of their relationship, was not a good idea.

"I need to get home."

"That was for real?"

She nodded rather than lie aloud. Although, it was real regarding her peace of mind. Travis was triggering her in a different way than before and she needed to figure out how to deal.

"In that case, I guess I'll see you tomorrow."

"Yes." Cassie opened her door as Travis started walking down the street toward his truck. "Good luck with the plumbing," she called after him. It seemed like a friendly thing to do and the more she practiced, the better she'd get.

He turned and took a few backward steps. "Since you won't drink with me, I guess I have no choice but to deal with it tonight."

"Such is life." She opened the door and settled into her seat, her muscles going slack against the cushioned leather as she watched Travis turn and walk down the empty street toward his truck.

He was right. Dealing with one another in a polite way was exhausting. But for her grand-mother's sake, she'd suck it up and make this thing work.

CHAPTER FIVE

TRAVIS CLOSED THE cabinet door under the kitchen sink and got to his feet. The fix was simple enough—the kitchen plumbing would have to be replaced and he imagined the bathrooms would be the same. He'd offer to do it, but with the haying coming up fast, as well as the wedding, it was possible that his grandfather would simply hire the job done. He could afford it. The ranch was doing well, and Will had been careful with his money, to the point that the McGuires offered a four-year scholarship to a deserving student every year. Cassie had been the first recipient, because Will had thought that giving it to Travis wouldn't look right. But the ranch had helped pay for Travis's education, and a rodeo scholarship had covered the rest. They'd both done okay, except that Cassie had used her education, while he only used facets of his.

As Cassie had said earlier when they parted ways, such was life. Situations cropped up; decisions were made. Cassie had chosen her career over family life and he'd done the opposite.

They'd both given up something.

Travis went upstairs to check the bathroom plumbing, his boots echoing on the wooden steps. Things looked good under that cabinet, but he was going to suggest that his grandfather change out all the sink plumbing to keep leaks at bay.

He came back down the stairs and stood for a moment in the living room, debating next moves. It was early and he wasn't ready to drive back to the ranch. Cassie might have said no to a drink, but there was no reason he couldn't stop by the Shamrock Pub and see if his old rodeo friend Gus Hawkins was tending bar. Maybe a beer would help take the edge off, because after his dinner with Cassie, he was just this side of tense. It had been difficult to carry on as usual when he really wanted to interact on a more personal level.

Why was he so drawn to her?

He'd decided long ago that it was more than the sense of protectiveness that had flooded him when she'd taken the facer during graduation, although that had been the turning point. After that, her face and mannerisms had become a source of fascination. He enjoyed the way her eyes narrowed and gleamed as she plotted strategy, and the suspicious tilt of her full lips when she thought he was playing her. More than that, he liked it when she let go and laughed and they shared a moment, however brief.

She hadn't laughed much tonight, but he had enjoyed it when the old Cassie peeked out from behind the professional facade Cassie had erected. He hadn't been kidding when he said that she came off as stiff, and that stiffness, he assumed, was a defense she'd developed to tamp down her natural impulses to accept every challenge, fight every battle. In the professional world, particularly education, an attitude like that might be a hindrance to career advancement, at least until a person reached the upper echelons, and Cassie was all about her career.

And there it was. Cassie. Career. That was what he was up against and a small part of him whispered that it was best to leave things as they were and not complicate both of their lives by engaging.

HAVING GROWN UP RURAL, Cassie did what everyone did when they made a trip to town—she stopped by Hardwick's Grocery to grab a few needed items before driving back to the ranch. Walking the aisles had been remarkably soothing after being on high alert with Travis for over an hour, and when she returned to her car with a bag of life essentials—microwave popcorn, chocolate and the diet soda Katie didn't like—she felt more in control. It was amazing how an hour with Travis had tilted her world. Even more amazing was the fact that she was still thinking about his fingers grazing her back and how she'd responded.

Unacceptable.

Right.

She started her car and headed out of the parking lot, telling herself that she had the situation under control and that tomorrow's session with Travis and the horse was no big deal.

She was approaching the Gavin city limits sign, set a hopeful half mile outside what one would consider the limits of the city, when her phone rang. She answered via her sound system, then pulled off the road as a familiar voice said hello.

"Darby?"

"Yes! I'm in town and I'd love to get together tonight. Is that possible?"

"You're in town? I thought you weren't due until next week." She had a note on her calendar.

"Kind of a spur-of-the-moment thing."

"Imagine that." Cassie's very best friend from high school was also her polar opposite. Darby used to joke that, between the two of them, they made a normal person. Maybe that was why they'd been inseparable.

"I got a call for an interview in Missoula earlier today, and given the current state of my company, I decided I'd better jump on this before my ship sinks."

"I can understand that." Darby worked in the corporate office of a major department store, but online shopping was putting a squeeze on them, and it was anyone's guess as to whether the store would survive. "I bet the job being in Montana doesn't hurt your feelings."

Darby had never wanted to leave Gavin, but career opportunities in their small hometown were minimal. At least Missoula was only a couple of miles away.

"I have my fingers and my toes crossed," Darby said with a laugh. "I know it's a drive for you, but I'd love to talk face-to-face."

"I think this was meant to be because I'm on the edge of town."

"Excellent! I'm at my brother's and he's in the process of going over my car because it's making a funny noise. He does *not* want to go out for a drink when he's done, but I do."

"I'm turning around now."

"Are you talking on the phone while driving?" Darby asked sternly.

"No. I'm not. I pulled off at the city limits. I'll pick you up in five."

"I can't wait to catch up."

It'd be more a matter of Darby catching up with Cassie than vice versa. Darby emailed often, while Cassie kept waiting for the perfect moment to write back. And, stunner, the perfect moment rarely arrived. She communicated, but not as frequently as her friend. For that reason, she would be buying the drinks. One each, because she had a long drive home.

Darby was waiting for her in the driveway and Cassie was struck by how little her friend had changed. Her reddish-brown hair was caught up in the artless bun that suited her angular face, and her bangs brushed her eyebrows as they had since she and Cassie had become besties in the fourth grade. When Darby wore makeup, she was stunning. When she didn't, she was striking. Tonight she was striking.

Cassie had barely gotten out of the car before she got a hug. "It's been too long," Darby said. "You look great."

There was a scuffling sound from under Darby's car and her brother Finn appeared on the other side. "Hey," he said with his easy grin.

"Hey yourself. Are you sure you don't want to come out with us?"

"Are you kidding? Every time I go out with you guys, I end up in trouble."

"Not true."

"Yeah?" He lifted his eyebrows. "Name a time."

"Funny," Darby said with a mock sneer. Then, as she walked with Cassie to the car, she said sotto voce, "You can think of a time, right?"

"Maybe…" Not really. Poor Finn had never done well with the two of them, having gotten into trouble more times than he should have. It wasn't that she and Darby had made trouble…it was more like they'd stumbled into it and Finn followed.

"I'm a rule follower now," Cassie said.

"You've always had a predilection for rules, but lately—" Darby opened the door "—I've noticed an alarming escalation." She grinned at Cassie as she closed her door.

"I can't be in charge of district-wide discipline policies and do some of the stuff we used to do."

"Guess we won't be toilet papering any houses or anything tonight."

"Nope. Not unless I'm certain we won't get caught."

Darby laughed, and Cassie noticed that it wasn't her full-on life-is-great laugh. Having a shaky job situation was stressful. "Where to?" she asked.

"Surprise me."

Cassie put the car in gear. "One surprise, coming up."

"YOU HAD DINNER with Cassie Callahan?" Gus Hawkins, half owner of the Shamrock Pub, set a draft in front of Travis, then wiped the polished wood with a damp towel, taking care not to make eye contact. Probably because he had a stupid smile on his face.

"Our grandparents are getting married, so Cassie and I are putting our rivalry behind us."

"You went to dinner to celebrate this new-found peace?" Gus lifted a skeptical eyebrow, then reached for his water bottle.

"It's a little early for celebration."

"Still have a few kinks to work out?" Gus guessed.

"It is Cassie we're talking about." Travis picked up his beer.

"But things have kind of softened between you, right?"

"Can you imagine them any more tense than they've been?" Back when they'd fed off each other, acting and reacting.

"Not without one of you exploding," Gus said before drifting down the bar to take an order.

"Is Thad okay?" Travis asked when he came back.

Gus frowned at the mention of his great-uncle, who owned the other half of the pub. "Yeah. Why do you ask?"

"I thought you'd given up bartending to ranch full-time."

Gus gave him a self-conscious grin. "Lillie Jean is kind of pregnant and I'm taking the occasional shift to make extra money for baby stuff."

"Kind of pregnant?"

"Not showing, but totally into it. The sewing machine is going full-time."

"And you?"

Gus's smile widened. "It's scary, but exciting. And Thad…" He laughed. "He's been waiting a long time for a great-grandniece or nephew. I think he's going to change the big wooden ranch sign to include the baby's name."

"Better hope he or she wants to ranch."

Gus tipped the water bottle again, then wiped his mouth with the back of his hand. "My kid will want to ranch."

A commotion at the far side of the room brought Gus's head up. Raymond Quentin was being his usual asinine self, trying to hit on Vince Taylor's daughter Mellie. Travis shook his head and focused back on his beer.

"I'll be tossing him out before the night is over," Gus predicted.

"My money is on Mellie. She'll toss him out."

Gus laughed. Mellie was a princess, but not someone to mess with. "More like neuter him. I think it's going down now."

Indeed. She said something to Ray, his face went red and then he made a sneering reply before heading back to his laughing group of friends near the pool tables. From the shoulder punching and finger pointing, it was fairly obvious that a bet had been made and that Ray had failed in his mission.

Travis turned back to the bar, but Gus watched for a few seconds more before turning his attention back to his friend. The place was busy, but not so much so that Gus couldn't carry on a conversation.

"I hope he's learned his lesson." Gus leaned his shoulder on one of the decorative columns behind the bar. "How are things on the ranch?"

"Busy." Travis tipped his mug. "And the wedding will be on the ranch, so that just adds to the…"

His words trailed and his beer mug didn't quite reach his lips before he put it back down again.

"What?" Gus asked, automatically looking to the door.

"Nothing." Except that his dinner date, the one who had to go home, wasn't at home. She was here. Cassie and her friend Darby stopped inside the door, exchanged looks, then made their way to a table.

"Right," Gus said. "Listen. If you guys challenge one another tonight, make it pool or darts. *Not* drinking, okay?"

Travis gave his friend a dark look.

"Old habits can be hard to break," Gus said before tilting up his water bottle.

Travis's mouth curled into a smirk. "Thanks for the moral support."

"Anytime." Gus punctuated the words with a couple of swipes of the bar rag, then headed down the bar to where a patron waited at the far end.

Travis had a couple of choices. He could have his drink at the bar and slip out, or he could amble over and have a pleasant word with Cassie. She hadn't gone home. Big deal.

But why couldn't she have simply said that she had plans?

Because her plans are none of your business.

He was about to turn back to the bar, when Cassie spotted him from across the room, and from the way her eyes widened and her lips parted for a brief instant, it appeared that she was having a small attack of the guilts. Travis stepped down off his stool. Best to clear the air. No hard feelings and all of that.

"No bar fights," Gus said in a half-serious voice.

Travis lifted a hand to indicate he'd heard, then wound his way through the tables toward Cassie and Darby. This was an excellent time to practice the fake politeness of which they spoke.

"I DON'T BELIEVE IT," Cassie said in a low voice. Darby—who was surreptitiously watching Ray Quentin, a man she'd once disastrously dated believing that he was misunderstood and redeemable—followed her gaze.

"Oh," she said simply. "It's Travis."

"It is. I had dinner with him and told him I was going home."

"I guess he knows that's not true," Darby said.

"Guess so." Did she owe him an explanation? In the name of peaceful relations, she might.

Darby gave her a perplexed look. "You had dinner with him?"

Cassie gripped her drink with both hands, the ice in the gin and tonic the server had just delivered chilling her fingers. "We are on the cusp of developing a new working relationship."

"Meaning?"

"When we're around family, we'll be nice to

one another." She didn't mention the part about spending time together to practice getting along, because she was still mulling over the situation in her head.

"That will be new and different."

Cassie gave her friend a look, then glanced up as Travis neared the table. "Hey," she said when he was close enough to hear. "Guess I owe you an explanation."

"Nope."

He honestly looked as if he didn't want to hear one, but she continued to explain, just so that the facts were out there. "Darby called as I was leaving town."

"You don't owe me an explanation," he said firmly, which made her feel more self-conscious than before, as if she was protesting too much, which she was.

"Right." She lifted her chin. "Would you like to join us?"

Travis shook his head. "I'm catching up with Gus. But thanks."

"Why'd you come over?" She had to ask, even though she had a feeling she was going to regret doing so.

"So that you wouldn't feel self-conscious about being here after saying you were going home."

Her cheeks began to heat as she said, "Oh."

She wasn't used to being thrown off her game by someone being nice, and it was kind of annoying. "Thank you."

"You're welcome. See you later." He gave her a cool nod, then smiled at Darby. "Good to see you, Darby."

"Yeah," Darby echoed with a smile. As soon as Travis was out of earshot, she leaned closer and said, "How is he still single?"

"I guess," Cassie said through her teeth so no one could hear her, "that the right woman hasn't come along."

"Huh." Darby took a sip from her drink. She glanced at Ray again. "I hope he doesn't notice me."

"Do you want to leave?" Because Cassie wouldn't mind leaving one bit.

"After my drink." She lifted her diet cola. "I'm not going to let a blast from the past keep me from doing what I want to do."

"Good for you." But having Travis and Ray there had put a damper on their moods. "When will you be driving back through Gavin?"

"The interview is tomorrow at one, if Finn gets my car up and running. If not, I'll borrow his. I'll be back tomorrow evening or early the next morning. I'm burning vacation days for this, but I'm afraid that if I don't, I'll be getting those vacay days in a severance package, so I don't mind."

"That's tough."

Darby drew in a breath and exhaled. "It's the way it goes. But maybe this is a silver-lined cloud. I'd really like to get something closer to home." She picked up her drink, then sipped through the straw. "I'd like to live here, so that I'm closer to family, but I'll never find anything in my field here." Like Katie, Darby had built a career in the human resources department of her company, but specialized in recruiting. Unfortunately, as business decreased, so did recruiting opportunities.

"Do you like your field?" Darby frowned and Cassie continued, "Katie quit her corporate job and started fresh. She's really happy."

"She also has a ranch to live on rent-free."

"True. I wasn't trying to make it sound easy. But if you're going to change jobs, you might take a long hard look at what you want to do for the next decade. Maybe you want to continue in your chosen field, maybe not."

"My job is my job. I'm happy working nine to five and starting my real life after the workday is over." She stirred the ice in her drink with the straw. "But you're lucky to have found something you love."

Something I love that is on the verge of giving me ulcers.

The thought crept into Cassie's head, and she ushered it right back out again. All jobs had their ups and down, their pros and cons.

"I am," she said simply.

"Hey, Darby. Knocked anything over lately?" Darby's hand jerked at the sound of Ray Quentin's voice from directly behind her, sending her diet coke flying. Ray started laughing as Cassie jumped to her feet while Darby sat staring at the cola-covered table as if in shock.

"Don't just stand there laughing like an idiot," Cassie growled. "Go to the bar and get something to clean this up."

"I'm not cleaning up." Ray gave her an incredulous look.

Cassie drew herself up to her full administrator height. "Yeah. You are. This is your fault. You need to help take care of it." From the corner of her eye she saw Darby shake the cola off her hands and then get to her feet.

"I'll get a bar rag," she said.

"Don't." Cassie spoke in a no-nonsense voice. Darby did not need to clean up her ex's mess, but her friend ignored her and headed across the room. But at least she was out of harm's way.

Cassie brought her attention back to Ray. She had to tip her head back to do so, but she'd stared down more than one big blowhard in her career. Most of them crumbled. Eventually.

Ray puffed out his chest and stepped closer. "How is Darby's clumsiness my fault?" he asked in a low voice.

Cassie raised her eyebrows. "You purposely scared her to get laughs from your friends. Kind of low-hanging fruit, wouldn't you say? Can't you do better?" All her training had taught her not to draw lines in the sand. Not to set up a situation where a person had to act in order to avoid being humiliated.

It felt good to ignore her training and go with her gut. This jerk had hurt Darby for the last time.

"You might be surprised at what I can do."

She sensed someone coming up behind her and gave a quick glance over her shoulder before immediately reestablishing eye contact with Ray. "I've got this," she muttered to Travis, who was now standing at her shoulder.

"You don't," he murmured back.

"Leave this to me," Cassie said. She meant it.

"You are in over your head," Travis whispered as they both stared down Ray. "Gus will take care of this."

"Then why are you here?"

Ray had watched their between-the-teeth exchange with a look of growing amusement. "Are you here to help, Travis?" he asked in a loud voice.

"Travis, please. Let me handle this," Cassie said without looking at him. She felt him move closer instead of farther away.

"Travis, *please*," Ray said in a mocking voice. "Go back to your bar stool and let the little woman handle this. Or should I say..." His mouth twisted into an ugly smirk before he completed the sentence with a word that few people said in public. Even in a bar.

Something snapped in Cassie's brain as the word left his liver lips, and before she was aware of moving, the contents of her glass covered the front of Ray's plaid cowboy shirt. Ice cubes clattered on the table and fell to the floor at his feet.

Cassie's gaze jerked down at her empty glass. Had she really just done that?

Another ice cube clinked to the floor.

Oh yes, she had.

Ray looked down at his shirt, took a moment to flick away the lime wedge caught on his trophy rodeo buckle, then slowly raised his gaze.

His eyes were like black bits of coal on the edge of igniting. Travis's hand settled on Cassie's shoulder as Ray shoved the table out of the way, leaving nothing between the two of them but air and anger. Travis pulled, Cassie dug in, more because her brain had frozen than because she wanted to stand in front of the human equivalent of an angry bull.

"Move!" Travis pushed her to one side and her shoe hit the spot where the drink had landed, causing her foot to skid sideways. She almost went down, hitting her elbow on the table before she clutched at it and righted herself. As she fought to catch her balance, she got bumped again, then heard the distinctive sound of a fist connecting with flesh. Travis's flesh.

Ray reared back to swing again, but Travis launched himself at the man, catching him off-balance. He grabbed ahold of Ray's arm as the man staggered and wrenched it up between his shoulder blades. Ray let out a roar, but Travis held fast.

"Back off, Cassie," Travis said from between clenched teeth.

For once in her life, she did as Travis said, moving numbly away from the two men. Darby took hold of her arm and pulled her to the edge of the circle of people who were trying to get a closer look at the action.

"Don't even think about it," Gus Hawkins said to Ray's friends as he came around the bar with his small bat. He needn't have bothered, as they were in the process of drifting toward the rear exit, abandoning their buddy.

"If he'll go peacefully, just let him leave with

his friends," Travis said, the strain of holding the man reflected in his voice.

"You have to call the authorities," Cassie said. "You can't let him get away with this."

"Let him leave," Travis repeated in a deadly voice.

"There's a deputy on his way," Gus said to Ray. "If I were you, I'd be gone before he gets here."

"You gonna file charges?"

"Am I going to see you in here anytime soon?"

"No." Ray practically spit the word.

Gus nodded and Travis slowly released the man.

Ray rolled his shoulders before turning to Cassie and giving her a look that made her back up a half step. Then the big man abruptly turned and stalked toward the door his friends had slipped out.

Travis was breathing hard. When the door closed behind Ray, he put his hands on his thighs and dropped his head to catch his breath.

"Sorry I didn't get out here sooner," Gus said. "I was dealing with a faulty tapline in the basement when Darby came barreling down the stairs to get me." He, too, was breathing hard.

"No worries," Travis said.

No worries if you didn't count the fact that his face was swelling up at an alarming rate.

"You should have pressed charges," Cassie said. "He assaulted you."

Travis raised his head to give her a cold look. "And you committed a battery."

"What?" She glanced at Gus, who nodded.

"Throwing a drink is assault," he said grimly. "You're an educator and with social media being what it is, and all his friends filming with their phones—"

Cassie raised her hands. "I get it." There was nothing the people she'd crossed in her school district would like better than to have some ammo against her. "I…I'm so sorry, Gus."

"You didn't start it," he said gruffly.

Travis said nothing. He simply stood with a grim expression on his rapidly swelling face. She couldn't tell if he was angry at her or Ray or the way things had gone down, but he was definitely fuming. "Do you want to go to the clinic?" she asked in a small voice.

"I do not."

"It's over, folks," Gus said to the gawking patrons who hadn't resumed drinking. "Sorry about the disturbance. The guy's lucky Thad wasn't here."

The mention of his elderly uncle got a few laughs and people once again settled into their seats. Darby and the server busied themselves wiping up the mess that Cassie and Ray had made, leaving Cassie to face Travis.

Before she could stutter out some of the words swirling through her brain, he met her gaze dead-on. "Don't say a word."

She said a word. "Fine."

His mouth flattened as he once again ran a hand over his swelling eye, causing a wave of guilt to wash over her. She'd allowed herself to lose control and Travis had paid the price.

"I'm so sorry," Darby said to Travis after the server had taken the wet cleaning towel from her and headed back to the bar. "I didn't mean—"

"This isn't your fault," Travis interrupted in a gentler tone. He briefly met Cassie's gaze, shook his head, then turned and walked back to the bar. Gus pushed the table back into place and righted a chair that had been knocked over.

"We need to leave," Cassie said to Darby, who still seemed to be shaking off the shock of what had happened.

"I'll walk you to your car," Gus said. "Just in case."

"Thank you," Cassie and Darby murmured at the same time.

As they reached the door, Cassie glanced back to see Travis accepting a plastic bag of ice from the pretty sever, which he then pressed to his face. He didn't look at her, but he must have seen her in the mirror behind the bar, because she swore his shoulders tightened before she finally pulled her gaze away and went out the door Darby was holding open.

"Not your fault," her friend said after they were safe in the car. "Things just…happened."

"Thanks."

But regardless of whose fault it was or wasn't, she owed Travis McGuire one big apology and that was not a comfortable feeling.

TRAVIS MUTTERED A low curse when he rounded the last corner before the ranch and saw that the lights were still on. Of all the nights for his grandfather, who was usually in bed by nine unless he went to a county commissioner meeting, to stay up, it had to be tonight, when Travis was in no mood to answer questions. His grandfather wasn't a man who was easily put off when he wanted answers, and Travis was fairly certain that he'd want to know why his grandson was returning from a date with a black eye.

Maybe Will had fallen asleep watching TV.

Travis shot a look at the dash clock. It wasn't that late, but Will was a creature of habit. In bed by nine at the latest. It was ten thirty. A whisper of hope went through him.

If Will was asleep, then he could slip into the

house and up the stairs to his bedroom undetected, and then he could deal with the inevitable black-eye questions in the morning, because they were coming. He'd still have the black eye, but he'd also have time to cool down. The slow drive home had allowed him time to fume and his anger was still simmering.

He was ticked at himself for not intervening as soon as he saw Ray Quentin leave his friends, his target obviously Darby, his former girlfriend. Maybe he could have headed the man off. And he was angry at Cassie for not backing down from a dangerous situation after Darby had removed herself from harm's way.

How hard would it have been to step back when he got there instead of facing off with that mountain? He might have been able to defuse the situation if she had. It wouldn't have been the first time he and Ray had exchanged pleasantries in the bar, and he'd always been able to bring the man around to his way of thinking. But no.

But he couldn't blame Cassie for throwing the drink. It'd been all he could do not to throttle the man when the filthy word left his lips, but instead he focused on getting Cassie out of the line of fire—which put him directly into it.

Mostly, though, he was angry with Ray Quentin and there wasn't anything he could do about it. If he'd had Ray charged, then Ray would have retaliated against Cassie, and Travis wasn't going to have that.

Better to have Ray banned from the bar.

Travis eased open the kitchen door, hoping the blare of the television would drown out the sounds of him slipping through the kitchen, but instead he heard the distinctive heavy tread of his grandfather's socked feet crossing the living room.

Excellent. Short of switching off the light and making a dash for the stairs under the guise of desperate times calling for desperate measures, he had no choice but to collect himself and calmly answer questions.

"How'd the date go?" Will asked as he walked into the room.

"Not exactly as planned." Travis pulled off his hat and raised his chin, and Will let out a sharp exclamation.

"Did Cassie Callahan do that?" Will's shocked expression would have been comical under different circumstances.

"Not purposely." He'd give her that.

His grandfather approached slowly, as if a bruised eye was contagious. He put a finger to Travis's chin and turned his head slightly.

"That's going to be one nice shiner. Who did it?"

"Ray Quentin. Long story."

"I have nothing but time," Will said, standing back and regarding his grandson with a perplexed frown.

Travis turned to hang his hat on the hooks by the door, then succinctly outlined the events in the bar. Ray had picked on Darby; Cassie had jumped to her defense. Ray called her a filthy name and Cassie had then assaulted Ray with her drink. Shortly thereafter, Travis was the proud bearer of a swollen eye.

When he was done, Travis idly rubbed his hand over the sore spot. There really wasn't much more to say than that he was pretty ticked off with Cassie taking her stubborn stand and Will didn't need to know that.

"Want to put a steak on that?"

"Maybe an ice pack," Travis allowed, heading to the freezer and pulling out a frozen bag of peas. Close enough.

"Do I dare ask how dinner went?"

"Well enough. Cassie didn't start any fights. There." Travis sucked in a breath as the cold plastic made contact with his tender flesh.

"Sounds like there were extenuating circumstances in the bar."

"Yeah. And if she'd backed down instead of drawing a line, then maybe... I don't know."

He wasn't going to get into it with his grandfather. "It's done."

"Is it?"

Travis pressed the peas more firmly to the rapidly numbing side of his face. "For now. Yes."

"And later?"

Good question. Excellent question.

"Don't worry. We'll work things out." He pressed the peas more firmly to his eye as the cold numbed the flesh.

Will gave a short snort. "I can't wait to see what that looks like."

Travis's mouth tightened but he refrained from giving a response, because frankly, he was of the same mind.

CHAPTER SIX

TRAVIS WOKE BEFORE the first pink streaks of dawn appeared above the mountains to the east, the throbbing on the right side of his face making it impossible to sleep. After a few mighty attempts to talk himself into feeling no pain, he lay staring at the ceiling, doing his best to think about anything but Cassie and Ray and the events of the previous evening.

Unfortunately, his sore face kept bringing up the subject.

They were going to talk today. Hash this thing out.

This muddled thing, because he had no idea what his objective was. To not get himself slugged again?

He rubbed a hand over the good side of his face. Cassie was driving him nuts, only in a different way this time. He was angry with her for stubbornly putting herself in harm's way, and the what-ifs had eaten at him during his restless night.

What if, after shoving that table aside, Ray

had taken a swing at Cassie instead of him? The thought chilled him.

Why had he taken so much time to get Cassie out of the line of fire?

And again, why had Cassie not just backed down when he'd told her to?

Because Cassie was never going to do what he told her to do.

The room was growing light when he heard his grandfather in the kitchen, clattering around as he made coffee. His head throbbed when he got to his feet, but felt better after a quick shower.

He inspected the bruise after patting his face dry. Yeah. It was a good one. His eye wasn't swollen entirely shut, but it would be a while before he had any real depth perception. After dressing in his work clothes, he followed the smell of the dark brew into the kitchen and his grandfather let out a low whistle when he saw Travis's face.

"That's bloomed nicely."

Travis gingerly ran his palm over the swelling. "Looks worse that it feels."

Will gave a disbelieving snort and poured Travis a cup of coffee. "What are your plans for the day?"

They started every morning this way. Shared coffee, then an outline of the day before Travis started morning chores. Will rarely ate breakfast, but Travis would grab something during his break between feeding cows and starting whatever was on the top of the to-do list that day.

"I'm heading out later this morning," he said.

"Any place in particular?"

"I…uh…mentioned to Cassie that I'd give her a hand with the McHenry mare."

Will's iron gray eyebrows drew together. "That's nice of you, all things considered."

Travis gave a careless shrug and sipped his coffee. The less said, the better. Will seemed to understand his tactic. He shot his grandson a few suspicious looks, as if wondering what good could possibly come of the two of them working together, but did not resurrect the matter.

After finishing his coffee, Travis put on his boots and hat, shrugged into a light denim jacket and headed out the door. The fresh air felt good against his battered face and he breathed deeply. There were times when the sameness of his days brought a sense of serenity and satisfaction, and other times when he needed something, anything, to break the cycle of boredom that stretched on between ranch emergencies.

Today fell somewhere in the middle. The chores didn't require a lot of thought, but whatever awaited him on the Callahan ranch would not be boring.

CASSIE WAVED GOODBYE to Katie and the girls as they headed out the door on their way to visit Rosalie and Gloria in town, then turned and reached for the coffeepot the second the door closed behind them. Caffeine. Glorious caffeine.

After pouring her third cup of coffee that morning, she leaned back against the counter and held the mug with both hands as she sipped. Despite her exhaustion, she smiled as she watched through the window as Katie loaded the chattering girls into the backseat of her truck. Kendra and Bailey were excited to tell their great-grandmother about the new flowers they'd planted. Katie was excited to meet with the owner of a soon-to-be-opened restaurant about supplying him with fresh herbs and salad greens.

Cassie was excited to be alone.

She'd barely slept, thanks to Ray Quentin and the events of the previous evening, but she'd managed to do a pretty good impersonation of a wide-awake, carefree person while she and Katie made breakfast for the girls and chit-chatted about the upcoming wedding. She and Darby had texted back and forth, both needing reassurance that the other was okay, and Katie had teasingly asked if they'd had a big evening.

Oh, yeah. The biggest.

Cassie closed her eyes and brought the cup

to her lips again. Now that she had the house to herself, she could collapse in peace.

Or not.

Try as she might, she couldn't put the events of the previous evening into perspective, and until she could, she wasn't going to relax.

She'd pushed things with Ray, yes, but she'd done it for Darby, and she hadn't expected things to get physical. In fact, in all her face-offs in all her administrative years, not once had things gotten physical, except for the time that Mrs. Walter hit her husband with her handbag during a contentious meeting. The poor guy had conceded a point Cassie had made and the missus had viewed it as a serious breach of their united front.

By the time Katie got back from town, she'd probably know what had happened in the Shamrock Pub, and then she'd demand to know why Cassie hadn't told her, and Cassie would explain, quite rightly, that she couldn't exactly bring it up while Kendra and Bailey were eating waffles.

For being a person who hated unfinished business, she certainly seemed to have a lot of it of late—her relationship with Travis being top on the list. Last night they'd fought over a door handle, then all but elbowed each other out of the way for the honor of dealing with the jerk who'd harassed Darby. They had a journey ahead of them.

Cassie gave her head a shake as she stared over her cup at the opposite wall. Travis wouldn't have gotten punched if he'd listened to her and let her handle things, but that small truth didn't stop guilt from twisting her gut.

You can't change the past.

Yeah? That unchanged past is going to put a very real spin on the present and you need to deal—just as soon as you figure out how.

A meeting was in order, but she needed to wait for the right time and circumstances. Obviously the horse-training thing wasn't going to happen, which was a shame, because at this point in her life, she was able to acknowledge something that her teen self never would have been able to—Travis knew more about horses than she did. He had more experience, and even back in their rodeo days, when she fearlessly climbed onto whatever mount she chose to ride, he knew more.

Cassie drained the last of her coffee and set the cup in the sink. Instead of feeling groggy, she was now officially buzzed, and she needed to occupy her hands while her mind worked. She rinsed the cup, then moved around the kitchen, wiping surfaces that were already clean, then checked the laundry basket, hopeful for a load or two that needed attention. Nothing.

The garden.

She walked to the window and stared out at the neat rows of greenery that abutted the drive on the far side. Even the most meticulously tended garden had weeds and she would tackle those suckers. A search-and-destroy mission would allow her subconscious to sort through the matters she needed to put in order.

Clouds were building fast to the north, so she slipped on a jacket before letting herself out of the house and heading for the garden. The wind was warm, lifting her hair, but it would no doubt turn cold once the clouds pushed closer. They were in for rain.

The soil in Katie's big garden was damp, but not too damp. Cassie was able to walk between the rows without her rubber shoes sinking too far into the rich soil, but she was also able to easily pull the weeds that she found snuggled in between the vegetables and herbs.

Cassie got to her feet at the end of a row of lettuce, stretching the kinks out of her back, feeling just as guilty as she had when she'd started. She was about to start on the next row when the sound of an engine caught her ear. She crossed to the garden gate and then her heart gave a jolt as she recognized Travis's truck. Automatically she glanced at her watch and saw that it was close to ten o'clock.

The horse? Really?

Or maybe he's come for another reason.

Cassie pushed her hair back as she considered that possibility. She wasn't ready for a face-to-face, but he'd protected her from having assault charges brought against her, and she owed him. The least she could do was to tell him that she was sorry things had turned out as they did.

Cassie's jaw muscles tightened as she made her way to the garden gate as Travis pulled to a stop. *Relax.*

Yeah, yeah, yeah. How was she supposed to relax when she could see Travis's black eye through the windshield of his truck?

Small droplets of rain began to wet the ground as Travis parked and Cassie worked her way along the row of lettuce to the gate. He was waiting for her when she got there and for a moment all she could do was to stare at his colorful and very painful-looking eye.

"Travis, I'm sorry."

It was as if she hadn't spoken.

The wind whipped over them in a sudden gust and Cassie caught her hair on either side of her neck until it passed. Fat drops of rain started beating around them, splattering on her light jacket and making dark spots on Travis's felt hat. He jerked his head toward the barn, and she nodded before letting herself out of the garden and following him to the old wooden structure. Normally she didn't accept being ordered around—even silently—but given the circumstances, she made an exception. He opened the main door and she followed him through.

Rain began to pound the roof in earnest as he shut the door. Cassie let out a breath and shook her arms to dislodge the water droplets.

"About last night," Travis started, and Cassie lightly shook her arms again, her stomach tightening now that they were about to get into the meat of the matter. "What is *wrong* with you?"

Her chin snapped up. "I said I was sorry you got involved. You should have let me handle it."

Travis's mouth opened, then closed again so hard that his lips went white. Cassie would have shifted her weight if she hadn't taught herself long ago not to give such an obvious tell.

"It's my fault?"

Her eyebrows lifted. "I didn't invite you over. You showed up."

Travis rolled his eyes to the ceiling. "You are a piece of work, Cassie Callahan."

"What does that mean?" she asked, planting her fists on her hips.

"It means—" he stabbed a finger at her "—that

you are so relentlessly sure of yourself that you are blind to reality."

Wind rattled the barn as she stared at him, searching for words. She had so many to choose from, so many withering ways to bring him down. She pushed them all aside. "What reality?"

"The reality of Ray Quentin doing you bodily harm."

"In a public place? With witnesses?" But even as she spoke, she knew her argument was weak. He'd practically thrown the table that had separated them.

Travis lifted his forefinger and lightly tapped his eye.

"Admit it. You got in too deep to save yourself."

"I don't think he would have hit me." She didn't. "I think he would have called me more foul names. He likes hurting women by humiliating them."

Travis threw up his hands. "I can't believe you."

"That goes two ways," Cassie said, her voice rising. That was a mistake. Yelling was a form of weakness, but she didn't seem able to stop herself. "I was dealing with matters. You butted in."

"I was trying to save *your* butt." Now Travis was yelling.

"You didn't *need* to save my butt."

A sudden gust of wind swept over them, and they turned toward the door, which must have blown open.

"You two should be ashamed of yourselves." Will McGuire stood in the doorway, the wind coming in from behind him.

"Grandpa—"

"I could hear you guys over the storm, for Pete's sake." He stepped inside and closed the door behind him.

"I thought you were working in your shop," Travis said.

"Rosalie called and asked me to bring her some things she forgot here." Will pointed a finger at Travis's chest. "I thought you were supposed to be helping Cassie with her mare."

Cassie shot Travis a look. That was news to her.

"We needed to talk," Travis said.

"Some talk." Will looked like steam was about to roll out of his ears. "I will not have Rosalie getting upset because you guys can't stop sniping at one another. Do you hear me? I won't have it." Now Will was yelling.

"Yes," Travis said.

Will turned a truly frightening look toward Cassie, obviously waiting for a response. "Yes," she muttered, feeling like she had when she was fifteen and had been caught toilet papering a house with Darby.

"I don't care how you work this out, but you *will* work it out. You guys need to figure out a way to get through this wedding without Rosalie suspecting that you want to tear each other's throats out. Got it?"

Travis's mouth was a hard, flat line, and Cassie suspected that he was as embarrassed as she was, being taken to task by his grandpa. He shot Cassie a look, which she met dead-on. "We'll work on it," she said directly to Travis. Challenge made.

"Then get it done. Duke it out after I leave. I don't care." He shook a finger. "Just…work things out." He let out one final ferocious breath, then turned and stalked out the door, banging it shut behind.

TRAVIS HAD THE OPTION of following his grand-father out of the barn, getting into his truck and driving away. Working things out with Cassie could be as easy as keeping a wide berth at family events. He had the self-discipline to do that.

But he wasn't going to.

"Well?" He tossed the word out to see if Cassie would take control of the situation.

Cassie squeezed her forehead, looking as if

she wanted to be anywhere but where she was. It was the first time he could honestly say he'd seen the fight go out of her. His grandfather had done in a matter of minutes what he hadn't been able to do in a decade of competition. He'd shut Cassie down.

"What do we do about this?" he asked when she refused to take the ball and run with it as he'd expected.

"Fake it." She spoke as if it was a no-brainer.

Travis shook his head.

"Why not?"

"Because," he said as he hooked a thumb in his pocket, "we'll do exactly what we did last night. Start off pretty decently, and then spiral into old habits."

That earned him a frown. "Do you really think we lack the self-control to make it through family functions?"

"Yeah. I do."

"Come on," she said in a scoffing tone.

He spread his hands in an are-you-kidding-me? gesture.

Her mouth flattened as she looked away. "We can do it. I don't see any other way."

So it seemed. Travis raised his gaze to the cobwebbed floor of the loft above him, debating next moves, and then it struck him. Either a possible solution or the beginning of a battle royale.

Regardless, it was a way for him and Cassie to spend time together without witnesses and do some good at the same time. Plus, Cassie hadn't thought of it.

He lowered his gaze and found Cassie studying him with a perplexed and somewhat suspicious frown. "We're going do something to convince my grandfather that we can cooperate for more than two or three minutes."

"Work with my mare?" He could tell from her tone that she knew that wasn't the answer, but she hoped it was.

He gave his head a slow shake. "That's not enough."

"What is enough?"

"It's supposed to rain the weekend of the wedding."

"I know," she said with a frown. "Grandma said that Will is hiring a crew to clean out the barn in case the forecast is correct."

Travis shook his head. "No. Grandpa was *going* to hire a crew, but I don't think he should do that when there are two able-bodied people who can do the job."

She gave him a sharp look and he nodded.

"You and I will clean out the barn. We will

work in harmony, demonstrating our ability to get along."

"We will." She spoke flatly, but it was more of a question than a statement.

"Yes."

Her full lips twisted dubiously, teasing out the dimple at the corner of her mouth. "Are you okay?" she asked with a sudden frown, and he realized he was staring at her mouth.

Heat rose from his collar as he shifted his gaze and cleared his throat. The push-pull he experienced with this woman was driving him nuts. He was drawn to her, but he didn't know how to interact with her. Old habits were getting in the way.

And maybe it was that realization that softened his voice as he said, "We suck at faking it, Cassie. Let's work this out."

To his surprise, instead of arguing, Cassie took a seat on a straw bale, loosely cupping her hands as she focused on the dirty floorboards beneath her feet. The wheels were spinning, but he had no idea what her response would be. If she said no, then they would fake it. What choice did they have?

"How much time do you think it will take?" She addressed the floor before raising her gaze.

"We'd have to assess together, but my best

guess is at least a week. Maybe more, maybe less."

"I'm giving you extra credit points for backing me into a corner."

"I don't want you in a corner, Cass. I want you to work with me on this."

"Very well." She got to her feet and held out her hand to seal the deal. And just like that, they were on the same page—but for how long?

"Two handshakes in two days," he said as he took her hand. Her skin was as warm and smooth as he remembered and he kind of hated to let go.

"Actually, less than twenty-four hours."

"I stand corrected." And he wondered how many more times he would be corrected until they finished with the barn. It didn't matter. What mattered was that they learned to deal with one another and what better way to do it than by mucking out the wedding barn?

CHAPTER SEVEN

THE MIXED SCENTS of hay and animal, topped with a healthy dose of dust, hit Travis's nostrils as he rolled open the big bay door on its squeaky runners. When the wheels hit the bumper at the end of the rails, he stood in the open doorway studying the dusty interior as the enormity of the task ahead of him sank in. What had he been thinking when he came up with the idea of tackling this jumble of junk with Cassie?

That he'd kill several birds with one stone. The barn would get cleaned. He and Cassie would know at the end of the project if she and he could work out their differences or if they'd have to agree to live several hundred miles apart and take turns showing up at family events. And they'd save the cost of the cleaning crew.

He'd explained all that to Will over dinner the night before and Will's only comments were that he was glad he and Cassie were working things out, and that he'd better not find blood on the walls when they got done. But Travis could tell that his grandfather was grudgingly pleased that they were making an effort.

But where to begin? The big stack of tires? The jumble of parts? All the piles of stuff that had nowhere else to go, but were too good to throw away? A cat appeared from between barrels, blinked at him, then backed out of sight. Travis wasn't familiar with the cat—as far as he knew they didn't have a black and white—but it wasn't uncommon for cats to move in and he wouldn't be surprised to find that she had a litter hidden somewhere in the junk they'd be moving. If so, she'd have plenty of time to cart them elsewhere, because it was going to take a while to haul it all outside.

He walked farther into the dim interior and stood next to the column that held up the partial loft. The ropes that he and his sister, Amanda, had swung on as kids were still on the small platform above the loft that they'd dubbed the crow's nest, pulled to the side and fastened to an upright. Their mom had had a heart attack the first time she'd seen them launch themselves over the loft. Their father had thought it looked like fun. He'd just started fighting his battle with rheumatoid arthritis and was fully in favor of taking every opportunity to enjoy life—even the risky ones.

Travis hadn't known then that his dad's illness would shape his own life as well as those of his parents. Arizona was kinder to his father's body than the brutal cold of the Montana winters, so his parents moved south close to the time Travis graduated college. Travis had returned home, and with the exception of the occasional jaunt to Arizona to visit the folks, he'd been on the place ever since. The odd thing was that there was never a time when it was a good time to leave the ranch and see a few things. Last spring, between calving and planting, he'd attempted a trip to Seattle to visit a college friend, but had been called back early by unexpected spring blizzards that stranded some of their cattle.

It seemed that whenever he tried to leave, the ranch called him back.

"And here I am," he muttered.

"I see that."

He jumped at the sound of Cassie's voice and turned to see her standing in the doorway, very much as his grandfather had been standing in the doorway of the Callahan barn the day before. "I didn't expect you for another twenty minutes or so."

"I got away early. Didn't you hear me drive up?"

He shook his head. "The house blocks the

sound. I've missed more than one signature delivery because of that."

"You need a dog to alert you." She smiled wryly. "Or a goat."

"I have dogs." He nodded at Will's two old Aussies sleeping next to the grain shed. "Deaf, both of them. And if I brought Wendell back to the ranch, it would break Lizzie Belle's heart." He'd given the dwarf goat to Katie a little over a year ago, to keep her little goat company.

"True. They are inseparable."

So far so good. No snarking.

And Cassie had on her business face. He imagined she'd spent as much time convincing herself they could do this job peacefully as he had.

Cassie walked into the barn and did the same thing he'd done just a few minutes before, settling her hands on her hips and turning a slow circle. "Wow. I kind of forgot what a really barnlike barn looks like."

"Yours is in much better shape junkwise," he agreed.

"My grandfather and dad were nuts about cleaning it out every spring. We did have the neatest barn of any of our friends. The thing is, yours is bigger and I don't think Grandma wants to get married on the ranch she came to as a new bride."

"Totally understood." And since Will's wife divorced him and remarried when Travis's dad was a kid, Will didn't have the same feelings about his ranch. He hadn't built a life there with anyone except for his kids, whom he'd raised.

"Overwhelming." Cassie summed up the situation with a single word.

"That's an understatement." He came to stand beside her, his unlikely partner. "By the way, I promised Grandpa no blood on the walls."

"We can wash the walls," she deadpanned.

He gave a short laugh. "I hope we won't have to do that more than once or twice."

She arched an eyebrow at him. "Well, it is us..."

Travis nodded. It was them.

He shifted his attention to the heaps of stuff, ridiculously aware of Cassie standing next to him, her hands resting lightly on her hips as she, too, studied the junk, no doubt developing a plan of attack and wondering how to get him to sign off on it.

Finally, she broke the silence. "In the old days I would have taken one half of the barn, you the other, and we would have raced to see who could get it done first."

"But this isn't the old days."

"No." She sounded almost wistful. "But wouldn't that have been fun and easy?"

He got it. Their old relationship hadn't required much effort. They simply fed off one another. It was irritating and invigorating and… predictable in an odd way. Now they had to come up with a whole new way to deal with each other and he'd be the first to admit that he had a lot to learn. More than that, he wanted to learn.

She gestured at the larger equipment parked in front of them. "Let's get that stuff out of here, then lay out a plan for the rest. What we can hide, what we have to move. Like that."

"What we have to wash down."

"Oh, that will be everything. Do you have a fire hose?" She craned her neck as if expecting to spot one somewhere.

"That's quite possibly the one thing we don't have."

"What a shame."

"But I have a pressure washer and we'll be using it."

"Do you have a plan in mind?"

"I thought we'd develop it as we go."

"That seems a little loose to me. I think we should have something concrete in place, because as I see it, our biggest obstacle is a mutual need to be the boss."

"You don't say," he stated dryly.

"The Ray Quentin affair perfectly demonstrated that need."

His eyebrows came together. "I wasn't trying to boss you in that bar, Cassie. I was trying to protect you."

She looked as if she expected him to suddenly say, "Ha. I'm kidding." When he didn't, she said, "It appeared to me that you were trying to take control of a situation I already had under control. I didn't need to be protected until you showed up."

"How, in a thousand years, could you have thought that?" he demanded. She hadn't had the situation anywhere near under control.

"I thought it because you pushed your way into the situation and tried to take over," she replied, missing the point entirely.

"Do you think I did it for fun?" He tapped his cheek beneath his sore eye, then, remembering his objective, dropped his hand. Still, it took him a second to ask, "What are we gaining by rehashing this?"

Her mouth tightened, but to her credit, she didn't push on.

"I have an idea," he said. It was getting late and he still had stuff to do that afternoon. "For today, and today only, you take that half of the barn and I'll take this one. We clear out the big stuff, then tomorrow we will come up with a plan of action." His lips twisted. "The concrete kind."

"Great," Cassie said on a sniff. "We've wasted enough time."

Because someone wanted to argue...

Travis kept the thought to himself. And that seemed to be the best strategy moving forward—to keep their mouths shut. Tomorrow, as he'd said, they'd give it another go.

He made a sweeping gesture. "Pick your side."

She pointed to the side she was standing on and he said, "Cool. We work until eleven, then I have to go to town."

"Fine."

"Okay, then."

For several long seconds they stared one another down, then Cassie did a pivoting turn and headed for the stack of old asphalt roofing shingles. Travis sucked in a breath, then turned and headed toward his side of the barn.

At least there wasn't any blood on the walls.

EVEN THOUGH SHE was driving, Cassie closed her eyes in relief as her truck bumped over the McGuire ranch cattle guard on the way home. She opened them again when the tires hit gravel.

The day was done.

Her clothes were dusty, her shoulders were

stiff and her jaw ached from not talking while working in the barn. Tomorrow they could talk, work out that concrete plan. Today she'd needed time to collect herself, and it wasn't only because they'd managed to morph their initial conversation into another argument about the Ray Quentin situation; it was because she was working out how to deal with a guy whom she found unexpectedly attractive.

Her peers would have laughed their behinds off at the idea of her, the great negotiator, having to have a self-imposed time-out because she couldn't control her mouth—or her eyes.

Being hyperaware of his black eye, she couldn't help but study it in the same way one touched a sore tooth. *Yep. Still there. Still appears to be painful.* And he kept catching her. Generally, she was immune to embarrassment, but that wasn't the case with Travis—thank you, unexpected attraction—and after the third or fourth catch, she almost said, "I'm watching your eye, not you, buddy." Instead she'd lifted something that was too heavy and almost fell over.

Saying she was only checking out his eye would have been a lie, of course. She also noticed the way his muscles moved under his T-shirt, the easy way he walked. The way the sunlight caught the brown stubble on his jawline and how his cheeks had hollowed under those ridiculously high cheekbones. She noticed things that had never been on her radar before, and the more she noticed about him, the more she was tempted to do something to drive a wedge between them.

Unfortunately, wedge driving was not on the agenda. They were working together to learn to do just that—work together; therefore, working in silence seemed her safest bet.

But what about tomorrow? They couldn't clear out the entire barn in silence, could they?

She toyed with the idea of being candid and telling him that, in a very technical sense, she found him attractive. Physically attractive. Therefore, if he caught her staring, that was all it was.

Right.

No way was she giving him that kind of ammo. He could just catch her staring and wonder why. Best-case scenario, he'd think she was plotting something against him.

The thought made her smile. A little. Then she was back at the conundrum.

She wasn't feeling herself—or rather, she wasn't feeling like the person who'd left Wisconsin for a visit home before classes. She didn't know if it was the time off, being back in Montana or being in close contact with her former nemesis, but she wasn't as securely buttoned-up as she had been only a few days ago.

Travis thinks you're stiff, and Katie thinks you're there but not, so at least you appear to be all buttoned-up. They didn't have to know that she was wrangling unfamiliar feelings and sensations. She was a good actress.

Taking comfort in the thought, she turned onto the county road. She might feel different inside, but it was just because of all the changes raining down upon her.

Her phone rang as she rounded a corner and seeing the name on the screen, she pulled over on a wide spot to answer the call from Darby.

After a quick hello, Darby said, "I didn't get the job."

"At least you heard back." In the current job market, it wasn't uncommon to not hear.

"I have a friend who works there, so that was probably why. There was no offer to keep my résumé on file."

"Maybe your current company can turn things around. They hired a new CEO."

"Death throes," Darby said darkly. "But I'll hang on until the bitter end, or until I find something else. I want to be back in Montana, but now I'm going to broaden my search. If my company goes south, I can't afford to be picky."

"You don't care what you do as long as you're close to home?"

"Let me put it this way—I currently live in a vibrant city with lots to do, and I still miss Gavin. Yes. I'd like to be closer to home." She hesitated, then said, "I thought about applying at Hardwick's Grocery store, but they only have part-time positions. I need more income than that."

"Something will come up." Cassie wasn't a huge fan of platitudes, but she knew when her friend needed to hear one.

"Thank you," Darby said softly. "I'll keep you posted. Have you seen Travis since…you know?"

"As a matter of fact, I'm leaving his place. He and I are cleaning out the barn in case it rains on Grandma's wedding day."

"You and him and no one else?"

"You mean like a referee?" Cassie asked dryly.

"Pretty much."

"Nope. It's just the two of us." And since she was still embarrassed at being taken to task by Will McGuire, she didn't delve into the details of how it all came about. "It needs to be done, and it saves Will and Grandma the cost of hiring a crew."

"I'm surprised that Travis has enough free

time to do that with Will living in town. Did they hire help on the ranch?"

"No," Cassie replied with a thoughtful frown. "We're only working a couple of hours a day." But Darby brought up a good point. On their ranch, Nick and Brady would start haying soon, and there were the pivots to tend and the fences to mend. When did Travis find the time? And why hadn't she thought of that?

Perhaps you are a little too focused on yourself...

Perhaps.

"How's his eye?"

"Swollen and colorful." And he was still ridiculously good-looking.

"No grudges?"

"We worked through that," Cassie said, hoping she sounded casual instead of shifty. There wasn't much that she kept from Darby, but this thing with her and Travis... It felt too personal to share.

"I bet that was interesting."

Cassie laughed, glad that her friend was letting her off the hook. "Keep me posted on your job search, okay?"

"Will do."

"And call me anytime you need to. Promise?"

"Only if you do the same."

"I will." Maybe.

There were some things, like negotiating peace with a former nemesis, that a person simply had to handle alone.

"THIS COULD PROVE INTERESTING," Rosalie said as she pulled the cozy off the teapot. She and Will had developed a nice routine of having beer or wine before dinner and tea after, often on the front porch of his new house, where they sat together and watched the world go by. Every now and then, Gloria would walk the two blocks down the street with her new rescue dog, Sylvia, and join them.

"Interesting in what way?" Will asked as he accepted the cup of tea and then leaned back in his chair. He hadn't been much of a tea drinker when they'd started seeing one another in a serious way, but he'd become a convert after she'd made him his first chai latte. He'd also sworn her to silence. "Travis would poke fun at me in an unmerciful way," he'd said. Rosalie doubted that, but she agreed that it would be their secret.

"I believe you know what I mean."

"Oh. The barn going up in flames."

"What?" She nearly dropped her teacup.

"Sorry. I didn't mean that literally. I meant the two of them working together could cause some friction."

Rosalie knew that Will thought Cassie and

Travis's habit of butting heads upset her, but the truth was that Will was the one who seemed to find it the most upsetting. She didn't know if he was projecting his feelings onto her, or if he was simply trying to keep her happy by negotiating peace between their grandchildren.

Rosalie took her seat next to Will and balanced her cup on the arm of the chair. Cassie and Travis were both grounded individuals, college educated, successful in their chosen fields...and they still triggered one another.

She waved at their neighbor across the street as the woman left her yard to go on her exercise walk, then glanced at Will. "I have a hard time, given Cassie and Travis's history, believing that they volunteered together for this task out of the blue." She gave Will a sideways glance. "Especially after the incident at the Shamrock." Cassie had called to explain how Ray Quentin had given Travis a black eye, but Rosalie was certain that she hadn't been told the full story.

Will shifted in his chair and Rosalie pretended not to notice. So much for them "volunteering." Will obviously had something to do with it, but if Cassie and Travis had agreed to the plan, she thought it was a great way for the two of them to get their mutual need to take one another off at the knees out of their systems. They hadn't been particularly kind to each other during their teen years and now, thanks to her and Will, they were going to be seeing more of one another.

On the plus side, anything that distracted Cassie from the job that was eating her from the inside out was A-OK in her book. Rosalie hoped it took two weeks to clean the barn. Maybe by that time, Cassie will have developed some perspective. Or maybe she'd continue her no-holds-barred career path.

"But here's the thing," Will said, drawing her attention back to him. "The hay is almost ready to cut and if we're looking at rain at the end of the month, we need to get it taken care of."

"And Travis is busy with the barn this week."

"Exactly. So I'm going to handle the haying."

"Do you have enough help?"

He smiled that smile that made her knees go a little weak. Will was one handsome man. "Lester has volunteered."

"In the same way Cassie and Travis volunteered to clear out the barn?" she asked mildly.

Will laughed. "Les offered to help." He patted her knee. "I won't be seeing you so much before the wedding."

"I'm going to be busy with preparations." And not only her own. Katie wanted her Christmas wedding to be a small affair, but there was still a lot to do. Two weddings in a matter of months did keep one hopping.

"I could drive into town, of course, but sometimes we work at night."

"I know the drill," Rosalie said with a gentle smile. She had reason to, having been a rancher's wife for over three decades. "And if you need help, I drive a mean swather."

"I thought you hated ranch work."

"I prefer town work, but that doesn't mean I don't have skills." She looked over her teacup at her man. "Skills that I am not afraid to use."

"Well, if Lester's wife isn't as understanding, then I may be calling on you."

She smiled at the man who'd somehow slipped into her heart. "You do that," she said softly. "Anytime you need me."

Cassie arrived at the McGuire ranch at exactly eight o'clock, ready to discuss next steps in the barn project, which meant negotiating and not arguing. She'd slept like the dead thanks to all the tugging and lifting and hauling she'd done the day before, and there was nothing like a good night's rest to help one gain perspective. Unfortunately, the perspective she gained when she was alone seemed to shift when she was with Travis. If that happened, she'd deal.

The driveway gravel crunched noisily under

her running shoes as she approached Will's old dogs, who were sleeping next to the stuff they'd stacked on opposite sides of the open bay door yesterday—her pile and his pile. She leaned down to stroke their heads, earning herself canine smiles, then cleared her throat before entering the building just in case Travis needed a warning to stop talking to himself. She needn't have bothered.

The barn was empty—of human beings, that is. Something small and furry scurried for cover near the rear door. Whatever it was, it had a lot of hiding places. Despite a good two hours of hauling things out the previous day, there was still plenty of junk to tackle today.

So where was the guy who'd been so gung ho to start at eight o'clock on the nose?

She heard another faint scuffling noise in the junk, but when she moved toward it, the noise stopped. She definitely had company. A cat or a rabbit maybe. It wasn't a pack rat, or she would have smelled it. Pack rat was possibly the only smell, other than skunk, that this old barn didn't carry. She hoped the pressure washing did its job.

The sound of an ATV caught her ear and she walked out of the barn to see Travis coming across the field. He stopped to open the gate, drove through, got off and closed it again before once again mounting the machine.

"Busy morning?" she asked after he pulled to a stop a few feet away from her.

"Fencing problem," he said after turning off the engine.

"Something you need to deal with now?"

He pulled off his gloves. "I'll handle it after we're done."

Cassie casually slipped her hands into her back pockets. "Need help?"

A surprised look crossed his face, giving her a whisper of satisfaction. She did love to catch him off guard, but that wasn't why she offered. She'd offered because that was what neighbors—and people who were trying to prove points to themselves—did. She could spend time with Travis and have a normal, non-contentious relationship. That was the perspective she'd gained from her good night's sleep. She only hoped it didn't change as she spent time around the man.

"I might," he allowed.

"Depending on how well we do today?" she guessed.

"Pretty much."

Great, because she planned to have a nice co-operative day. "I came up with a tentative plan of action."

"So did I."

"After you," Cassie said with a gracious gesture, even though it was harder than it should have been. He was right. She did love to take control, but there were times and places and she needed to differentiate between needing to take the helm and wanting to. At work she needed to. With Travis she wanted to.

"My plan is to not mention Ray Quentin or anything relating to the Shamrock Pub."

So, he'd done some thinking, too. Her gaze strayed to his bruised eye, which looked only slightly less swollen than the day before, and for some unknown reason her cheeks began to warm. Guilt? She shook it off and drew herself up another half inch or so. "I agree."

Not only had the incident itself gotten in the way of their truce, rehashing it had done the same. Plus, there was no way she was ever going to get him to admit that if he'd simply stepped back when she'd asked, none of it would have happened. Even Darby agreed that while Ray might look scary and shove furniture, he was unlikely to hit someone weaker than himself. But in the long run, as much as she loved being right, what did it matter?

"And your plan for the barn?" she asked.

"Pretty straightforward. We move everything out and pressure wash the heck out of the interior, sort through the junk and put the essentials back."

"And we'll hide the ugly stuff with some kind of paneling," Cassie added. She simply couldn't see a wedding venue with the things a barn kept out of the weather in plain view.

"Do you have panels?" Travis asked.

"We can come up with something."

His eyebrows rose as he silently mouthed, "We?"

Somehow his lips were even sexier when no sound came out.

Get a grip.

"Yes, *we*, working cooperatively," she said, sounding very much like a substitute teacher who had no idea how to talk to kids.

Travis frowned at her overly bright tone, giving her the uncomfortable feeling that he could tell that she was playing a part in the hopes that acting would become reality, as in, she was here to do a job and she was not attracted to a guy who drove her nuts.

Her defenses started to rise, and she firmly squished them back down again. "No blood on the walls, remember?"

Travis's forehead cleared at her more normal tone of voice. "Right. I guess we can brainstorm on that later." He gestured with his chin toward the upper part of the barn. "We'll also have to clean the loft so that dirt and debris don't rain on the guests when the kids run around up there."

"Kids…" Cassie glanced up at the loft above them, thankful that (a) he wasn't looking at her so that she could get that grip, and (b) her normal voice had come back. "I don't suppose we can block entry?"

"Could they have kept you out of the loft with a mere barricade back when you were a kid?"

"Unlikely," she agreed. Especially if she'd been dared to do something. She kind of missed those damn-the-torpedoes days.

She glanced up to find Travis studying her, and again her cheeks began to warm. She couldn't remember the last time she'd blushed, but here she was, two blushes in and the day had barely begun. It was putting her in a bad mood.

"Tell you what," he said thoughtfully, "if you help me string the wire for the fence when we get done, if there's still no blood on the walls, I'll go to your place, haul your mare back here and work her when I have some free time."

Cassie stared at him, wondering what had prompted the out-of-the-blue offer.

"Well?"

She cleared her throat as self-conscious blush number three threatened. "That would be excellent. I'd pay you, of course."

He looked like he was going to give her a flat

negative to the payment option, but instead he said, "We will come to some kind of a cooperative solution in that regard."

She mouthed a silent "We?" and he grinned, his eyes crinkling at the corners.

"Look at us. We've made a couple of decisions that haven't involved raised voices or fisticuffs."

The unexpected intimacy in his voice tugged at her a little too strongly and she once again felt the need to drive that wedge, protect herself, before she freaking blushed again.

But before she took action—or talked herself down, she wasn't certain which would have happened first—Travis stepped back and turned to face the interior of the barn. Cassie let out a silent breath.

"Where do you want to start?" he asked.

"There," she said, pointing to the corner closest to them which was jammed with metal containers holding who-knew-what.

"Fine with me. Unless you want to work on separate areas again."

He shot her a questioning look and she shrugged, even as her brain was shouting, *Yes, yes, yes*.

"I think it'll go faster if we work together."

He gave a low laugh. "One would hope anyway."

"Yes. One would hope." And she hoped she got through the day without either picking a fight or making a fool of herself. She had a lot to learn about navigating these new waters, but as he said, they were doing better.

CHAPTER EIGHT

CASSIE PULLED THE fencing pliers out of her back pocket and skillfully pried the rusted staples out of the wooden post. Once done, she bent and collected the staples off the ground, tossing them into the metal container in the back of the side-by-side UTV.

Travis brought his attention back to the wire stretcher, which he clamped onto the broken ends of the top wire. Once he had the wire stretched, Cassie hammered a new staple into the post, holding the wire in place while he slipped a narrow metal sleeve over the broken ends and crimped it. They worked well together—when they didn't speak.

Once the top wire was secured to the other posts, Cassie pushed her blond hair back from her forehead and stared out over the pasture, making Travis wonder what she was thinking. She seemed more relaxed in the open air, surrounded by the country she'd grown up in. Who wouldn't be happy in knee-deep grass with a gentle breeze ruffling their hair?

Did she like living in the city?

He'd thought he'd be okay with it back in the day, but the job he'd given up before returning home had been with an agriculture-consulting business funded by the government. Although he'd have been based in a small city, he would have spent a lot of his time in rural settings advising ranchers and farmers.

Cassie spent all her time in town. In fact, it sounded like she spent all her time in her office.

She shot a look his way, her expression distant, as if she was pulling herself out of deep thoughts. "I can't believe you didn't lose any cattle through this break. You could have driven a truck through it."

An old post had gone over—Travis suspected a moose might have been responsible since all the cattle were accounted for—taking out a good twenty feet of wire. They'd reset a new post, then managed to fix the broken and stretched wire without having to add more.

"My good luck." He set the wire stretcher into the back of the side-by-side, then held his hand out for the fencing pliers.

"Mmm." She took a last look around, then got into the side-by-side. They'd barely spoken that day, which was one way to keep from sniping at one another, but despite the lack of conversation, the air between them had practically crackled whenever their gazes connected.

A pent-up need to engage? Or something else?

The third time Travis caught her studying him, he decided it was something else.

When he'd caught her staring the previous day, he'd assumed that the guilty shift of her gaze had to do with feeling bad about his black eye.

But two days of black-eye guilt?

He didn't think so. Cassie didn't operate that way. Putting together the clues—surreptitious looks coupled with the way she looked totally ticked off when he caught her—he suspected that she found him interesting in a way she hadn't expected.

Funny, but the exact same thing had already happened to him.

"I have an idea," she said as he started the side-by-side.

"Yeah?" He gave her a sideways look. Her hands were settled in her lap, loosely clasped, giving her a prim look that he would have never seen on Cassie's face back in the day.

"I'll load McHenry's Gold tomorrow morning and bring her over when I come to work."

Travis put the machine in gear and started

across the pasture. "I take it you've spent enough time in my company?"

"Yes," she said simply, and he couldn't help smiling.

"Sounds good." Because he wasn't about the push things.

Yet.

CASSIE DIDN'T LIKE the way Travis kept studying her, as if he knew something about her that she didn't want him to know, especially when she couldn't keep her eyes off the guy—or keep herself from getting clumsy when they worked together hauling a barrel or some such thing out of the barn. She was so concerned about Travis discovering her unfounded fascination with him that she was self-sabotaging.

And she was going to stop doing that.

She squeezed her hands together in her lap, wishing she wasn't so ridiculously aware of the guy driving them across the bumpy field.

He's winning...

It's not a contest.

When had things not *been a contest with him?*

Now. Things are no longer a contest.

She glanced over at him. "Things are no longer a contest."

He shot her a bemused look in return. "Good to know."

"Just stating a point out loud. Getting myself on track in the name of peaceful relations."

"Thank you for including me."

She nodded at the windshield. "Anytime."

Travis drove the rest of the way to the ranch with his eyebrows knit together. Cassie knew because of her excellent peripheral vision, which she'd developed during her early teaching days. Mission accomplished—he was no longer giving her those see-into-her-head looks. Instead he was wondering what her new tactic was.

When in doubt, divert. Of course, she should have known that Travis would not be diverted for long. After parking the side-by-side, Travis hesitated before opening his door.

"Are you sure you don't want me to drive over and pick up the mare? The trailer's hooked up."

Indeed, there was a long gooseneck cattle trailer hooked to the ranch flatbed truck.

"That's okay," she said. They'd had enough together time for one day. They got out of the side-by-side and he walked her to her car.

"I plan to put her in that pen there." He pointed to a corral next to the barn. "Just in case you get here before I get back from feeding."

"She can get to know her sisters over the fence." The corral abutted the pasture where Travis's three McHenry mares grazed. If McHenry's Gold didn't work out, he might have four, and she would have to let the mare go for less than she'd paid for her. Depressing thought, but maybe what she deserved for letting impulse and her competitive nature get the best of her.

He cocked his head at her as if he was about to comment on the horse situation, but instead he reached for her with one hand, and Cassie, having no idea what was going on, leaned away from him. Part of her wanted him to touch her and the other part was afraid of what that might lead to. Impulsive behavior with Travis had led to her downfall more than once and this—

"Hold still," he said gruffly, interrupting her analysis. "There's a spider."

Cassie made a startled exclamation, then abruptly pressed her lips together and did the impossible, clenching her fists and holding stone-still as Travis gently swept the spider from the shoulder of her shirt with the backs of his fingertips. The little beast landed in the gravel and scuttled away, thankfully in the opposite direction.

"Wolf spider. It was probably on you since we left the barn. We have a lot of them in there."

Cassie's eyes probably doubled in size. Logically she knew that a wolf spider wasn't a threat, but the thought of the creepy, crawly thing clinging to her for hours…

"On that note, I think I'll just go home," she said in a choked voice.

"Do you want me to check for more spiders?" he asked blandly.

Now her skin was crawling as if there were spiders everywhere. "No. Thank you. I'll just go home and burn these clothes, and everything will be fine."

"I never knew you were afraid of spiders."

"Not afraid, creeped out," she said as she opened the car door. She looked at him over the top of the door. "I dare *you* not to be creeped out by the thought of a spider riding around on you for an hour."

One corner of his mouth quirked up. "Remember, Cassie. This is not a contest."

Cassie made a face at him and got into the car, shushing the small voice that once again whispered, *He's winning.*

"I WOULD APPRECIATE help with the haying," Travis said after he and his grandfather settled into their chairs on the front porch. His grandfather seemed suspiciously enthusiastic about a chore he once said made him want to put a stick in his eye. Will had never made a secret about preferring cow work to farming, and had been unreceptive to Travis's suggestion to invest in headphones and listen to music or podcasts.

Will propped one foot up on the wooden box he used as an outdoor footstool. "I think it's important to get that barn cleaned out ASAP. Rosalie will rest easier once it's done."

Travis tipped up his beer instead of saying, "Only Rosalie?" Because as he saw it, his grandfather was just as invested in the wedding plans as his bride-to-be.

They sat in silence, watching a flicker peck away at the pine tree closest to the house. The air was warm and heavy with humidity. Another storm was brewing.

"How are things going in the barn?" Will asked a little too casually.

Travis gestured at the piles stacked on either side of the barn bay door. "I can't believe how much more we have to do."

"Yeah," Will said conversationally. "There's about a century worth of collecting there."

"The Callahans cleaned their barn yearly," Travis pointed out.

"They had more manpower," Will said without any hint of taking offense. Rosalie had softened the man.

The ranch had kept Travis, his dad and his grandfather busy to the point that there really wasn't a lot of barn-cleaning time.

They'd hired help after Travis's dad had started to lose his mobility, but while Will was an excellent bronc-riding coach who volunteered with the local high school rodeo team, he was not an easy man to work for. After three guys had been hired and subsequently quit, Travis had decided he needed to put his career on hold and come home to help his father and grandfather through a difficult time. By the time his father had to depend on his wrist crutches and made the decision to move to Arizona, Travis knew he was staying on the ranch. Some things were meant to be, and this was one of them.

"Nice afternoon," Will murmured as he reached down to the cooler at his side and pulled out another beer. Travis shook his head when he offered it up, and Will closed the cooler before popping the top.

The flicker moved from the pine tree to the eaves of the barn, hanging sideways as it picked at insects hiding in cracks between boards. Now that his grandfather spent more time off the ranch than on it, Travis enjoyed these sit-downs with him. And he enjoyed watching how the old man changed as new things came into his life. Funny that Will's life was taking new turns, and with the exception of Cassie, his continued on the same path.

"Are you and Cassie getting along all right?"

"Fair to middling," Travis replied, hoping his grandfather wouldn't ask for details.

"Rosalie's worried about her. Thinks that job of hers is eating her alive."

"There are signs of that." Travis took a drink as the flicker disappeared into the trees near the barn. "But she's kind of reverting back to her old self as we work together." Or rather pingponging back and forth. Sometimes she was the Cassie he'd grown up with, and then, as if she caught herself being herself, she was back to wearing her administrator hat. He didn't like that hat and felt a striking urge to knock it off.

"Probably no chance of her deciding not to go back."

Travis shook his head. "She seems committed to her career."

"Careers can be modified."

Travis gave his grandfather a sideways look. "You know that you can't give Rosalie a smooth path in all things."

"Nope," Will agreed affably. "But where I can, I will."

"It probably won't happen in the Cassie arena."

A few seconds of silence ticked by, and then Will said, "Do you want her to go back?"

Travis gave his grandfather a sharp look. "What kind of question is that?"

Will met his gaze placidly. "A reasonable one, given the circumstances."

Travis pulled his gaze away and searched the trees for the flicker while he dealt with his grandfather's question. He wanted to ask what circumstances, but decided it was better to let the matter drop.

Will was not of like mind. "My feeling is that someone can't set you off like that unless there's some kind of spark between you."

"What if it's the spark of irritation?"

"Is it?"

Travis scowled at his grandfather. "You aren't going to let this drop, are you?"

"It's dropped."

Will focused on the barn, leaning back in his chair, the picture of nonchalance.

Travis did the same, but he was pretty darn certain that he could hear the old man humming under his breath.

MCHENRY'S GOLD WALKED the peripheries of her new enclosure as Cassie coiled the lead rope and halter. The horse had loaded with only a minor amount of balking that morning, which gave Cassie hope. The mare was smart and maybe with a few Travis lessons, she'd be good to go. If not, then Cassie had spent a whole lot of money keeping Travis from having something he wanted. Something he probably couldn't afford to buy from her, since he'd given up bidding and let her win the horse.

"Thank you for doing this." She hung the halter, which was old and had spent a lot of time out in the weather, over the fence post so it would be available when Travis needed it.

"Looking forward to seeing what she can do."

Cassie didn't doubt that. Travis had a way with horses, just as she had a way with high school kids. She'd enjoyed her emergency substitute stint in the high school English department. There was a lot of energy, angst and flat-out goofiness. Several of the kids in the AP class had a deliciously dark sense of humor and they'd played off each other nicely after she'd established who was in control of the classroom. It wasn't the job she wanted to do eight to ten hours a day, but it'd been nice to know that she hadn't lost her knack with kids.

"Do you like working in an office?" Travis asked conversationally. "Being indoors all the time."

"It keeps the rain off." Travis took hold of the handle and rolled the gate open. When the squeaking wheels came to a halt, she asked, "Why?"

"You seemed more...I don't know...relaxed... when we were fixing the fence yesterday."

It had been pleasant working in the pasture

with the sun on her back, the scents of grass, pine and damp earth filling her lungs. "I enjoyed it, but trust me, I can relax in other circumstances."

"When?"

"When you aren't around."

He shot her an amused look and she felt like smiling back until he said, "Why haven't you been home for a significant visit in the past years?"

Not an attack, she reminded herself. Merely a question—on an issue she was touchy about.

Cassie ran a hand over her opposite arm. "To begin with, I was on a probationary period with my job. I couldn't come home."

"And when it was over?"

She dropped her hand. "Things happened. You have no idea what it's like having so many irons in the fire."

"I don't," he agreed easily. "But I know what it's like to be in the moment instead of plotting minutes, hours and days ahead."

"I think you've done your share of plotting, or you wouldn't have been so successful in academics," she pointed out.

"But I can also do something that hasn't been written into my daily goals."

"As can I."

"Once upon a time you could, but can you

still?" He raised his hands. "Not sniping. Just asking."

No. He was trying to get her to demonstrate.

Cassie tucked her hair behind her ear. "I've worked hard to rein in my impulsiveness, but that doesn't mean it's not there."

"Merely lying dormant?" His lips formed another fascinating half smile.

"Unfortunately," Cassie replied; she glanced down at the gravel, wondering how in-depth she wanted to get with this man who put her so on edge, and why she felt twitchy about answering questions she would have freely answered had anyone else asked.

She wasn't secretive about the changes she'd made as she worked her way into a management position. She had always been organized to the max, and been driven to succeed, but she'd also sabotaged herself by not being shy about sharing her opinion or taking action without fully considering consequences. It'd taken a while to understand that there were other ways to achieve a goal than full-frontal assault.

She shifted her weight as she brought her gaze up to his. "Being impulsive, firing off my mouth without thinking, jumping into the fray without a plan of action, tended to get me into trouble professionally, so it seemed wise to adjust to circumstances. Now it's a habit."

"I kind of like impulsive you."

"Do you? I always thought that impulsive me was the bane of your existence."

"It was. Once."

"What does that mean?"

"I think the meaning is clear." He turned to face the interior of the barn, leaving Cassie to fight a sudden urge to grab him by the shoulders and turn him back toward her and demand a real answer.

The real answer doesn't matter. He's just saying something—again—to put you off-balance.

And it's working.

Cassie rolled her shoulders as if physically shaking off the thought. "We should get to it."

"Right." He jerked his chin in the direction of some dilapidated wooden storage bins propped against the wall on what was his side of the barn. "Let's get those out. I'd like to load them onto the trailer while it's empty." He'd backed a utility trailer close to the barn at some point.

"Right." Cassie pulled her gloves out of her pocket and buttoned the top button of her chambray shirt. Two days in the barn had taught her to keep everything buttoned as closely as possible to keep the fine dust that coated everything from clinging to exposed skin and drifting in through open collars.

Together they manhandled the first set of

bins out the door, making it almost to the refuse trailer before one of the boards gave and it fell, pitching Travis sideways. He regained his footing and took hold of a more solid support.

"Good to go?"

He nodded and they awkwardly carted the broken storage unit the rest of the way to the trailer. "One down."

And only one to go.

The second was wobblier than the first, but they got it to the trailer without incident.

"What's next?"

"More awkward stuff." He pointed to the pieces of an antique hay rack and other bits of equipment that would never again see service. "Grandad says he's going to put the rake together and use it as a lawn ornament."

"Nice idea."

"Still strongly in the idea stage."

Cassie smiled, then made her way to the tangle of curved metal tines, some still attached to the framework, others lying nearby. Concentrate on the task at hand, not the man who created so many conflicting emotions.

She was concentrating so hard that when she turned to pick her way out of the jumble of tines, she caught her pant leg and pitched forward. Travis made a grab for her as she went down, somehow catching her before she hit the metal rake frame. She clutched at the front of him as he hauled her upright.

"Are you okay?" he asked gruffly.

"My foot is still caught." She pulled it free from the tangle of metal, using her hold on the front of his shirt for balance. His grip tightened on her arms, sending a curl of warmth through her.

"You good now?"

"Uh-huh." But as their gazes connected, she found she wasn't in any hurry to let go of the front of his shirt. *Almost as if you've been looking for an excuse to touch him.* Her heart started beating double time as he studied her face in a lazy way, then his gaze slid down to her mouth and there was no mistaking the direction of his thoughts.

"Well?" he asked softly.

"Well, what?" Cassie asked, somehow pushing the words out of her throat. What would it be like to kiss that mouth, which drove her to distraction? That mouth, which was now curved into an overly confident half smile. Really? "Do you think I'm going to kiss you?"

"I hope you're not going to bite my nose."

Cassie shoved her hands against his chest, sending him stumbling backward. He caught hold of a wooden upright before going down.

She gave him an unsympathetic look as he

regained his balance, but her heart was hammering. He'd read her perfectly and she wasn't ready to be read like that. "You are one cocky man, Travis."

"Just calling things the way I see 'em."

"Tell me how you 'see 'em.'"

"There's a reason you keep watching me."

Prickly heat warmed her cheeks. "I'm watching you because we're the only two people in the barn. Who else am I going to look at?" She gritted the words out from between her teeth. "Besides, I feel bad about your eye."

"I think it's about more than my eye."

He lifted his eyebrows, silently encouraging her to unburden herself, but Cassie's survival instinct, honed during many, many meetings in which she had to keep her personal feelings to herself, kicked in. She wasn't going to utter a word until she knew exactly what she wanted to say, and since logical thought escaped her, that could be a while.

The silence stretched on and it began to feel as if the atmosphere between them would crack before either of them made a move. Finally, as Cassie was reaching her breaking point, Travis shifted his weight and glanced past her to the junk behind her. "We'd better get to work."

The atmosphere didn't crack. It diffused, leaving Cassie feeling oddly deflated, but her heart was still beating too hard of a rhythm against her ribs.

"Yes." For once she was happy to leave unfinished business unfinished. And she was *not* going to look at him today. Not unless it was in the line of duty. She straightened her shoulders, and settled her hands on her hips, doing her best to look as if she'd had enough of this nonsense and it was time to go to work.

Travis stuck his thumbs into his front pockets, looking so much cooler than she felt, but looks, she reminded herself, could be deceiving.

"Opposite sides of the barn again?" she asked.

He nodded. "Seems safest."

"No thanks to you."

He tilted one corner of his mouth up into a yeah-right smirk, then reached for the gloves in his back pocket. Cassie did the same before turning and striding off to her side of the barn.

She only hoped the time passed quickly so she could get out of here and back to her own ranch, where she could indulge in some primal scream therapy.

CHAPTER NINE

BY THE TIME eleven o'clock rolled around, Travis was covered head to toe with the powdery dust that permeated old barns. He beat his hands on the front of his chest, raising a small cloud.

"Quitting time?" Cassie wiped the back of her hand over her forehead, leaving a smear. It was the first time either of them had spoken since they'd retreated to their neutral corners, which had its benefits. They both had stuff to work through, and it had kept them from arguing about who started what.

"A little after."

They still had a ton of work to do, but a lot of junk had been moved out of the building, including the hay rake and the jumble of tines, as they wrestled with their private demons.

"I think we should work together tomorrow," Cassie said as she pulled off her gloves. "I have stuff over here I can't handle alone."

She hadn't asked for help with anything that she could tug, pull or push at least an inch at a time, and she'd extended him the same cour-

tesy as he'd strained to maneuver a grain barrel full of traps and other metal miscellanea out
the door.

"I'm good with that."

She lightly slapped the gloves into her palm.
"You took me by surprise earlier."

"It wasn't an ambush."

"No. You were right. I have been watching
you."

He'd wondered as he'd worked if Cassie
planned to recap the situation before she left,
or if she was going to let it slide into the never-
to-be-discussed realm. Now he had his answer.

"And you've been watching me," she added.

He'd thought he'd been pretty slick about that,
but apparently not slick enough. Was that heat
creeping up his neck?

"Don't want you sneaking up on me."

"Right. And I'm only concerned about your
eye." She gave him a long, thoughtful look, one
that put his nerves on edge. "What if by some
crazy happenstance I do find you physically attractive? Where does that leave us?"

He bit the inside of his cheek, wondering if
he was stepping into a trap. "Exploring new
territory?"

She slowly shook her head.

"So be it," he said. "You won't find me pushing."

"I'll believe that when I see it."

"I don't push."

She put her hands on her hips and in a mock deep voice said, "Stand back, little lady, while I handle big bad Ray Quentin."

"Funny." He started to touch the sore spot on his face, then realized what he was doing and dropped his hand. "I was trying to protect you."

She let out a breath as she fixed him with another thoughtful gaze, as if wondering what to do with him. Or rather with whatever feelings he stirred up in her.

"You know, we can pretend none of this is happening," he said, "but it isn't going to solve anything."

"There's nothing to solve."

He let out a choked laugh. "Dream on."

She rolled her eyes. "I can't believe this."

"Kind of took me by surprise, too."

Her gaze crashed into his. "That's not what I meant." She let out a sharp breath. "It's time for me to go." She started toward the bay door.

"I don't think you should leave until we settle this," he called after her. It seemed that for once in her life Cassie was retreating in the face of a challenge.

"Look, if you need thinking time—"

She stopped dead under the frame of the bay door.

"You want to settle things?" she asked as she gave him the challenge-accepted look he knew so well. Eyes narrowed, mouth tight. "Do you?" She sounded like Dirty Harry facing down a punk kid. "Shall we get the inevitable kiss over with?"

"Well, when you put it like that—"

She closed the distance between them with quick steps, took his face in both hands and tilted it down so that she could meet his lips in a full-on closed-mouth kiss. A totally fake kiss, meant to make a point.

A totally fake kiss that stirred his blood.

When she released him, he managed a cocky half smile.

"That's all you got?" he asked, knowing full well he was treading into dangerous territory.

To his surprise, instead of exploding, Cassie gave him a look he'd never seen before—and he'd thought he'd seen every expression she was capable of during their years of competition.

"Oh, no," she said in a low voice that made him distinctly uneasy. "I have this, too." She reached up then to slide her palms over his cheeks before pulling his mouth down to hers, only this time her hands were gentle and her lips were soft and warm, inviting in a way he hadn't expected.

They were both breathing in less-than-perfect

rhythm when their lips parted minutes later. For one long moment they stared at one another, then Cassie stepped back, still holding his gaze as she said, "I think that's enough exploration for one day."

"All right." An inadequate response, but his brain was still coming up to speed. Cassie, however, seemed to be back on her A-game.

"Let me rephrase," she said briskly. "That is enough exploration for *all* the days we're working on this barn."

He gave her a dubious look.

"And things will *not* be awkward between us."

Did she really think they could regulate such things?

"Right."

"I'm serious."

He let out a small scoffing laugh. "Do you think we can kiss like that, then just walk away?"

"I do and we are."

He shook his head and then gave her a rueful half smile. "Good luck on that, Cassie. I don't think it can be done."

She gave him a look. "I think it can."

"Let the games begin."

CHAPTER TEN

"HOW WAS YOUR DAY?" Katie asked as she took a seat at the table where Cassie was coloring with her little nieces. Cassie's shoulder muscles stiffened at the innocent comment and she made a conscious effort to relax them.

Well, I kissed Travis...

"McHenry's Gold is settling in at the McGuire ranch." The mare had been nuzzling one of her cousins over the fence when Cassie got into her car, wondering if she dared ever come back to the ranch. Yes, she'd held her own nicely after kissing Travis, but she didn't know for how long she could keep it up.

The man could kiss.

"And how did barn cleaning go?"

"Messy." In more ways than one. She gave Katie a bright look as she latched onto a distracting element. "I heard kittens today. I think the mama was in the process of moving them as Travis and I worked through the junk."

"Do you think Tigger would like a friend?"

"That would be fun," Cassie said. Maybe she

should have gotten a kitten instead of a horse. Cheaper, easier to care for—but it wouldn't get her out into the sunshine, so she was still hoping that her McHenry mare would work out. "As to the barn, I think we'll be done in a matter of days and then it's a matter of how much decorating do we want to do?"

"The long-term forecast hasn't shifted. A solid week of rain."

"It's Montana. Anything can happen."

Kendra reached for the metallic gold crayon that was just beyond her fingertips and Cassie rolled it her way. The little girl smiled her thanks and began to tackle a buckle on a dog collar with careful strokes.

"I want to color good like Aunt Cassie," Bailey muttered as she inched her crayon closer to the outline of a butterfly.

"Go really slow," Cassie said. There was no use telling her young niece that her motor control had yet to fully develop and that coloring inside the lines would get easier as she got older.

"I used to scribble, too," Kendra said as she colored just up to the dark lines on her picture, taking care not to cross them.

"I'm not scwibbling."

"Scr—" Kendra started to correct her sister,

but stopped and glanced at Cassie, who gave her an encouraging smile.

It was good to correct correctable behavior, but she'd had to explain to Kendra that some things would correct themselves with age. Nagging wouldn't help.

Cassie was familiar with nagging, because she'd nagged Katie when she'd been young, doing her best to turn her little sister into a clone of herself. It hadn't worked in the way she'd expected. Katie had become an over-achiever, just like her two older siblings, but she'd never been happy with her traditional career. It wasn't until she'd moved home and started the herb business—which had truly concerned Cassie—that she'd come into herself. She still overachieved, but in a different way.

"That's a beautiful butterfly," Cassie remarked when Bailey held up her picture. She'd been so careful of the lines that there wasn't much color within half an inch of the boundaries, but she'd accomplished her goal. And Cassie had to admit that her niece had an eye for color.

"What color should I make my puppy's collar?" Kendra asked.

Cassie considered, then said, "What's your favorite color?"

"Purple, but I make everything my favorite color," Kendra said.

"Ah." Cassie pulled out her phone and brought up a picture of a color wheel. "Then let's try the complementary color of purple."

Kendra gave her a bewildered look and Bailey leaned closer to look at the phone.

"This wheel has all the main colors," Cassie said.

"Where's pink?" Bailey asked.

"Pink is a hue…" Cassie bit her lip. "They don't have the light colors. Just the dark ones."

"Oh."

"If you add white, you get the light ones," Kendra said importantly. "We did that when we painted at school."

Bailey was jealous of Kendra going to school and didn't reply.

"Okay. Find purple." Two small forefingers stabbed at her phone. "Now, let's go straight across the wheel and what color to you get?"

Kendra traced the path. "Yellow."

"That's right. Yellow and purple are complements. If you mix them together, you get black."

"Ick." Kendra made a face.

Cassie laughed. "You don't have to mix them. But these complementary colors are special buddies. They go well together." She moved her phone in front of Bailey. "Pink is really light red, so find red." Bailey pointed, then moved her finger across the screen to green and then smiled up at Cassie.

"That's good. Green and red. Now, let's do blue…"

Her phone rang, startling them all, and when she saw her assistant Anna Lee Novak's number on the screen, her heart skipped. They'd agreed that Cassie would be out of all loops except for in a dire emergency.

She gave her nieces an apologetic smile. "This might be something important. We'll talk more about colors later. Anna Lee, hi."

"I'm sorry to bother you, Cassie, but I need to give you a heads-up."

"Sure." Cassie kept her voice bright as she looked over her shoulder at Katie and then strolled down the hallway out of earshot. "What's up?"

"I don't know, but something is going on. There've been a lot of school board members going in and out. Closed-door meetings. Stuff like that. And you know how you can just tell that something is wrong?"

"Oh, yeah."

"Something's going on. Everyone is on edge. Even the people in Payroll, and that department has been cut to the bone, so you know that they aren't worried about being laid off."

Cassie pressed a hand to her forehead. If the

higher-ups—Doug Everett, the superintendent, and Rhonda, who had the job that Cassie would move into after sabbatical—were dealing with something behind closed doors, it had to be serious. Cassie was not so foolish as to pooh-pooh office vibes.

"There's one more thing, and it's why I'm really calling."

There was a note in Anna Lee's voice that had Cassie gripping the phone a little harder. "I heard Rhonda talking on the phone in her office when I came in early from lunch and I very distinctly heard her say, '*If* I retire. That may not come about given the circumstances.'"

Cassie's heart skipped. What circumstances? "You're sure that's what she said?"

"It was plain as day. She didn't realize I was in the outer office."

Rhonda made no secret about the fact that she loved her job, and Cassie had secretly wondered just how happy she was about the way things had worked out. She didn't have as many years to give the district as Cassie, but she was only fifty-six. She could easily give them a decade more if she so desired, but her husband had retired and wanted to travel, and Rhonda had grudgingly agreed to work one more year and then retire herself.

"She might have been joking," Anna Lee

added weakly. "You know how hard it is to tell with her."

"Yes." As in the woman rarely joked, so when she did, it took people a while to catch on.

"That doesn't sound like a joke to me."

It had seemed like Rhonda was on board when they made the deal with the superintendent and the board members, who had seemed relieved to have a difficult decision taken out of their hands. But what if Rhonda changed her mind? She had seniority and Cassie would get squeezed out of her job after putting everything she had into it.

"No," Anna Lee said apologetically. "I thought you should know, which is why I broke my promise to you and called."

"Feel free to break it again. Anytime. I'd like to be kept abreast of what's going on if at all possible."

"I'll keep my ears open and if I find out anything, I'll call."

"Thank you, Anna Lee."

"Hey," she said softly. "I'd rather work for you than Rhonda. I always know where I stand with you."

"Thank you. Talk to you later." Cassie had barely ended the call when Katie walked into the sitting room.

"Don't say it," Cassie muttered.

Katie, of course, ignored her. "I thought you were on sabbatical."

"I am."

"Then you have no business taking calls from school."

"This is important."

"Do you want to know how many times I've heard that over the past two years? You know, when you had to miss Christmas and stuff."

"I can't fix the past."

"Exactly. But you can fix the present."

She'd fallen into that trap neatly enough. Cassie tried the big-sister scowl. It didn't come anywhere close to working. From there she worked into, "Katie, I appreciate your concern, but this is none of your business."

Katie made a rude noise in return. "Try to keep me out of it." She unfolded her arms. "Cassie, wake up. You are wasting your life."

"I am not."

"Not your career. Your *life*. There's a difference. You wouldn't be on sabbatical if deep down you hadn't recognized that you were having an issue separating your life from your job."

"I'm on sabbatical so that I can further my education, spend time with my family and so that my colleague can retire without penalty." A colleague who'd better not screw her over.

"But you can't keep your finger out of the

pie. I may be the youngest," Katie continued, settling her hands on her hips, "but I've gone down this path and I see things that I don't think you are seeing."

"I'm building a career. I've been working in this direction since I left college and I'm seeing returns on my investments."

"At what expense?"

"An expense I'm willing to pay."

Katie gave her a sad look. "I think your jawbone is about to shatter." Then she turned and walked down the hall to the kitchen, where Bailey and Kendra were still talking colors.

Cassie blew out a breath. She and Katie were different people. Cassie could no more imagine leaving her career than she could imagine washing all the colors of her laundry together into one load. She wasn't wired that way. Katie was. But, if her career left *her*, then what?

You roll with the punches, girl.

But so far, professionally anyway, she hadn't faced any real setbacks. She'd had bumps and obstacles in the course of her career, but no real setbacks or detours. She'd told herself that it was due to careful planning, keeping her finger on the pulse of the school district and adjusting her professional course accordingly.

Now it occurred to her that maybe that hadn't been enough.

Maybe she'd been fooling herself.

Maybe things were going to be taken out of her hands, and she was going to spend a year eating up her savings, only to find herself without employment at the terminus. Maybe Rhonda was going to try to stay and force the school board to decide between them—the local woman whose family went back generations, or the woman who had no community connections other than having worked there.

And suddenly kissing Travis McGuire seemed like an easy-to-deal-with problem by comparison.

CASSIE ARRIVED AT the McGuire ranch earlier than usual, but Travis was already working when she got there—not out of a sense of competition, but because there was so much to be done in a short period of time.

"Morning." Travis looked up from the metal tray where he'd dumped a can of miscellaneous hardware and was now sorting through it. When they put the stuff back in the barn, it would be organized.

"About that kiss yesterday."

Travis's hand stilled before dropping large bolts into a Folgers coffee can. "What about it?"

"Be on notice that if I'm preoccupied today,

it's not because of you or the kiss or anything along those lines."

"It would be bigheaded of me to think that," he agreed solemnly.

Cassie laced her fingers together and stretched them in front of her as if cracking her knuckles, making him wonder if he needed to do some warmup exercises of his own.

"Given yesterday's finale, no. It wouldn't be." She dropped her hands. "I'm fighting on too many fronts, Travis. It's taking a toll."

Travis wasn't used to Cassie discussing matters she held close, and the honesty of the unguarded words had him abandoning the bolt sorting and moving a couple of steps closer to her.

"What's going on?" he asked. The sunlight slanting in through the open door spilled across her face, illuminating shadows beneath her eyes. Shadows that had not been there yesterday.

"I got a call from work. I'm still gnawing on it."

"Whatever the problem is, is it something that you need to worry about while on sabbatical?" He put more emphasis on the last word than he'd intended.

"Yes."

"But—"

She closed her eyes, looked like she was

counting to ten—or reviewing her mental list of what she wasn't going to do. "It's not an actual problem. Yet." She opened her eyes, fixing him with a serious gaze. "It's the potential for a problem. A big one if it plays out the way I'm afraid it's going to."

"How so?"

"My school district has lost population—the tax base is shrinking, and we now have too many upper administrators. I am one of two assistant superintendents. One assistant has to go. Rhonda, my counterpart, had one year to go before she could take retirement with no penalty. We hammered out a deal with the school board where I would take a one-year unpaid sabbatical and she would finish her year. I'll step into the position when she retires next June."

He shifted his weight and crossed his arms, mirroring her position. "What's going on now?"

"I don't know for certain," she said slowly. "My administrative assistant called me to say that something was off, and that she heard Rhonda discussing the possibility of not retiring."

"What happens if Rhonda doesn't retire?"

"The board would have to choose between us, I guess." She let out a breath. "I need to know what's going on."

"You aren't going to abandon your grandmother before her wedding."

Cassie gave him a hard look. "I know my track record sucks, but no. I'm not." She dug her hands into her hair on either side of her head, closed her eyes again. The situation was truly eating at her.

At least she hadn't verbally coldcocked him for suggesting she'd abandon her grandmother.

He frowned at her, but she didn't look his way as she dropped her hands loosely back to her sides. Her hair stuck out from her hands raking through it, giving her the wild look he remembered from back in the day when she'd accepted any challenge he tossed her way.

She studied the gravel between them for a long moment, then glanced out over the field where his McHenry mares grazed. "My job is really important to me."

"You hide it well."

Her laugh ended almost before it escaped her lips. "Thanks."

"Are there other fronts besides me and your job?"

"Katie. She's relentless in her nagging about my job and priorities. All for my own good in her mind, but she doesn't understand."

He wondered if anyone understood, including Cassie.

They stood facing one another for a long silent moment, but unlike yesterday, it wasn't a silence that might shatter at any minute.

"I want a truce," Cassie finally said. "A real one." There was something in her solemn tone that dug at him.

"What if I think it might do you good to be distracted from the things you can't control?"

She shook her head, her faint half smile telling him that she wasn't interested in being distracted. "A truce. Please."

When he didn't answer—not because he didn't want a truce, but because he was coming up with a caveat—she cocked her head to one side. "You are an attractive guy, Travis Mc-Guire. Black eye and all." She kicked her toe against the ground, but didn't break her lock on his face. "That said, I need an ally right now, not more things to drive me crazy."

Travis gave a slow nod and managed not to say what he was thinking, which was, *Well played.*

"All right. Consider me an ally."

There wasn't much else he could say. Cassie had done a masterful job of taking away his option to say anything else.

CASSIE GLANCED UP after hefting a wooden box of old leather strapping and found Travis studying her—again—which meant it was time to address things. She needed an ally, not someone stressing her out by looking concerned.

She stood patiently holding the box in front of her until he looked up. "I'm fine," she said as their gazes met.

"Okay." He stacked a couple of bolt cans on a plastic storage bin.

"Don't make me sorry that I shared."

He set the bin back down again. "What are you talking about?"

"You look like you're worried about me." She shifted the box in her arms.

He let out a soft snort. "*You* look like you're worried about you."

"One of us worrying is enough," she said shortly. After her mother died, she'd come to realize that having people worry on her behalf was a burden she did not wish to carry.

"Don't obsess over things you can't control." She was about to reply when he added, "It doesn't help."

He sounded as if he spoke from experience.

You don't want to know. You've got your own issues.

She wanted to know.

"What does help?"

"Time. Perspective."

"It's too early for that."

"Then why tie your gut in a knot?"

"Because that's the way I handle these things." Cassie carried the box out into the sun and set it with its buddies before stretching the kinks out of her back. Travis was right. She needed to stop creating nightmare scenarios about her job and Rhonda staying, which might mean that she had to leave. She pushed the hair back from her brow, grimacing at the fine grit on her forehead. Too bad they couldn't have pressure washed first, then hauled stuff. But some of the junk was so rusty it might have welded into one solid tangle if it got wet.

She turned a slow circle and wondered what on earth Travis was going to do with all this stuff. Some was going back into the barn, some to the landfill. Rosalie had claimed the old wooden barrels for her store, but first they would serve as part of the wedding display.

Cassie pulled out her phone and snapped a photo, then sent it to Darby with the caption "Does this remind you of anything?"

The driveway looked very much like Darby's lawn had looked after they'd hauled all of her belongings outside so that the people who were about to rent her place could move in. There'd been a mix-up with the rental truck company, so her belongings had sat on the lawn for hours before her boyfriend and the truck showed up.

So many people had stopped, thinking it was a yard sale, and one person offered her so much money for her brass headboard that she'd sold it.

Cassie dropped her phone into her pocket. She wouldn't get a reply from Darby until her friend went on break at work.

Back to Travis.

He was waiting for her.

"I'm not trying to boss you, Cassie."

Oddly, she hadn't considered that possibility, which would have been her first thought less than a week ago. *Don't tell me what to do...*

"I know. You're slipping."

The corner of his good eye crinkled attractively. The other eye...well, it was less swollen and now more shades of yellow and blue than black and purple...but it was still too puffed up to mirror its buddy. Maybe that was good, because one eye crinkling in silent amusement was doing a number on her. Imagine what two would have done.

"Are you heading out to work on the fence again?" She needed to ground herself. Think about...anything...except the unknowns connected to her job and the fact that Travis seemed to be growing more attractive every day. The latter was made all the more difficult by the fact that she'd kissed those gorgeous lips.

"For a bit. I'll ride your mare this evening and give you a progress report tomorrow."

Cassie pushed some gravel with the toe of her shoe. "I wondered last night if you were still on board for that. I almost brought the horse trailer this morning."

"I'm on board." His gaze was direct, sincere. He hadn't planned to bail.

"I appreciate it."

"Hey. One less front for you to fight on."

Unless the mare didn't work out, and then she'd have to make some hard choices and possibly take a financial hit.

"You know," he said slowly, once again meeting her gaze, "I understand how things can eat at a person. I apologize for telling you to just move on."

"I imagine you're trying to help me skip a step."

"I think that might be it," he agreed.

An unexpected warmth flowed through her at the thought of him being concerned enough to do that. "Are you working from your own experiences?"

He gave a noncommittal shrug. "Maybe we'll have a beer sometime and discuss."

But not now.

Fine. She would accept that.

"I assume it won't be in the Shamrock Pub?"

His mouth curved, creasing his cheeks. "That goes without saying."

"THE KIDS ARE making headway with the barn?" Rosalie asked as she cut two very thin slices of store-bought chocolate cake. She simply didn't have time to bake anymore, and truth be told, she didn't miss it. She'd had her baking years and now she was having her entrepreneurial years. *A time for every purpose.*

"The darned thing is almost empty, and the driveway is full of ju…important ranch equipment." He let out a long breath and he considered the task ahead of him. "Now I have to make decisions about what to put back and how and, well, all that kind of stuff."

"Maybe this rain was a good thing," Rosalie said. "And since we're going to be ready for rain, maybe we'll get sun."

"I'm sure that'll make the kids happy, spending all that time cleaning for no good reason."

"Clean barn and, as far as I know, they haven't done one another bodily harm."

"True." Will leaned back to give her room to put the plate in front of him. "Looks good."

"I was at the stove all day."

He laughed and lifted his fork. She loved that even dusty old jokes like that made him laugh. He was very different than Carl, but different was good. There was no way she could have found another Carl, so she found a Will instead.

"I was thinking about the kids," Will said after wiping a few crumbs off his chin with a napkin. "And how they set one another off."

"Understatement," Rosalie said in a low voice.

"I think that something has changed there—for Travis anyway."

Rosalie gave him a sideways look. "Changed how?"

Will set the fork back on his plate. "I think that Travis might—" he sucked in a breath "—have a thing for Cassie."

"A thing? Do you mean feelings?"

"Maybe."

Rosalie put her own fork down. "Oh, my." She frowned over at Will. "Do you have any evidence?"

"I've been reading the boy for years," Will said gruffly. "Something is different."

"Have you seen them together often?" Because as far she knew, he hadn't, so what was he basing this on?

"No. Not since the argument in the barn, but things are different."

Rosalie didn't ask which argument in which barn, because there'd probably been several.

"You're certain this isn't wishful thinking on your part?"

Will blew out a breath. "I can't say that's not so. Travis isn't getting any younger and while he's done his share of dating, no one seems to fire him up like Cassie."

"Another understatement," Rosalie murmured before giving her husband-to-be a thoughtful look. "I wonder how Cassie feels?"

"That would be an interesting thing to find out," Will said. "Not that you can just come out and ask her."

"No," Rosalie agreed. "Cassie's not a big sharer in that regard." She'd kept her personal life private even when she'd been living at home. Rosalie thought it had something to do with losing her mother at a young age and people encouraging her to share her grief. That wasn't the way Cassie operated, but they hadn't discovered that until after the damage had been done.

Will took another bite of cake. "I guess we'll have to keep an eye on things. Hope for the best."

"I guess," Rosalie agreed, thinking that Travis might be in for a grandfatherly talk soon.

"So, if you see Cassie looking all moon-eyed—"

Rosalie burst out laughing and Will grinned

back at her. He reached out and covered her hand with his.

"Anyway, let's keep an eye on things. If we see one of them making a tactical error, maybe we can guide them down the right path."

"Will...you're an optimist." Cassie was never one to be guided. "That said, I would love it if she had a reason to come home more often, so I'm going to keep my fingers crossed that things are different with her, too."

CHAPTER ELEVEN

CASSIE GAVE A choked cough as dust swirled around her, then stopped sweeping to let the worst of it settle. She'd been vibrating with pent-up energy when she'd returned home from the McGuire ranch an hour ago, and, since she was still dusty from cleaning the barn, it seemed like the perfect time to tackle the shed where she stored her old belongings. The bubble gum–pink fake-fur coat, which was now in the donation box, had convinced her that she probably had other items that could be parted with. Her life was in Wisconsin and it wasn't fair of her to take up space on the ranch with things she was never going to use again.

At least, she *hoped* her life was in Wisconsin.

Cassie attacked the floor with renewed vigor. Travis was right. She needed to let this go.

She and Rhonda and the school board had made an agreement. She had to move forward under the mindset that all parties would honor that agreement, regardless of what Anna Lee had heard Rhonda say into the phone.

But she couldn't help wondering if there was anyone else she could call to get a little more perspective. A friendly school board member? The principal whom she'd defended against serious, yet bogus, accusations last year? Someone who might have more information or a different perspective?

It wouldn't look good to be out of the loop and begging for information, especially since it might get Anna Lee in trouble for contacting her in the first place. Her best strategy was to wait for Anna Lee's next call and assess her strategy when she had more facts.

"Hey, Cass?"

She stopped sweeping and went to the door. Katie stood behind the closed front gate with the two little goats peeking out from either side of her.

"What's up?" she called back. The air outside the shed was wonderfully dust-free.

Katie held up her phone. "When will you be done with the barn? Grandma wants to know."

"We're pressure washing day after tomorrow. It'll have to dry, and we have to figure out what to do with all the junk, but she can look the place over and make plans."

"Thanks." Katie put the phone to her ear and headed back to the house.

Cassie turned back to the shed, grimaced at the dust still hanging in the air, then decided to call it a day.

After sweeping the mound of dirt and debris into a scoop shovel and carrying it out to the corral, she returned to prop both broom and shovel against an interior wall. If she had time, she'd start sorting tomorrow. Or maybe the next day. Pressure washing might be more involved than she expected. On the other hand, if she and Travis had another day like today, where he was unexpectedly understanding and even concerned about her well-being, she might once again return home with a need to dive into some therapeutic cleaning.

She headed back into the house, stopping to give the little goats a couple of head rubs. They followed her up the porch steps, but Cassie shook her head apologetically as she took hold of the door handle. "Sorry, guys. You're staying out here." Two sets of golden eyes blinked at her, but Cassie remained unmoved.

Katie was just ending her call as Cassie slipped into the kitchen, expertly keeping Lizzie Belle and Wendell at bay as she closed the door. A few seconds later the goats clattered back down the steps and into the grass.

Katie tucked her phone into her pocket and reached for a glass of water sitting on the counter. "I'm going to meet Brady in town to look at some better furniture for the manager's house." Katie and Brady planned to make the small house across the driveway from the main ranch house their home after they married. "Do you want to come?"

Cassie glanced down at her dust-covered shirt, but instead of asking if she had time to shower and change, she said, "I think furniture shopping is better left to the people who will be sitting on it." She wasn't going to be good company.

"Brady wants leather. I want something soft and squishy." Katie set down the glass.

"What makes you think I'd take your side?" Cassie asked.

"Because behind your all-business exterior, you're soft and squishy." Katie's eyes danced at the ridiculous statement.

"Am not," Cassie replied in mock disgust. "And I really don't want to get in the middle of this."

"Okay, but when I end up with man furniture, I'm blaming lack of squishy backup."

"I bet the delivery truck will bring a nice compromise of leather and squishiness."

"I hope." Katie gathered up her jacket from

where it was draped over a kitchen chair and pushed her hands into the sleeves. "You know, when you get done with the shed, the basement could use some attention."

"See you later," Cassie said pointedly, gesturing toward the door with her chin.

"See you," Katie said on a laugh.

After her sister's truck disappeared from sight, Cassie poured a cup of coffee, turned off the pot, then leaned against the counter as she sipped. The house felt empty and she couldn't decide if that was good or bad. There was no one there to see if she indulged in job obsession, but there was no one there to distract her from it either.

The little girls were in town with Rosalie; Nick was installing custom cabinets he'd built into his girlfriend Alex's kitchen and Cassie needed to find another less dusty project.

The garden?

Katie and the girls had been weeding when Cassie left that morning, so probably not. She glanced around the spotless kitchen, then concentrated on the coffee, which was much better than the instant stuff she made for herself because she didn't want to take the time to make a decent pot.

Time, time, time.

When she'd been on the job, every minute

of her day had been filled with something and she'd returned home with just enough energy to nuke something for dinner, watch something mindless on TV then fall into bed. Her social life had sucked, and she hadn't minded one bit.

What did that say about her?

Cassie cupped the mug with both hands, savoring the warmth as she considered the answer.

It said that she found a lot of satisfaction in her work.

It said that she didn't care about what she might be missing. Nope. No fear of missing out for her.

It said that she might have buried herself in her work to keep from thinking about what she was missing.

The last thought didn't sit comfortably, but no one was perfect.

So how was she going to feel living a time-choked solitary existence when she got back?

Different.

Another uncomfortable thought that she was saved from considering too deeply by the sound of an engine. She leaned across the table and looked out the window as her brother was pulling into his usual parking spot.

Funny thing that no one seemed to care that Nick worked his butt off, just as she did. His number one job was fathering his kids, but he also handled the ranch with Brady, did custom work for local contractors and he spent a lot of time in his shop building cabinets. Yet did anyone harp at him about overdoing it? No.

"Hey," he said as he opened the door. He stopped before coming inside and brushed some sawdust off the front of his shirt.

"There's coffee. I turned off the pot so it wouldn't burn, but it should still be hot."

"Coffee sounds good." He shrugged out of his jacket and hung it on the handmade hooks near the door. Small particles of sawdust clung to his dark hair and the back of his shirt—in other words, he looked like he usually did while working on a carpentry project.

"What are you doing back so early?" She handed him a cup and he took a seat at the kitchen table, while she leaned against the counter.

Nick had been ridiculously busy finishing an independent contracting job, leaving early and working late. He usually rolled in close to dinner time, then spent his evenings with his daughters, reading and playing games. Cassie often joined in, but there was a limit to how much the two of them could discuss in front of very curious little girls and there were a few things she was curious about—like how serious his relationship was with Alex, the woman next door, whom his girls thought was some kind of a princess.

Not that she would stick her nose into a sibling's private affairs and ask nosy questions… but she might hint at the matter since Alex appeared to make both him and his girls happy.

"My lumber order didn't come in at Cooper's Building Supply, leaving me at a standstill, so here I am."

"How much longer on the job?"

"I'm almost done. About a week if this order comes in." He pushed a hand through his hair, making it stand up. "This is the last time I stack contracts like this. I hate spending this much time away from the kids."

"You'll finish in time to start haying," Cassie pointed out. "I bet the girls will like riding in the swather."

Nick laughed. "Probably. I do prefer jobs where I can take them."

"I heard they went with you when you fixed Alex's house."

"Couldn't keep them away." Nick smiled, but didn't bite at Cassie's subtle tell-me-about-Alex opening. He lifted the cup to his lips and after he drank, he said, "I heard a new story at Cooper's about how you gave Travis a black eye. It doesn't match the one you told."

"Really?" She reached around to empty the

coffeepot into her cup even though she hadn't planned on drinking any more. "How did Travis get his black eye?"

She'd shared a slightly edited version with her family the day after the incident, so she didn't feel as if she had anything to hide. In a town the size of Gavin, there was no way they wouldn't hear about what had happened that night at the Shamrock, and it was much better for her to get her own story set in their brains before they began hearing the inevitable variations of the truth.

"You pulled back to throw a punch at Ray and hit Travis in the face with your elbow."

"Ah." Cassie fought a smile as she sat down at the table. "I kind of like that version."

"I thought it was colorful." Nick leaned back in his chair, stretching his legs out in front of him. "How are things going in the barn-cleaning area of your life?"

"Not bad. We got the last of the stuff hauled out today and we'll start pressure washing tomorrow."

"I never got the story as to why the two of you ended up being the barn cleaners." Nick said.

"Well, Travis needed help and I owed him for that elbow in the eye," Cassie replied with a half smile.

"Not going to give me a straight answer, eh?"

"Truthfully, Will caught us in the middle of a huge argument the day after the black-eye incident and shamed us into working together."

Nick made a silent O with his mouth. "*That* explains a lot."

"I didn't tell Katie about the argument because she's been going all mother hen on me."

"She's worried about you."

Cassie leaned forward. "Do you know how stressful that is?"

"I know what it's like to have people worried about you."

"Touché." Cassie leaned back again. After his wife died, they'd all worried about him and the girls, had tried to do what they could, which wasn't much other than to be there if he needed support. "Are you worried about me, too?"

Nick focused somewhere on his cup as he considered the question. "I'm not worried." He brought his gaze back to hers. "I think you're making some mistakes, though."

Cassie's jaw tightened, but she was ready to hear his take on matters. She had asked, so she wasn't going to blow him off. "I'm listening."

"I understand why you've had to sacrifice holiday visits and such, but I think your original—and valid," he added quickly, "excuse is gone. Now it's becoming a habit."

She opened her mouth, then closed it again. "I like my job. I want to do it well."

"I know."

When he didn't argue with her, or tell her that she was sacrificing her life for her job, she felt emboldened to admit, "I have approached work with a sort of tunnel vision."

"Goal-oriented people do that."

She gave a nod.

"Are you going to keep doing it?" he asked gently.

"I'm going to try not to, but…" She pushed her coffee cup aside and leaned her forearms on the table. "The problem is that I conditioned the school board to expect that from me. If I slow down to a normal workload, I'll look like I'm slacking." She let out a breath that lowered her shoulders. "And I got a call yesterday. Something may or may not be brewing at work."

Nick raised his eyebrows, so she explained, laying out what her associate had told her, finishing with, "Of course, Anna Lee may have misinterpreted."

"But you prefer to fear the worst."

"Yep." One corner of her mouth tightened.

"Not much you can do about it either way."

She patted the table with the palm of her hand. "That's what's driving me nuts. I'm not on the school district payroll. It's as if I don't exist until next July. I have no say. No clout." She collapsed back into her chair. "Travis essentially told me not to die the thousand deaths, but it's kind of hard not to."

"I understand. And I also agree with Travis."

Travis, who appeared to be speaking with the voice of experience.

Cassie pulled her cup back toward her, more to have something to do with her hands than because she was interested in finishing the coffee it held. She raised her eyes to meet her brother's gaze. "Does Travis have some secret thing in his life I don't know about?"

"Probably quite a few," Nick said dryly.

Cassie scowled down at her cup. "The only reason I ask is because he seemed to understand what I was going through today."

"He knows about the job situation?"

"I told him."

Nick seemed mildly surprised. "You guys are moving forward."

"Not everything is a competition," Cassie quoted. "Anyway, when we talked, I just had this feeling that something was up. Something he wasn't going to talk about."

"It might concern his dad. I'm sure Dan's condition is difficult for those who love him."

"Yes."

"You know, Travis only came back to the

ranch because no one else could work with Will after his dad's RA took a turn for the worse. I think Will was stressed-out and taking it out on the guys he hired."

Cassie frowned at him. How could she have not known this?

"You weren't here," Nick said, reading her thoughts. "They hired and fired three or four guys when Dan was getting ready to move to Arizona. Travis came back to fill in and never left."

Cassie narrowed her eyes at him. "You're saying that he's there out of duty?"

"I'm saying that we all make choices and he made his."

"Huh."

Nick put his hands on the table and pushed his chair back. "And on that note, I'm going to take a shower."

Cassie nodded at the table as she digested this new information. "Don't clog the drain with sawdust," she called absently.

"Yeah. I'll try not to."

After he'd headed down the hall to his bedroom, Cassie got to her feet and paced over to the dining room window, which faced the direction of the McGuire ranch. She'd always assumed Travis was right where he'd intended to be all along. He'd studied agriculture. The family owned a ranch. It made sense.

Or maybe it had just *seemed* to make sense. Cassie knew of only one way to find out.

CASSIE ARRIVED EARLY on their last day of junk hauling and, after parking her brother's truck, went straight to the small corral where her mare happily munched grassy alfalfa.

"How'd she do?" she asked after Travis tossed hay to a heifer he'd brought in yesterday due to a limp.

He wondered if he should soften the blow or just state facts. He went with facts.

"She needs miles put on her, Cassie. A lot of miles. You're not going to plunk along a trail and enjoy yourself. She's really skittish."

"Ever?"

"I don't know." The mare had shied several times and twice she'd attempted to spin and head back to the ranch. She was testing him, seeing what she could get away with, and she needed to learn that she wasn't going to get away with anything. He had no doubt that Cassie could ride the mare, but she was looking for a pleasure mount to relax with.

Cassie looked past him to the field where his McHenry mares were grazing, foals by their sides. The wind ruffled her hair and she smoothed it without breaking her gaze. "You're saying she might be out there next year, making babies."

"I can't afford to pay what you paid for her."

She shifted her gaze his way. "You almost paid that price."

"I was very afraid I was going to have to. When you made that last bid, I could have kissed you."

She took a long look at his mouth, stirring up memories of when they had kissed; memories that were pretty close to the surface, because every now and again he revisited them.

"And you did," she said as she lifted her gaze.

"Well," he said with a half shrug, "I owed you."

"Actually—" she shifted her weight as she considered the matter "—I kissed you."

He smiled a little. "If I still owe you, we could fix things."

"Uh—" she shook her head "—I don't think so." She didn't step back, but she turned her body so that she wasn't fully facing him as she once again studied the mare.

They'd come a ways, he and Cassie. She trusted him to a point. He wished she trusted him more. He wished she saw him differently—not as someone she shouldn't kiss, but maybe someone she should.

"Last day before the big pressure wash,"

she said conversationally. Talk of kissing was now officially off the table. He couldn't help but think that he might find an opportunity to bring it up again.

"It is," he said as he started walking slowly in the direction of the barn. Cassie fell into step and the vibe between them was remarkably relaxed, despite kissing talk. "Feeling better about the stuff that was eating you yesterday?"

She gave a soft snort. "I was until you brought it up."

He played along and rolled his eyes, even though he could see that she was more herself today. "Sorry."

"Tell me about staying on the ranch."

He glanced down at her, but she didn't meet his eyes. "Staying on the ranch?"

"Did you always plan to run the ranch?"

"Who have you been talking to?" When she shrugged, he narrowed his gaze and said, "Nick?"

"I'm not naming sources."

"But you've been talking about me."

Her cheeks flushed a delicate rose. "I was trying not to think about my job."

"And I was the next thing on your mind?"

"Don't get a swelled head," she muttered. "Did you want to do something else?"

"I had a job," he said as they came to a stop at

the open bay door. Inside, the last of the equipment waited. They didn't have a full day's work, but he had some other chores before they geared up for pressure washing.

"Did you?"

"I did. But my dad's condition was going south fast and I decided to come home."

"Any regrets?"

"Who doesn't have regrets? I would have liked to have worked for a while, experienced something new." Reynaldo kept calling him and asking him to do just that. "But I like my life just fine."

"I never guessed that you wanted anything but to be on the ranch."

Neither had his grandfather, and Travis wasn't about to clue the old guy in.

"I don't talk about it, because of Grandpa."

He could see from the look she sent him that he didn't need to worry about her discussing the matter. "Gotcha."

She shifted her attention to the interior of the barn, giving him her profile. Her jaw muscles were relaxed, softening the line of her chin, making him believe that she had gotten a handle on the job problem.

She turned her head suddenly, and caught him staring. "That's not a look of concern, is it?"

He shook his head. "Today you can worry about me."

Her mouth curved into a gentle smile and he was smacked with an almost overwhelming urge to kiss those beautiful lips.

"Naw. I have faith in your abilities."

"Thanks." He gestured toward the barn. "Shall we?"

Cassie sucked in a breath, then buttoned the top button of her shirt. "Yes. We shall."

WILL SHOWED UP about an hour after Cassie had left for the day. Travis straightened from where he was sorting through random garden equipment.

"What are you doing here?" Last he'd heard the plumbers were coming that afternoon.

"Jake, the plumber, had an emergency. He won't be able to come until tomorrow." Will propped his hands on his hips. "Amazing how much space there is in an empty barn."

"And how little space there is in the driveway." Travis gestured at the piles that surrounded them.

Will gave a grunt of agreement. "Rosalie wants to see the space. We're coming out tomorrow evening."

"The interior should be drying by that time."

"Good." Will studied the dusty interior for

another couple seconds, then said, "Going to be one heck of a mess behind the barn with all the runoff."

"We'll make sure the wedding guests don't venture back there."

"Most of our guests have seen worse," Will said. He jerked his head toward the house. "I need to pack up some more clothes."

"Or buy a washer for your town house."

"Oh, that's coming. The plumbers are going to put in a more modern drain system tomorrow after fixing the other problems."

"I bet Rosalie will enjoy being able to wash her clothes."

"So will I." Will grinned. "I kind of like doing laundry."

"I have a pile—"

"No."

When they got to the kitchen, Will automatically pulled two beers out of the fridge, holding them up as if he'd never seen beer before. "Ultra hops?" He made a face and looked back into the fridge. "Where's my beer?"

"Gone. Be open-minded," Travis said.

"So Rosalie keeps reminding me."

Travis had a feeling his grandfather loved being managed, and it definitely took a special person to do that.

They settled on the porch and Travis watched

as Will took his first sip. He lowered the bottle and scowled at it, then drank again.

"Different."

"In a bad way?"

Will shook his head. "I could get used to it."

"Once you have a decent IPA, you never go back."

"Oh, I'll go back," Will assured him before tipping up his bottle. He wiped his lips with the back of his hand, then said, "How are you and Cassie doing?"

Travis gestured at the barn in front of him with his bottle. "You saw the inside of the barn. Not a single drop of blood on the walls."

"Walls can be washed."

"Exactly what Cassie said."

"Did you have to?"

Travis frowned at his grandfather.

"Wash the walls," he said impatiently.

"Did we fight? Oh, yeah." Travis smiled at the memory. He sensed his grandfather studying him a little too intently and turned his head in time to catch Will midstare. "Nothing that would upset Rosalie. We've learned to—" he tilted his chin as he considered the words most likely to end this conversation "—work together without sniping."

"That's good."

"Yes, it is."

"Is that all? No sniping?"

Travis gave his grandfather a full-on frown. "What are you getting at?" *And why aren't you letting this go?*

Will cleared his throat. "I don't want you guys to light into each other at the wedding. That's all."

Travis didn't believe for one minute that was all. Not when Will was acting so darned weird.

But hey, maybe it was just a case of pre-wedding jitters.

"We won't light into one another. You have my word."

"All right, then." Will took a very long drink.

Travis raised his own bottle. "Okay."

Yeah. His grandfather was definitely being weird.

CHAPTER TWELVE

"You understand that there will be no water fights," Travis said as he plugged the pressure washer into a heavy-duty extension cord and then took hold of the wand. After dressing in rubber overalls and coats with hoods, they'd made a loose plan of action. Cassie would spray down the upper walls, the underside of the loft and the columns with the garden hose, getting rid of not only dust but half a century of dirty cobwebs. He would use the pressure washer to get the serious grime off the wooden planks of the barn floor and the lower walls. They'd spray as much debris as possible out the back door where no one would see it once the doors were closed. And if someone did venture back there during the wedding celebration, then they did so at their own risk.

Cassie gave him a bland look, then pulled the trigger on the nozzle of the garden hose she held, squirting his rubber boots.

"Really?" he asked as Will's old dogs, who'd been sleeping in the sun near the bay door, seemed to sense danger. They got to their feet and ambled a good distance out into the driveway, where they settled in the warm gravel.

When Travis glanced back at Cassie, she gave him an unrepentant shrug, looking very much like the girl he'd never have dreamed he'd fall for. But he had and every day they spent together hammered that home. "You do realize you're outgunned…although, come to think of it, you never realized that before."

She mock sneered at him, a mere shadow of the sneers she used to send his way while they'd trash-talked.

"I'll pressure wash you right out of the barn," he warned. "In your dreams." Cassie squirted his feet again and he gave her a sharp look before turning on the machine. She held up a hand in surrender as it rumbled to life, and he grinned at her as it continued its threatening chugs. It didn't seem like a good time to tell her he'd never seen her surrender before. She was relaxed, but not that relaxed.

"Ready?" he asked.

"As always."

They started working on opposite sides of the barn, and soon droplets of water filled the air, dampening their skin and hair. Despite the rubber clothing, there was no way to stay dry with a task of this magnitude. But there was also no other way to remove years of grain dust, silt and other broken-down organic materials than to wash them away. Despite wearing a hood tied under her chin, tendrils of damp hair were already sticking to Cassie's cheeks.

Focus on the job.

He blasted the dirt in front of him, turning it to a muddy stream that he directed toward the door. The noise of the motor muffled the other sounds in the barn, so he barely heard the sharp cry that came just before a stream of water shot over his face, sending rivulets of cold water down his neck.

He turned to Cassie to have a word, but she wasn't looking at him. Instead she was practically dancing in place, staring at the floorboards in front of her, wearing a horrified expression.

"What?" he demanded, wiping a hand over his face.

"Snake." She kept her gaze on the floor, as if expecting the animal to materialize out of nowhere.

"I don't see a snake." He'd seen a couple of kittens peeking in through the rear door that day, but not one single snake. "Are you sure it wasn't a kitten?" There were kittens in the vicinity. They saw the black-and-white mama, who was obviously nursing, on a daily basis.

"I know the difference between a snake and

a kitten," Cassie said in a deadly voice before pointing to the planks a yard or so away from her boots. "He went through that big knothole in the floor. I almost stepped on him."

"You're wearing rubber boots. He couldn't have done you harm."

"He could have gone up my pant leg." She shook her loose-fitting overall leg.

"The chances of that…" The words trailed as she fixed him with another killer look. Fine, she didn't want to know the odds.

It was then that she seemed to notice that he was wetter than he should have been. "What happened to you?"

"I got sprayed by a woman reacting to a reptile."

"No."

"I didn't spray myself," he said sourly.

Cassie looked down at her hose, then up at him. "Sorry?"

"Yeah." He hooked a finger in the collar of his wet T-shirt and pulled it away from his skin. "Not a problem."

"It won't happen again."

"If it does, I will suspect that there was no snake."

"There was." She looked again at the knothole. "We might want to cover this with something."

"That's probably not his only portal."

Cassie wrinkled her nose at him. "Thanks. But now that I know he's there, I'm okay. Snakes don't bother me."

"Are you sure?" Because she was looking bothered not that long ago. "You went nuts over a spider."

"It was *on* me." She spoke through gritted teeth before abruptly turning and resuming her spraying.

Travis hesitated for all of a nanosecond and then squirted the ground next to her feet. Cassie let out a squeak and jumped, then whirled toward him, hose gun at the ready. "You will regret that."

He started to laugh and held up a hand. "I already do."

She lowered the hose instead of spraying him, then, just as he relaxed, brought the hose up and squirted him square in the chest, splattering the underside of his jaw.

"Psych." She laughed before giving him another blast.

There was no way he could squirt her back with the pressure washer, so despite having the gnarlier weapon, he was at a distinct disadvantage. He held up his arm to protect his face. "Truce."

"Ha!" She gave him another blast, but this one was at his feet. "Truce that."

"Don't squirt me, Cassie." There was a distinct warning note in his voice that he hoped she recognized as being serious…or at the very least, kind of serious. He had lobbed the first volley.

"Don't squirt you? After an unprovoked attack?"

"We'll never get done if we have a water fight."

"There's always tomorrow." She gave him a blast in the chest.

"Cassie…"

She gave him a wicked look that made him want to smile. Smile and pull her against him. He started forward and she held her ground, holding the hose gun in front of her, one finger on the trigger.

"One more step and I'll—"

A movement caught his eye and he risked annihilation by glancing out the bay door to where the old Australian shepherds were getting to their feet, their tails wagging as they stared in the direction of the house.

"Are you expecting guests?" Cassie asked.

"I am expecting no one."

Cassie set down her hose and together they walked to the open bay door. The voices grew louder and a second later, Will and Rosalie, who weren't due until that afternoon, came around the corner of the house.

"You really can't hear cars from here," Cassie said.

He gave her a look. "Did you think I was putting you on?"

"I thought my hearing was better than yours."

"What do you think now, Super Ears?"

"The pressure washer is loud."

He rolled his eyes, then pasted a smile on his face as his grandfather and Rosalie approached, winding their way through the mountains of equipment and junk that had to be sorted and stowed before the wedding.

"My, but this is wet work," Rosalie said, her sharp gaze traveling over their rubber suits, then lingering on Travis's dripping wet hair and face.

Travis shifted a little as his grandfather—who was well aware that normal pressure washing, even in a closed environment, didn't cause one's hair to stick to their head, or water to drip off their nose and eyebrows—gave him a dark look.

"It is," Travis agreed.

"I accidentally squirted Travis when I saw a snake," Cassie said.

"In the barn?" Rosalie put a hand to her chest.

"He went down a knothole," Cassie explained.

"Well, if he shows up at the wedding," Rosalie said, "it'll be at his own risk."

"Snakes don't bother you?" Travis asked innocently.

"Not if I know they're there," Rosalie said.

"I thought you were coming this afternoon," Cassie said as she shook water off her sleeves.

Rosalie shook her head. "We decided to take a drive while the plumbers work on the house. I wanted to find willow branches to paint for some floral displays and Will wants to look at the haying equipment." She pulled out her phone. "I also wanted to get some photos so that Gloria and I can start planning."

"Here. Let me, Grandma." Cassie held out her hand and Rosalie gave her the phone. Cassie snapped about a dozen shots of the dripping interior from all angles, then returned the phone to her grandmother.

"Thank you." Rosalie took a couple more shots, then slipped the phone into her jacket pocket. "Will said you have a lot of stuff to sort through before the wedding, and he was not kidding."

"We'll get it done. Don't you worry," Will muttered.

Rosalie gave him a look. "With the hay almost ready to cut?" She patted his arm. "I think Katie and I will clear the calendar for a day or two and help get this done." She shifted her attention back to Travis and Cassie, then glanced at Will, who put a light hand at her elbow. "We'll leave you to it," she said.

"Yeah. Don't drown each other," Will added. He bounced a look between Travis and Cassie, shook his head, then escorted his bride-to-be through the junk and across the wide gravel driveway.

Travis turned back to Cassie. "A truce. For real. Let's get this done."

"Yes." Cassie bent and picked up her hose. "I don't think your grandfather bought the snake story."

Travis risked the spray and reached out to wipe a droplet off the side of Cassie's face, then moved the hood aside to smooth a tendril of damp hair behind her ear. Her eyes widened at the gentle touch, but she didn't move away.

"It doesn't matter. As long as we're not killing one another in front of Rosalie, he'll be happy."

"I don't feel like killing you," she murmured.

"Why is that?"

Her lips parted in that tell of hers, then she gave her a head a slow shake. "I don't know."

Travis looked over his shoulder at the house, then back at Cassie. It seemed like the most natural thing in the world to lean in and touch his lips to hers in a light kiss. Her hand came up to splay over his wet chest as she briefly met his kiss, then eased back.

"Truce accepted?" he asked.

"Yes," she said in a husky voice. "Truce accepted."

"Do you see what I mean?" Will said as he opened the kitchen door and then stepped back so that Rosalie could precede him inside.

Rosalie had to admit to sensing a vibe between their respective grandchildren. One that they were doing their best to hide by acting overly nonchalant.

"Okay. There might be something there."

Will leveled a serious look her way. "And *we* need to do something about it."

"Will…"

"If we don't, then trust me, they'll ride this out without doing anything about it. Cassie will go to school and then back to her job. Travis will bury himself in ranch chores and his horse-breeding program, and then what?" He leaned closer. "We may never have an opportunity like this again."

"There are the family holidays and events," Rosalie pointed out.

"If Cassie comes home for them."

"You have a point," she said in a sigh. Cassie had changed since arriving home; she was more relaxed, more centered, which gave Rosalie hope that maybe her perspective had shifted to the point that she wouldn't make her job the be-all of her existence after returning to Wisconsin.

But she also knew how once one was back in their old environment, old habits began to creep in and take over. She was certain that they'd see more of her oldest grandchild, but probably not for more than a few days at a time.

Will pulled open a drawer and started rummaging around, then came up with a serious pair of wire nippers. "These should cut willow branches."

"I think you could cut bolts with them," Rosalie stated as she took the heavy pliers from him and turned them in her hand.

"I might have." He pushed the drawer shut. "What about it, Rosalie? Shouldn't we do something to help them along?"

She blew out a breath as she lowered the heavy nippers. "Interfering often backfires," she pointed out gently.

"I don't want to interfere. I want to haze them in the right direction."

She let out a low laugh at the cattle-herding term, and then raised her hand to touch his cheek as she looked into his very blue eyes. "Can we haze without being too obvious?"

Will's face lit up. "Sure we can."

"And not be pushy? These are their lives we're dealing with."

"I don't want to push. I want to give them opportunities to see what's right under their noses."

"I think they're seeing it, Will."

He pushed his chin out. "Fine. I want them to act on it. And they can't do that if they don't spend more time together."

CASSIE UNSNAPPED THE FRONT of the rubber coat she wore as Travis rolled shut the back door of the barn, effectively hiding the river of mud and debris they'd washed out of the interior. She slipped off the jacket, then let out a gusty sigh as cool air hit her damp cotton shirt.

"Nothing quite like being encased in rubber on a warmish day," Travis said as he undid his own jacket.

Cassie pulled the suspenders off her shoulders, allowing the rubber overalls to drop to the ground. "Double ah," she said as she stepped free of the last remnants of the sweat tent she'd worn. Honestly, she might have been better off just letting her clothing get soaked.

The barn was practically steaming as the afternoon sun warmed the roof and the water began to condense, but it was also clean. Remarkably clean.

Ready for a wedding.

"Would you like a beer or something?" Travis stepped out of his overalls and then gave them a shake, sending droplets flying.

Cassie gave him a questioning look. He'd never offered refreshment before, but they'd never put in such a long day. And their relationship was so much different than it had been that day Will had found them arguing in her barn. They'd worked through some thorny matters. Kissed twice—three times if she counted the first mock kiss that had triggered the second hot kiss. She now knew things about Travis that she hadn't known before, and he knew things about her.

"*No* is a perfectly acceptable response," Travis said, misreading her silence.

"I'd like a beer." There. No misinterpreting that statement. She also wanted to spend just a little more time in his company. When she was with him, it was easier to let job concerns drift to the back of her mind, and to accept that there wasn't a thing she could do while on leave.

That had been the hardest thing to accept. If Rhonda decided to stay and the board decided to let Cassie go, it was a done deal.

"It'll make Grandpa happy to see us being sociable," Travis said as they started across the driveway.

Rosalie had left for town about an hour ago, leaving Will at the ranch, the backseat of her car loaded with willow branches gathered from the banks of the creek that flowed through the pasture. He'd stopped by the barn to check on their progress and, seemingly satisfied that they were minding their manners, went to work on the swather and make certain all systems were go for haying.

"Will he even know?" Every now and then a metallic clang sounded from the direction of the haying equipment parked behind the grain sheds.

"The guy has eyes in the back of his head," Travis said darkly.

Cassie laughed and then bundled up the rubber gear.

"I'll take that stuff," he said when they got to the house. Cassie handed over the rubberwear, and he gestured to the chairs on the porch. "Have a seat. I'll bring the beer back with me."

Cassie had a seat, scooting her chair out into the sun and closing her eyes. She felt different than she had only a day ago. Closer to a point of acceptance and peace.

Perhaps this was the way one was supposed to feel while on a vacation. She didn't know, because she'd never taken a real vacation.

That might have been a mistake.

She could see now that stepping back cleared one's head, something she'd suspected was a myth put forward by people who weren't serious enough about their jobs.

Yet another shift in perspective.

The storm door opened behind her and her biggest shift in perspective stepped through. She opened her eyes and reached for the beer he held out, before he sat next to her.

"To a job well done," he said.

"Let's hope the junk sorting goes as well." Before leaving, her grandmother had suggested that perhaps she and Cassie and Katie could help sort through the stuff to hurry the process. Cassie offered her bottle and Travis gently tapped it with his own.

"I appreciate the help."

"It isn't like I have a lot of other stuff to do until the wedding decorating kicks off." Besides, it kind of felt right to continue working with Travis.

What would your younger self have said?

"Empty afternoons?" he guessed.

"I have to go through my belongings in the storage shed." She made a face at him. "I don't want to."

"Confronting the past… Yeah. I get it."

"I still own a bubble gum–pink fuzzy jacket."

He surprised her by laughing and saying, "I remember that jacket."

"Very fashionable, wouldn't you say?" she asked.

"Just as much as my acid-washed rodeo jeans."

She cocked an eyebrow at him. "*I* remember those jeans." She did. He'd looked hot in them and she'd hated it because her nemesis wasn't supposed to look hot.

He grinned at her, then fixed his gaze back on the barn. "Have you ever thought of getting a job closer to home?"

The simple question sent a frisson of alarm through her, but it shouldn't have. It was…a question. Not a hint that she should move closer to home, give up all she'd worked for. Be closer to him.

Did he want her closer to him?

It was a conclusion that one could reach after considering the facts, but she wasn't ready to go there. Instead she gave him a casual look and said, "When I first entered the job market, the school districts in this area weren't very financially stable. You could have a job one year and the next be out on the street. So I went to a place where they held on to teachers and administrators with the idea that I could work my way to the top. I'm almost there."

Travis nodded at the barn. "Understood."

She almost said sorry, but she wasn't going to apologize for doing what she had to do. But when he set his hand on hers where it rested on the arm of her chair, she didn't slide her fingers from beneath his or try to tamp down the warmth that flowed through her at his touch.

But she did have to take care not to lose her grip on the reality of her situation.

"We're okay, right?" Cassie swallowed after she spoke.

"What do you mean by okay?"

"Not getting ahead of ourselves because of a few kisses."

His grip tightened. "We will not get ahead of ourselves."

Cassie nodded, relieved that they were on the same page, while telling herself that she'd only imagined the note of disappointment in his voice.

CHAPTER THIRTEEN

AFTER FINISHING HIS morning chores, Travis found his grandfather in the barn, inspecting the interior. The place needed work, but it was so much closer to being weddingworthy that he felt a swell of satisfaction as he approached. Not only was the barn in great shape—he and Cassie had worked through some thorny issues during their days of junk hauling.

He was hopeful that they would continue to move forward, without the excuse of the barn to bring them together, although in some regards, she was almost as skittish as her mare.

She didn't want them to get ahead of themselves.

He wasn't entirely certain what she'd meant by that, but he totally intended to get clarification.

"I think this will work," Will said under his breath.

"It had better," Travis said through the open bay door. "It's the only barn we have."

Will didn't appear to hear him, so Travis

whistled. His grandfather jumped and turned toward him. "You shouldn't be sneaking up on a guy."

"I didn't sneak. You were miles away. Since you're swathing today, I thought I'd better ask if there is anything in these piles you're married to?"

Will shook his head. "Use common sense." He glanced at his watch, then craned his neck to look out the open bay. "Did you say Cassie is coming today to help you sort?"

"They're all coming. Katie, Cassie, Rosalie. First they have some kind of wedding meeting."

"Ah. Good." Will gave Travis a quick look, as if he was about to launch into something, then just as quickly looked away.

"Is everything okay?"

"It's fine. Why?"

"You're acting weird lately."

Will let out a snort. "I am not. I just wanted to know if you had help today." He turned and walked out of the barn, then stopped next to a pile of metal odds and ends. "You'll need it."

Travis picked up a chain saw chain that looked as if it had been used to cut through a steel beam and tossed it into the scrap-metal trailer, parked next to the wood trailer. Some stuff would be saved for recycling, but the stuff that didn't qualify would go the landfill. "I have lots of help." And he was certain his grandfather was aware of it.

"Things are going pretty good with you and Cassie now."

Travis slowly raised his gaze. "For the last time, Cassie and I will not upset Rosalie at family functions. We will not have a knockdown-drag-out at the wedding. Put your mind at ease."

"All right."

If Travis didn't know better, he would have thought his grandfather was flushing guiltily. Then a thought struck him. "Are you nervous about the wedding?"

Will shot a sharp look his way. "Getting married at my age is intimidating. I don't want to mess this up. I want Rosalie to be happy."

"I understand." Yet he still had a strong feeling that there was something else at play.

"Lester will be here soon. I'm going to see if I can get the swather started."

"You do that." And since Will had had the swather purring yesterday, he wondered why that was a concern.

Before Will got to the swather, Cassie, Katie and Rosalie arrived. Will met the car, then escorted the women past Travis and the junk piles and into the barn, where the ideas started flying.

"Now, that area over there," Will said, "will

have stuff stored against the wall. Things that have to be out of the weather."

"How big of an area?" Rosalie asked.

"Let me pace it off for you..."

Travis stayed outside, focusing on sorting trash from treasures, until Will called his name five or six minutes later.

"Yeah. Coming." He dropped a peavey with a broken handle into the "keep" pile, hoping he could find a new handle to fit it, and then continued into the barn.

Will made a gesture toward the area where they would be storing the essentials. "We're thinking that we'll rope off the area, but it might be nice to have some barriers of some kind—"

"Screens or dividers to hide things," Rosalie said. "Rustic, of course."

Just as Cassie had suggested to him earlier.

"Katie thinks she might have her wedding here, too, so if we could come up with something kind of permanent and picturesque," Rosalie added.

"Won't it be kind of cold?" Because last he'd heard, Katie planned to have a Christmas wedding.

"We'll rent propane heaters," Katie said. "The kind they use on restaurant patios."

"Ah."

His grandfather stepped forward, rubbing

the back of his neck thoughtfully before saying, "I thought maybe you could run up to the line shack and harvest that nice weathered wood and we could build dividers from it."

Travis shrugged. "Sure. Um…when?"

"Tomorrow?"

"They thought I might like to come with you," Cassie interjected with a lift of her eyebrows, clearly indicating that a lot had gone on while he was sorting.

"Are you coming with me?" he asked point-blank.

"Of course."

Will's face broke into a triumphant grin, which abruptly disappeared when Travis looked his way.

No way.

Travis let out long, low breath. Just what he needed. A matchmaking grandfather.

CASSIE WAS BEGINNING to wonder if she would ever cross the McGuire ranch cattle guard on her way home without being dusty or wet. Despite washing her hands at the standpipe and dusting off her clothes, there was still barn grime clinging to her shirt and jeans, only this time it came from sorting the stuff sitting in the driveway into "keep" and "toss" piles, rather than from packing it out.

"I feel gross," she muttered to her sister.

"We made some major headway." Katie used her look-on-the-bright-side voice. "And frankly, you're looking pretty good today. A couple of times you came home looking like you'd rolled on the floor."

"Thanks." But it was true.

"Hey, I totally appreciate the effort," Katie said. "I feel bad not helping to haul stuff out since I'm going to use the barn for my own wedding."

Cassie was glad her sister hadn't been there to help. If she had been, then she and Travis wouldn't have made so much headway getting to know and understand one another.

Maybe you've made too much headway...

She shoved the thought aside. That was a matter she would mull over later, when she was alone. "I don't think you would have had time with the herbs and Kendra and Bailey."

"Probably not. If I'd brought the girls, one of us would have had to watch them."

"To keep them from getting into the same kind of trouble we did?" Cassie asked with a smile.

"To keep them from getting into the same kind of trouble you and Nick got into. I was the homebody, remember?"

It was no secret that Katie had preferred staying with Rosalie and tending to more domestic matters, but if push came to shove, she could cowboy with the best of them. She just didn't like it as much.

"Brady really likes the idea of using the Mc-Guire barn for our wedding," Katie said as they drove across the bridge over the Ambrose River. "Especially since Will kind of brought us together."

Cassie frowned over at her sister, who made an eyes-on-the-road gesture before saying, "It's true. When Brady was headed off to Las Vegas to work at a bucking school there, Will talked sense into him and sent him back to me. There was a rabbit involved, too."

"Why didn't I know about this?"

"We don't tell a lot of people about the rabbit."

"I mean why didn't I know that Will had a hand in bringing you guys together?"

Katie gave her a look. "Because when you call, you talk about your job, ask about everyone, then hang up. Of course you're going to get superficial information."

"We used to tell each other stuff."

"Right up until you went to college. Then it was eye on the prize."

Cassie wanted to contradict her, but thinking back, she couldn't. She'd always assumed there'd be time for deep conversations later, after she'd achieved the next big goal.

Katie gave a small sigh. "I'm in no position to talk. I was the same way."

And now she seemed very happy that she wasn't that way.

"When I go back to work, I'm going to try for greater balance between my personal life and private. That's why I bought the horse."

"How's that going?" Katie asked.

"Time will tell," Cassie answered noncommittally. Right now it didn't look good, and she was beginning to wonder if she and Travis should go into a partnership with McHenry's Gold and raise a couple of babies. Cassie could trade the babies for the mare. Or maybe she'd trade one baby for the mare if Travis trained the baby.

Something to think about, talk about. They'd have time to do just that when they traveled to the far end of the sprawling ranch to collect boards.

Those "special" boards.

She gave her sister a quick sidelong look. "Did it seem to you that Will and Grandma seemed inordinately interested in getting a very particular kind of board for the paneling when we have a lot of pretty weathered boards in the boneyard?"

"Apparently these are goldish instead of silver gray and pretty cool-looking."

"All the same…"

"If they're pretty, I want them for my wedding," Katie said with mock sternness as they drove into the ranch. "Don't go ruining my chances to get cool wedding boards."

"Wouldn't dream of it. And it seemed important to Will," she said as she pulled to a stop.

"It's Will's wedding, too." Katie undid her seat belt after Cassie parked, but didn't reach for the door handle. Instead she half turned toward Cassie. "Do you think something is going on?"

"No," Cassie said a little too quickly. "Of course not. These must be some boards, that's all."

Katie gave a satisfied nod and opened her door while Cassie did the same.

There was definitely something going on.

ROSALIE STOOD ALONE in the barn with her eyes closed, trying to envision it as a wedding venue. It smelled of damp wood, but that would fade and soon she and her crew would start decorating.

She'd always loved the juxtaposition of the rustic and the elegant, and while she wouldn't have called herself elegant, she possessed a certain grace and Will was rustic to the bone, so the venue and the theme made perfect sense. Having the wedding on the ranch was special to Will, and Katie was all about having her own wedding there, too, so it worked out. Plus, cleaning the barn had brought Cassie and Travis together, but not in a way she'd expected when they first began.

Two grandchildren had forged happy relationships under her watch, but she wasn't certain what was going to happen with her eldest, most headstrong grandchild. Was Cassie going to head back to that pressure-cooker job of hers? If she did, that was her choice, and so far, Cassie had made the right choices in her career path—for her professional health anyway.

Rosalie would like to see Cassie take a job that wasn't as all-consuming, but she did her best not to butt into her children's and grandchildren's lives. Will didn't have the same standards of conduct, but she was beginning to be swayed to his way of thinking. What was wrong with her and him shooing the grandkids in a certain direction? Headstrong as they both were, they were fully capable of fighting back—if they cared to.

When her son, Pete, had called from Australia to discuss travel details the night before, Rosalie had mentioned that Cassie was working with Travis clearing out the barn and that she suspected that Will was trying to bring them together as friends.

Pete had laughed and said if Will could manage that, then he deserved to win a peace price.

After watching Travis and Cassie watch one another, however, Rosalie wondered if Will might get that prize. If so, then her Cassie had some choices ahead of her.

She turned as she heard Will's footsteps behind her.

"What do you think, Rosalie?"

"I think this barn is a perfect blank canvas," she said, spreading her arms out and doing a turn as if to embrace the emptiness.

"Yeah. It is," Will agreed gruffly. "And as a bonus, I'm getting rid of a lot of stuff that should have gone by the wayside a long time ago. I'll probably make some money on the scrap, too."

"Win-win," she said as she stepped closer and he settled an arm over her shoulders.

"You know," he said, "I think this thing with the kids is working out."

She thought he'd been a little too obvious when he'd set things up for Cassie and Travis to collect the line-shack boards, but neither of them had balked at the task, so perhaps they wanted to spend time together. "You old romantic," she murmured.

His cheeks started to go red, but he didn't deny it. "Who are you calling old?"

Rosalie leaned her head against his solid shoulder. "That would be us, my love."

Old and in love was as good as young and in love and, in some ways, a lot less complicated.

"Now?" Kendra asked as she leaned closer to the mixing bowl where Cassie was whipping the butter and sugar. She and Bailey stood on kitchen chairs on either side of Cassie, each holding an egg.

"I think we're almost there. Do you have your little bowls?" Which helped ensure that the cookies didn't have extra calcium from shell fragments.

"Mine's ready," Kendra said importantly.

"Me, too," Bailey added with a happy smile, pulling the bowl a little closer.

"I'm ready for eggs," Cassie said, taking a step back.

The girls tapped their eggs on the counter, then split open the shells, carefully dropping the contents into small glass bowls.

"Any shell pieces?" Katie asked.

"I don't see any," Bailey said, frowning down at the contents of her bowl. "But my yolk is broken."

"That's fine, sweetie." Cassie moved closer

to make certain there were no shells as her phone rang. She glanced to where it sat on the counter, then her heart skipped. Anna Lee.

"I'll take care of the eggs," Katie said, reading her sister's expression.

Cassie mouthed a thank-you, then stepped into the living room to take the call.

"There's definitely something happening out of the ordinary," Anna Lee said as Cassie said hello. "School board members are meeting with Rhonda. They look grim going into her office and even grimmer coming out. I caught a glimpse of the district lawyer once, but he might have been here for that accessibility issue."

Cassie almost asked how the accessibility matter was progressing, but didn't. One issue at a time. "Only Rhonda's office?"

"Doug is in Hawaii, using his vacation days before they expire. Rhonda is probably keeping him posted, but he left the day before things started to get strange, so he hasn't been personally involved. I hope this doesn't ruin his vacation."

"Me, too." Dr. Doug Everett had done an incredible job of keeping the school district running smoothly during difficult times. He was Cassie's mentor and role model and she owed him for all the support he'd given her.

"The board retreat is tonight. I'm sure some

information will break loose then. I'll call you afterward," Anna Lee promised. "It should be around nine your time. Is that too late?"

"Not at all."

"Good." Anna Lee hesitated, as if not yet ready to end the call. "So how are things out West?" she asked brightly.

"I'm enjoying time with my family." A safe enough answer. She couldn't really say she was torn between her need to follow her original plans and a primal urge to head back to work and deal with whatever was brewing. She didn't have that option.

"Family will keep you sane." Anna Lee gave a small laugh. "Unless they're the kind of family that keeps you insane."

"Right," Cassie laughed. "Thanks for the call. I have little girls waiting for me in the kitchen, but if anything else goes down—"

"I'll let you know."

Anna Lee said goodbye and Cassie slowly lowered her phone. Something was happening, but there was nothing she could do.

At least Anna Lee hadn't said anything more about Rhonda hinting that she might not retire, and in the name of being able to sleep at night, Cassie had decided not to ask.

"Is everything okay at work?" Katie asked in a voice that belied her pleasant expression when Cassie came back into the kitchen. The girls were watching the beaters blending flour into the butter, sugar and eggs, but they both looked up at Katie's question.

"I don't know," Cassie said honestly. "But given the circumstances, it has to play out without me, so I'm not going to worry about it."

Katie shot her a suspicious look, then her brow cleared. "Good attitude."

"Was that Grandma on the phone?" Kendra asked.

"No, honey. It was someone I work with."

Kendra made an O with her mouth, then scrambled down off her chair. "I'll get the plastic wrap to cover the cookies."

"Great idea," Katie said, then in what appeared to be a sisterly show of support, she changed the subject. "Brady got a second job offer today."

"No kidding." Cassie tilted her head. "Were you keeping it a secret?"

"Nope. Got a text while you were dealing with your call."

"That is great news." Cassie took the plastic wrap from Kendra and set it on the counter next to the churning mixer.

"Yep. The guy who had no training now holds his advanced welding certificate and two places in Gavin have offered him a job. Now all he has to do is choose."

"Fantastic. He's worked hard and he deserves this. You deserve this, too."

Katie shot her a smile. "Behind every good man, yada yada."

"Uh-huh."

"The only thing is that we are going to need another ranch hand if Brady takes the town job and Nick's contracting business continues to snowball."

This year hadn't been a problem because it had been a great spring and every cow they owned was on pasture. The fences were in good shape and Nick had cleared his calendar during haying, so with Katie's help, they could get the job done. But contracting brought in a lot of money, and since Nick was also leaning toward marrying Alex...

"Yes. We might need another hand."

"Do you care to fill the job?" Katie asked in an overly casual voice.

Cassie gave a sputtering laugh. "As much as I love all things ranch, no."

"Just checking."

"You've checked. I've answered." Cassie moved her eyes sideways, indicating their nieces, who were watching their aunts with the same interest they'd given to the whirling beaters of the mixer. Adult stuff could be fascinating.

"Yes, indeed," Katie said briskly as the last of the flour was worked into the dough. "We'll let these chill while we eat dinner, then we'll roll them out and you guys will have cookies to take to Aunt Gloria tomorrow."

"And for us to eat," Bailey announced.

"Exactly," Cassie agreed.

It was supposed to rain the next day, so rather than mow more hay, since it was disastrous to have the hay down during a rain, Will and Rosalie and Katie were going to help sort the barn junk, while Cassie and Travis went to the line shack and retrieved the wood before it was soaked.

To get those special boards.

Cassie shot a look in Katie's direction, but her sister did not look back.

Something was definitely up.

CHAPTER FOURTEEN

"WE'RE GOING TO have to work fast," Will said as he nodded at the nearly cloudless sky.

Travis wasn't so sure. The weather apps indicated that the rain wasn't due until the early evening hours, but Will did have a knack for sensing weather—a knack that Travis hadn't inherited, so he relied on the weather services.

"Bring back more boards than you think we'll need."

"Will do." The corners of Travis's mouth twitched as he met Cassie's eye. Will was taking great pleasure in lining out his crew.

"I guess we should take off before the storms hit," Cassie said. Sunlight glinted off her hair as she turned her head toward him, but Travis nodded solemnly in agreement.

"Right." Will pulled his gloves out of his back pocket and when no one moved he said to no one in particular, "What's everyone waiting for?"

"Nothing," Travis said. He started for the flatbed truck and Cassie fell into step. They went to their respective sides of the vehicle, opened the doors and climbed in.

"My grandfather is suffering from pre-wedding jitters. How's Rosalie doing?"

"My grandmother is positively serene. She's sure about what she's doing." Cassie gave him a sharp look. "Is Will having second thoughts?"

"Definitely not. He's afraid of disappointing her."

Cassie gave a small laugh. "That's kind of hard to believe. I was always kind of intimidated by him when I was a kid. He was so gruff and unsmiling."

"You? Intimidated."

She made a face at him. "So do you think your grandfather's huge interest in having us get the special boards is to make my grandmother happy?"

"Nope," he said easily, shifting down as they approached a hill.

"Then what?" she asked in a voice that made him think that she already knew the answer, but was hoping she was way off base.

"I believe that these boards *are* very cool—" he shot her a look "—and that they're being used as an excuse to give us more alone time together."

Cassie let her head drop back against the rear window, something she couldn't do in a newer truck. It made a hollow thunk, but she didn't seem to care. "I had the same feeling."

"It's not so bad."

She gave him a sour smile. "I hope that he's doing this in the name of solidifying our friendship."

"I'm sure that's it."

"And nothing more." She spoke to the windshield.

He almost said, "Would that be so terrible?" Instead he reached out and took her hand, giving it a warm squeeze. She squeezed back and held on for a second longer than necessary, then slipped her fingers out from his.

"Family," she said on a note of mixed exasperation and amusement.

"Exactly."

CASSIE ONCE AGAIN leaned her head back against the rear window, then raised it again as the truck hit a bump. Enough head banging. "All we have to do is ride this out." She spoke more to herself than to Travis.

"Sure." There was a note in his voice that caught her attention.

"You *do* want to ride this out, right?"

"Of course." He spoke flatly, and she decided to believe him. They'd talked just yesterday about not letting circumstances get out of their control, essentially establishing a verbal contract, and she was going with that. If Travis had second thoughts, he could voice them plainly so that she could shoot them down.

Travis slowed to a stop in front of the gate leading to the high pastures and Forest Service land and Cassie automatically reached for the door handle.

"Careful with the door," Travis said, and, sure enough, the wind caught it and tried to pull it out of her grip.

"Your grandpa is a good weather predictor."

"Yeah. I should have believed him."

Cassie slid out of the truck, the wind whipping her hair as she opened the gate and then shut it again after Travis drove through. The dark clouds the wind was pushing were just visible over the tops of the mountains to the west, which meant they might be driving back in the rain.

"How far to the line shack?" she asked as she got back into the truck, slamming the door against the wind.

"Almost five miles."

"And why the chain saw?" Which was lashed to the flatbed railing with a strap.

"Because there was a tree across the road the last time I came up to check cows."

"Does Will know about the tree?" As in, did

he plan on them dealing with the task together, as they'd dealt with the barn?

"I don't think so. I don't bug him with small details."

Cassie settled back in her seat. "I'm looking forward to the days when my grandchildren will protect me from the realities of life."

"I doubt that."

"You don't think I'll have kids and grand-kids?"

"I don't think you can give up enough control to allow someone to protect you from reality," he stated in a reasonable voice.

"I could if I didn't know it was happening," she pointed out.

"Somehow I can't see you not being aware. And in control." The track was narrowing in front of them and he slowed to drive around the end of a fallen tree. "Do you delegate at work? Or do you try to take care of everything on your own and your associates work around you?"

The truck hit another bump and she automatically clutched the dash to steady herself.

"Sorry about that," Travis muttered.

"The tactless question or the bump?"

"The bump. I'm curious about the answer to the question."

"Of course I delegate." But she did like to be kept up-to-date on everything.

"Just asking."

"And my people like working for me." Those in the immediate office, anyway, who knew her and occasionally saw her funny side. Like Anna Lee. Teachers and administrators on other sites…maybe not so much. But she was a fair boss and her performance reviews reflected that. So what if teachers jumped a mile when she walked into their classrooms unannounced?

"How do you know?" he asked in a curious voice.

"I get excellent reviews from my staff. And those reviews are anonymous."

"Cool. Any areas where you can improve?"

She frowned at him. "Why do you want to know?"

He had the audacity to smile at her. "I have some ideas. I want to know if I'm close to right."

Cassie let out a long breath. "Fine. I have areas to improve upon."

"Let me guess—"

"I intimidate the staff. Sometimes," she added. "Not all the time."

He shot her an amused look. "What are you doing to remedy that? Team-building activities? Stuff like that?"

Cassie sucked air in through her teeth. "Being scary kind of helps me run things." She couldn't say she liked that about herself, but it did make her job easier.

"Is that good?"

"No. But it's effective." She shot him a look. "Could we maybe drop this subject? Because I'm done talking about it."

CASSIE SAT STARING straight ahead, making no further effort at small talk as he followed the narrow track leading to the line shack. The occasional unavoidable bump had them both bouncing in their seats, but Cassie would silently right herself and continue studying the road ahead.

He was fairly certain that she wasn't angry with him because he'd asked about her weaknesses in her job reviews. She was preoccupied—but with what? His best guess was that she wasn't thrilled at the idea of his grandfather pushing them together, but there wasn't much they could do about that short of confronting Will. And that, Travis imagined, would make for an interesting conversation. It appeared that she was fine with the occasional kiss, but that anything more was out of the question.

Why? Was it him? Her? Her job? His job?

Was he up against impossible odds? Before she left, he wanted her to know how he felt. He didn't expect it to change anything in the short term, but she'd have facts that may have a bearing on the long term.

Or was he deluding himself?

Lots of questions, no satisfactory answers. The one thing that was certain was that his gut twisted at the thought of Cassie walking out of his life.

Cassie snapped back to the present as he slowed to stop in front of the big ponderosa pine that had fallen across the road during the winter storms. Earlier this year he'd ridden around it, but now he had to deal with it, or they would not be collecting old wood.

Travis grabbed the ear protectors that hung on the gun rack, got out of the truck and grabbed the chain saw out of the bed as the wind tugged at his coat. "You might want to wait in the cab. Better for your ears."

Cassie didn't argue. He wondered if he needed to worry about that.

Once the truck door was shut, he fired up the chain saw and began limbing the tree prior to cutting it into manageable rounds. After he shut off the saw and set it down, Cassie got out of the truck.

He cleared his throat. "Sorry I touched a nerve earlier."

She gave a noncommittal shrug. "It's kind of what you do, right?"

"With no plans to stop at any time in the near future."

"Thanks for the warning."

He hooked his thumbs in his front pockets. "Feel free to do the same."

"Do you have any nerves that can be touched?" She propped a foot on top of a round. "Any bad habits or dark secrets?"

"I probably won't be telling you if I do."

"I'll see what I can ferret out," she said as she once again started maneuvering the log round toward the side of the road. "And for the record, I'm not bothered by admitting that I have areas where I need to grow." She gave him a quick sideways look. "But you're the only person I've told about using my perceived scariness to my advantage."

"As long as you're fair."

"I'm fair." She pushed the last of the wood out of the way, then turned to face him.

The wind continued to pick up as they cleared the road, lifting and swirling the sawdust around them. And sure enough, dark clouds were rolling over the mountains with astonishing speed.

"It doesn't bother you when people don't like you?"

"I can't afford to let it."

"You're tough, Cassie."

"I have to be."

He gave a nod of agreement, then headed to his side of the truck. He only hoped she wasn't too tough, because they still had a few issues to iron out between them.

TRAVIS DIDN'T APPEAR one bit concerned about Cassie ferreting out a nerve to touch, which was a silent challenge if she'd ever seen one, and if she hadn't been so preoccupied with convincing herself that things were cool between them, she would have put more effort into coming up with something to make him squirm a bit.

They drove a couple more miles on the twisting road, winding between overgrown Douglas firs and tall lodgepole pines, before coming to another gate at the edge of the sweet little meadow. Beyond the gate was a newish wooden shed with a metal roof adjacent to a jumble of boards and debris that had probably been the original shack. A sturdy corral with a lodgepole loading chute stood behind the wrecked cabin along with a large metal water trough fed through a pipe connected to a spring on a distant bank with black plastic pipe. The cow camp.

Cassie got out to man the gate, then waved Travis on after he drove through, preferring to walk the fifty or so yards. She breathed deeply as she walked, filling her lungs with the cool mountain air and staying in the truck tracks so she didn't have to fight the deep grass. The rain was coming, as Will had predicted, and it was coming fast, but hopefully she and Travis would have their cache of boards loaded and be on the way home before it hit.

Travis swung the truck in a circle in the meadow and backed close to the jumble of boards and roofing. She hoped he didn't run over a nail, because the last thing she wanted was to help change a tire in the rain; although, perhaps that was part of Will's master plan.

Was her grandmother in on this scheme of Will's?

Cassie couldn't see her live-and-let-live grandmother sanctioning such a thing.

She hoped. Rosalie could be a force to be reckoned with.

Travis got out of the truck and came around the hood to stand next to her.

"Okay," Cassie said as she picked up a broken board. "I concede. These are cool boards." The long rough-cut planks that had made up the siding of the collapsed shack were weathered to a beautiful coppery gold with streaks of brown and black.

"We've talked about collecting these for a long time, but you know how that goes."

She gave him an innocent look. "Kind of like cleaning out the barn?"

"Exactly. Tomorrow is always a better day to start."

Cassie pulled her gloves out of her pocket and slipped them on. "Where shall *we* start?"

"I'll knock boards loose with a hammer and you can drag them out. I figure we want as many as we can get."

"Was this shack standing when you were a kid?"

"Yeah, but a tree came down on it, so we logged the adjacent area and built again."

"Where's the tree?"

"Burned in the stove of the new shack. We dragged it off with the truck, cut it up."

"Excellent use of resources."

A blast of wind lifted Travis's hat and he barely caught it. He pulled it lower on his forehead. "We'd better get moving."

Indeed, a charcoal-gray wall was coming at them over the not-so-distant mountains.

Travis started lifting and untangling the jumble of boards, occasionally knocking one free from an upright while Cassie dragged anything that was unattached out of the pile and laid it parallel to the truck to load later.

The wind was starting to get serious when the first drops of rain stung her face. She wiped her coat across her face and tugged at another board. Travis joined her and together they pulled three boards free before the rain began pelting them, hitting Cassie square in the face and then running down the front of her coat.

"Let's go," Travis shouted.

Cassie started for the truck, thinking they would wait out the storm in the cab, but Travis caught hold of her arm and led her to the shack, which was closed with a simple hasp and a combination lock that was hanging unlocked. He slipped the lock out of the hasp, then threw the door open. Cassie stumbled inside, pushed by the buffeting wind. Travis followed, pushing the door against the wind, which howled through the cracks until he managed to shove it into place.

Cassie swept her wet hair back with both hands. "What is it about working with you where I end up soaking wet?"

He shook the water off his hands. "I could ask the same, because I always end up being a lot wetter than you." He pulled off his ball cap and hit it against his leg, then set it on the table. "This is more of a squall than a real storm. It should blow over pretty fast."

"I hope Will gets his essentials into the barn in time."

"I'm sure he will. He was bossing his crew pretty well when we left."

Cassie took a turn around the one-room shack. "This is actually pretty nice." It even had vinyl flooring to make it easier to sweep out the dirt.

"When we built this shack, I took care to make it as rodent-proof as possible. So far so good."

"You spend the nights up here instead of going back home?"

"Sometimes. I like it here." He pulled an enamel teapot out of the small cupboard unit, then opened the lid and looked inside. "No spiders. Do you want some tea?"

"Let me see that." She put her hands over his as she peered down into the sparkling-clean pot, then she stepped back. "Tea would be nice." It would take that chill off, maybe give them something to focus on besides each other.

He opened the bottom unit and pulled out a gallon jug of water and filled the pot.

"You really are equipped for an emergency stay."

"We've had hunters shelter here in storms."

"That's why it isn't padlocked."

"Exactly."

"Has the place ever been vandalized?"

"Not so far. I hope that continues. Since the

only road access is via the ranch, a person needs to be on foot to access from the other directions. Not that many hiker-vandals in the area."

"Nice."

Travis dropped a teabag into each cup as the rain began to hammer on metal sheeting above them. He glanced up as if worried that the roof might collapse under the weight of the pelting rain.

"Some storm," Cassie said from under her breath as he closed the metal container that held the teabags. "Will did a good job with this."

Travis gave her a half smile. "I don't think Grandpa controls the weather. Not that he wouldn't like to." He gave her a look. "He's a control freak, too, you know."

Cassie pressed a hand to her chest as if shocked at his statement. "Are you suggesting…?"

"Uh-huh."

She made a dismissive noise as she leaned against the edge of the wobbly table, then thought better of it and once again stood upright, hugging her arms around her. "Do you guys work together well?"

"We do."

"You just disregard the controlling stuff?"

He considered for a moment. "I don't react to it."

"Ah. Just like with me."

"Right."

She smiled a little, then hugged her arms just a little tighter. "Is that how you handled coming back to the ranch when you'd had other plans? By not reacting?"

"I…uh…" He'd obviously never tried to articulate how he'd handled the shift in his life. "There wasn't a lot of sense in reacting or resenting or anything."

"Really?" She would have reacted and resented if her plans had been side-railed.

"Life is all about choices and I made mine."

"Or was it made for you?"

A shadow crossed his face before he pulled in a long breath. "That's not important. You work with what you're dealt." Travis turned his attention back to the stove.

Cassie gave a slow nod that he didn't see since he was studying the kettle as if it was about to tell him the secret of life. The nerve had been located and now the question was, did she touch it twice?

The kettle spout started to steam, and Travis turned off the burner, then poured water over the teabags. Cassie took her cup after he poured, then set it back down again.

"Hot."

"Due to one of those crazy laws of physics, no doubt."

"I was always better at chemistry." Cassie went to the window to stare out through the smear of water that blurred the outside world, wondering if she wanted to bring the conversation back to what he dreamed about—or had dreamed about before life interfered.

The floor creaked as Travis came up behind her. "Tell me what your plans were," she said without taking her gaze off the window.

"Later." His hands came up to rest on her shoulders, then his thumbs started doing magical things to her tight muscles.

"Are you attempting to distract me from sussing out the truth?" she asked.

"Totally. I don't want my nerves touched." His fingers hit a tight knot in her shoulder. "Do you ever relax?"

"Something about you keeps me on edge." She bit her lip to keep from moaning as he worked the tension out of her muscles.

His thumbs stilled. "Good edge or bad?"

"I don't know." Raindrops smacked into the window in front of her in little kamikaze splatters. "I don't want to get trapped up here." An obvious change of subject, but Cassie wasn't worried about finesse.

"We'll get home," he said in a way that made her believe it.

"I don't like waiting."

Somehow, she knew he was smiling and his thumbs started working again. "Nobody likes waiting."

She wished his thumbs weren't working such magic, but she kept leaning into them. "I hope the road doesn't turn into gumbo."

When he didn't answer, Cassie turned and found herself in a loose embrace. Travis brought his face closer to hers, so close that she could see the flecks of white and gray in his blue eyes. "You are trying to distract me."

"Is it working?" he asked in a low voice.

"I don't…"

But whatever she didn't was of no import when his mouth met hers in a long, slow kiss. He wrapped his arms around her more tightly, their damp jackets pressing into one another. Through the fabric, she could feel his warmth.

"I do," he murmured when he lifted his head.

"I have no idea what we're talking about."

"Then don't talk." His mouth met hers again and this time Cassie's hand slid up around his neck, allowing her to push her fingers into his dark hair. It was so easy to lose herself in his kiss. Never had she felt anything that approached this degree of…right.

She wasn't ready for right.

She leaned back, her palms trailing down the front of his coat, but stubbornly refusing to fall back to her sides. A crack of thunder made her jump and Travis put his hands on her shoulders to steady her.

Cassie dropped her forehead against his chest and once again his fingers started working their magic. "If you're doing this to keep me from worrying about my job, it's working."

"That isn't exactly why I'm doing this," he replied in a low voice. She gave him a dark look, and he touched his forehead to hers. "It's not the best circumstances, granted, but sometimes, no matter how hard we try, we don't get to pick our circumstances. We have to work with what we got."

The words echoed his philosophy about his return to the ranch. "You want to work with this? I thought we agreed not to get ahead of ourselves."

"Define *ahead*."

"I don't know." She stepped away, instantly missing his warmth, then half turned toward the window and raked her hand through her damp hair.

He gave a slow nod. "Like it or not, you've been a big part of my life ever since the first day we met, when you beat me in that footrace and rubbed it in so badly."

"Only because you said those embarrassing things about me to save face."

"Okay, I laid down the first challenge. Then you laid down yours. Um…"

"Calf riding at the junior rodeo. I beat you."

"And then the essay contest."

"You talked smack about me again. And I beat you again."

"While you abstained from talking smack, correct?"

She bit her lip and stared up into his handsome face. The bruise around his eye was fading. But even with the bruise, he was nearly perfect—in her eyes anyway. "I might have uttered a word or two."

"I recall. My point is, I think we owe it to ourselves to see where this takes us."

Her heart started beating harder. It was one thing to kiss him, another to see where things took them. What if things took a turn she wasn't prepared for?

Oh, you mean like right now?

She definitely meant like right now. Especially when he lifted his eyebrows in a very serious way and said, "No plans. No strategies. No overanalysis."

"What?"

He lightly kissed her lips. "Let's just let this flow. You know…relax…and see where this is taking us."

"With your grandfather watching us like a hawk. Uh-huh. That'll be really comfortable."

Travis dropped his hands and shook his head. He was about to speak when Cassie cocked her head, then raised her gaze to the ceiling. "Listen."

"The rain is slowing down."

What had been a steady drumming was now more of an intermittent patter.

Momentary reprieve. She'd take it. "Looks like the waiting is over."

"Looks like it."

Neither of them moved.

Finally, Travis lifted his hand to trace the backs of his fingers along her jawline in a move so tender that it made her throat tighten. "I know working without a net is hard for you, Cass. It's no picnic for me either, but I see no sense in driving ourselves crazy during wedding prep. Let's just see how this all plays out. No pressure."

"Do you know me at all?"

He smiled, his cheeks creasing in a way that made her want to trace the lines with her fingertips. "I do. And I care for you. But I also know that we can't ignore this any more than we were able to ignore our rivalry."

She prided herself on being a straight talker, but she wasn't ready to admit that she cared for him, too. Not when it would cause already choppy waters to churn.

You do more than care. You're falling for him, and you're scared to death of the ramifications.

Ample reason to step back.

But Cassie did not step back.

"I'm not at a good point to rearrange my life." Unless Rhonda broke her promise. Then all bets were off, and Cassie would be searching for a job in upper administration.

"I'm not asking you to rearrange anything. I'm asking you to let us explore for a week or so and see where we are at the end."

Just go with the flow. See where things end up.

Why was that so terrifying?

Because, like Travis said, she was performing without a net, venturing into territory she couldn't control.

You're risking being hurt. Or hurting him.

But if she didn't take that risk, where would she be? Wondering. Debating. Probably feeling as frustrated and scattered as she did now.

She met Travis's gaze and asked herself one simple question. Did she trust him?

Probably more than she trusted herself right now.

"I… Okay. Let's do this."

"Let's," he agreed, gently touching her lips.

She loved the feel of his mouth on hers. The warmth, the promise. It was borderline overwhelming.

Cassie pulled back. "But I want the option of stopping at any time."

"Sure."

"Okay, then." A flash of nervous energy shot through her.

"Okay," Travis repeated with a smile. He jerked his head toward the door. "Ready to load boards before the next squall?"

Cassie pulled her gloves out of her pocket. "I'm ready for anything."

She wasn't, but if she said it out loud enough times, maybe it would be true.

CHAPTER FIFTEEN

"I SAW THIS COMING from a mile away," Darby said in a *duh* voice.

"There's no way you saw this coming." Cassie reached back to adjust the pillow behind her knot-free neck. Then, because her curiosity got the better of her, she asked, "How?"

"Oh, I don't know. Maybe the way he stepped in to try to protect you from Ray."

"He was just…"

"What? Putting himself in harm's way for you?"

"He would have done it for anyone."

Darby's silence said more than a contradiction would have.

"I'm starting to regret this call," Cassie murmured into the dark bedroom.

"Uh-huh. What's your plan?"

"We're not supposed to have a plan."

"You guys laid out parameters to not have a plan?"

"Travis laid out parameters. We're going to

go with the flow and see what happens until the wedding."

Darby started laughing. "I want to see that."

Cassie bit her lip to keep a wry smile from forming. This wasn't a laughing matter. It was serious stuff. "I can go with the flow." The smile broke through as Darby snorted in response. "I can fake it," she amended, even though she wasn't very good at faking anything with Travis. He had a magical ability to make her utter deep truths.

"I'm curious to see where this takes you," Darby said.

"Me, too. And a little afraid." Total truth. She was afraid of wading deeper into a situation that could end in any number of ways.

"Take things as they come. Roll with those punches. I know you can do that."

Cassie pressed a hand against her forehead as she stared up at the dark ceiling. "I'm supposed to embrace chaos?"

"It doesn't have to be chaos."

"No. I think it'll be chaos."

"It could be an adventure. If it doesn't work out, then you fake it at family functions. And honestly, how many of those will you actually attend?"

Ouch.

"Have an adventure, Cassie."

Cassie closed her eyes and rolled over onto her back. Maybe she could have her adventure and control things, too. Or maybe she could let go for a while. She wanted to let go, to not think of consequences, but her brain was hardwired into cause and effect.

"I'll think about it."

"Check back in with me regularly. It gives me something to think about while I wait for a job offer to save me from this sinking ship."

"Sorry I hogged the entire conversation. How's the job search going?"

"It goes and you don't get to deflect. I want you to focus on loosening up. I'll expect a progress report soon." There was a brief silence, then Darby said, "Relax. Embrace. Enjoy."

Cassie let out a breath and squeezed her forehead again. "I'll try."

"Atta girl. Progress report. Soon."

Cassie set her phone on the nightstand and rolled over, folding her arm under the pillow. An adventure. Right.

TRAVIS PICKED UP a board from the jumbled pile the wood had been dumped into when they dragged it off the flatbed the previous day. He sighted down the length of the board and found it to be surprisingly true, considering the number of Montana winters it had been through. Recycled wood of this quality brought a premium price and they had at least two or three more loads they could collect. He wasn't certain what they'd do with it, but maybe it was time to get it out of the weather.

After setting the board in what was to be the good pile, he took hold of the broken end of a wider board and started working it free. Cassie's car pulled around the house, pulling to a stop on the opposite side of the driveway from the barn, under the elm tree that hung over the backyard fence.

He had no idea how the day would play out. Yesterday, the rain had started coming down in sheets again as they started for home with the load of reclaimed lumber. He'd focused on keeping the truck on the slippery road, while Cassie had braced herself to keep from being tossed sideways when the truck bumped and skidded. By the time they'd hit the Forest Service gate and drove into the high pasture, neither of them seemed to have anything to say.

Will stepped out of the back door as Cassie got out of her car. She waved to him, and he raised a hand in greeting before continuing on his way to the tractor idling near the barn. Travis breathed a silent sigh of relief. At least his grandfather was acting a lot more like his old self. He hadn't casually grilled Travis about his trip with Cassie yesterday evening, and he'd been equally silent on the matter that morning over coffee.

Maybe he thought his job was done…or maybe Rosalie had had a word.

Either way, Travis was good with it.

He laid the broken board onto the not-so-good stack, evening it out with the toe of his boot as Cassie entered the barn. What effect would her night of deep thought have on their plan?

That plan being no plan, of course.

Cassie pulled her gloves out of her back pocket as she came to a stop next to the damp wood pile. Then she glanced back over her shoulder at the sunny sky. "Wouldn't you know it? No rain today."

"According to Grandpa, we're good for several days." Which was why Will wanted to start cutting hay as soon as possible.

"After yesterday, I believe him." She tapped her gloves in her palm as if she was about to launch into something.

"What's up?"

One corner of her mouth twisted up. "I'm off my game."

Not what he expected. The Cassie of old would have never announced a weakness.

"Maybe because it's not the same game as usual?"

"I did a lot of thinking last night." Her forehead wrinkled. "Most of it in circles."

"You need that plan."

"I've never done much without one."

"Except the impulsive stuff."

"I'm talking big picture."

"I'm talking not talking."

She frowned at him and he reached out to take her hand and lace their fingers together. "We have mundane stuff to focus on—wood to sort, panels to build. And…good news," he said in an encouraging voice, "that involves a plan."

She fought a smile and lost, and Travis had just decided he might have to kiss that mouth when the tractor engines coughed and sputtered and then died, followed by a colorful curse.

He met Cassie's gaze, lifted his eyebrows, then stepped back as Will came stalking around the barn.

"Trouble?" he asked.

"Dash lights are flashing like crazy. And right when I need this thing to behave," Will grumbled. He nodded at Cassie. "Good morning."

"Morning," she said as he headed past them to the toolshed. He disappeared inside, but left the door open.

Travis nudged the pile of lumber in front of him with the toe of his boot. "I sorted the boards into those that will need damaged parts cut off and those that are usable as is. And I set up the chop saw." He jerked his head toward the make-shift bench where he'd set up the power saw and other tools. "I'll show you what I have in mind."

"What will happen to all the stuff outside?" she asked as they crossed to the bench.

"Grandpa has it separated, and most of it will go to either the landfill or to scrap. I'll load a trailer using the tractor bucket after he gets done in the field today. *If* he gets out in the field, that is."

"If you have to help work on the tractor, I can handle the woodworking."

"You just want to show off."

"My skills are considerable," she said. She lifted a rusty hinge that he'd set on the table that held the chop saw. "You've been gleaning. I saw these in the scrap trailer earlier."

"Guilty. I have enough to make hinged dividers, which means that they'll be easier to set up than those that need other means of support, and they'll look cool."

"Kind of getting into this, aren't you?"

"I am," he said in a voice that clearly indicated he was speaking about more than a wood-shop project. "And you?"

She took a step closer, holding her hands behind her back as if she was afraid of what she might do with them. He took a quick glance at the toolshed, was about to reach for her when his grandfather popped out again. Instead he dropped his hand and rolled his eyes as Cassie laughed.

"You'd best lay out the plan for me, just in case you end up mechanicking."

"Lester's on his way and he is a mechanic." Travis smiled and reached out to tap her chin. "Fine. You can have your plan. I'll show you what I have in mind."

And he was more than a little amazed that she wasn't pushing in with her own construction ideas.

LESTER ANDERSON, Will's longtime buddy, arrived not long after Cassie did. He parked next to Cassie's car, then slowly got out of his truck and ambled toward the barn. He'd been Cassie's 4-H leader for years, although his hair had been dark then, and he'd walked a lot faster.

She started toward the bay door to say hello, but had barely taken two steps when Will came barreling around the corner.

"I'm glad you're here," he said, jerking his head in the direction he'd just come from. "That piece of junk beside the barn broke down on me. Did you bring your tools?"

"Don't you have your own?"

"We've been cleaning," Will said shortly.

Translation—he'd dumped all the tool-related stuff into a shed near the barn to be sorted later.

"I have tools."

"Great." Will turned and headed back the way he'd come, leaving Lester shaking his head as Cassie closed the distance between them.

"Good to see you, Cassie."

"Likewise," she said with a smile.

"I'm going to take care not to get too close to those elbows of yours."

It took Cassie a second to catch on, and when she did, she laughed—something she might not have done a week ago when she was a lot touchier about Travis's injury.

"You'd *better* take care. I'm deadly." She pointed an elbow in Lester's direction and he pretended to duck.

A metallic clatter came from the direction of the tractor and Lester motioned toward the noise. "I'd better go see what's what."

"Good luck," Cassie called. Travis had already taken a look and come up blank, but Lester was a mechanic and had a better chance of getting to the root of the problem fast.

"Good luck, Les," Travis echoed once the sound of the saw died down. He raised a hand in a salute as Lester disappeared.

Cassie picked up the board she'd set down and carried it to the chop saw.

"I hope Lester brought his tools," Travis said as she started measuring the board. "He's the best mechanic I know."

"It sounds like he got here in the nick of time," Cassie said.

"He probably did." He glanced toward the bay door.

"You want to be out there, don't you?"

He fixed her with a candid gaze. "It is my job."

"But you drew wedding-decoration duty and Will isn't going to let you escape."

"That's it. Rub it in." He started tacking together strips of pine for the frame that would support the weathered wood. "When I first came home, I thought about escape a lot."

Cassie's hand stilled before she marked the measurement on the board. "And now?"

"Now I'm good."

She wondered.

"I love the life, Cass. What's not to love? A lot of people would give anything to be doing this."

But it would be a choice those people made.

Lester wandered in a few minutes later. "I need a place to plug in my extension cord," he said as he went to the junction box. After plugging in the cord, he wandered over to take a look at what Cassie and Travis were building.

"Those will be cool," he said.

"Rosalie is really happy about them," Cassie said as she hooked the measuring tape on the end of yet another board. She wanted to get all the cutting done for all the panels, and then they could assemble.

The plan for the dividers was simple—weathered boards in a simple pine frame, two of which would then be hinged together. The hinges didn't match, which, to Cassie, only added to their charm. After Lester left, they began construction, and, as expected, they had a few things to adjust as they made the prototype.

After tweaking the height and the amount of space showing between the boards, the others came together more easily. During the construction of the third set of panels Cassie realized that she and Travis were working together, barely exchanging a word, yet somehow agreeing as to who did what. Travis measured and marked the boards, Cassie cut them. He screwed together one side of the frame and Cassie the other, passing the cordless drill back and forth with neither of them vying for control.

They worked well together for two people who'd made careers out of being at each other's throats.

She was considering pointing out that small fact when a quick movement behind Travis caught her eye. "Look at that." She pointed at the tiny little bundle of fur peeking into the open back door behind him.

"Not another snake, I hope," he said as he turned.

"It's one of the kittens you thought I mistook for a snake."

"That's pretty common, right?"

"Come here, baby..." Cassie slowly approached the little tabby puff ball, but it turned and skittered toward the old building behind the barn, disappearing underneath it. "Darn it." She turned back to Travis.

"Thinking a kitten might work out better than a horse?"

"All signs point to yes." Travis had ridden McHenry's Gold two more times, and while the mare was fine for someone who knew what they were doing, and enjoyed being on alert full-time, she wasn't shaping up to be a pleasure mount. Cassie had enough battles at school. She did not need another during her trail rides.

He reached out to tip up her chin. "I'll keep putting hours into her."

"I don't want to waste your time."

"It's a challenge," he said.

"And you do love a challenge," she murmured.

"I think that's why I like hanging around you."

A warm feeling flowed through her at the softly spoken words. She was about to step closer when a loud bang had her wincing instead.

Travis laughed lowly, then stepped back. "We need to get to work before Grandpa catches us and thinks he's a genius for bringing us together."

"For now."

Travis scowled down at her and Cassie wished, really wished, she could pull the words back in. "You do know how to enhance a moment."

"Hey," she said stubbornly. "You have to take the good with the bad."

"I think 'for now' can last awhile," Travis said in a low voice.

"Talking about the future is not *letting things flow*," Cassie said stubbornly. "You're changing the rules. Just like you did in that stupid pig-catching game."

"I'm not changing the rules. I'm being realistic about my feelings. It's part of the flow."

"Your feel—" Cassie pressed her lips together, then when she had control of herself, she said, "I thought we were just going to…" That was when she realized she couldn't articulate what she'd thought going with the flow meant.

"What? Flirt? I'm good with that." He rubbed a hand over the back of his neck. "Look. I understand that you have a lot of reasons not to get involved with a guy like me. But could you at least come to this with an open mind, instead of being absolutely certain that nothing will come of it?"

"I'm scared to do that." The words came blurting out. "And I don't want to be scared."

Travis studied her for a long moment, then slowly opened his arms. Cassie walked into them as if she was coming home, hugging him tightly.

"This is nuts," she muttered against his chest as he closed his arms around her, bringing a hand up to cup the back of her head.

"Yeah. I know. And I also know that in about ten seconds Lester or Grandpa is going to walk through that door."

Cassie gave a choked laugh and pulled back. "Okay." She pulled in a breath as she tried to determine exactly what was okay. "Start again?"

"Start again," he agreed with a half smile, his gaze locked on to hers. "And as long as we can do that, I think we're okay."

ROSALIE PARKED HER CAR next to Cassie's car near the McGuire main house, then glanced over at Gloria, who was regarding the barn with a sour expression, while the girls began unbuckling in the backseat.

"Are you sure about this?" Gloria asked.

"I am." Rosalie pulled the keys out of the ignition and set them on the console.

The weather forecast hadn't shifted even one day, so her wedding day was going to be a wet one, and at that very moment, Will and Lester were in the fields, swathing hay in an attempt to get it bailed before the rains. Thankfully, Lester had finally managed to get the stubborn tractor running. Rosalie only hoped that Will took her words to heart yesterday after she'd explained that he was being too obvious pushing the kids together. "And with two stubborn people, that simply isn't going to work," she'd said.

Will had grudgingly agreed, but she didn't know if he could successfully rein himself in.

"You're certain the roof doesn't leak," Gloria said, eyeing the barn suspiciously. "Because it looks like it might leak."

"It rained like crazy the day we carted all that stuff back inside, and I didn't see one leak." Her friend didn't have a lot of experience with ranch buildings and had been slow to convince, despite many journeys through Pinterest, that the barn would be a suitable venue for the wedding.

These are refurbished barns, she'd pointed out more than once while looking at the photos. *Yours is pressure washed. It's not the same.*

"Grandma," Kendra said as she and Bailey scrambled out the rear car door. "Can Bailey and I go exploring?"

"You'd better come to the barn with me and Gloria."

The girls didn't quibble because, after all, they were going to get to run around in a barn. The high-pitched whir of a saw came and went as they approached, and in the dim interior, Rosalie saw Cassie pass a board she'd just cut to Travis.

"There was a time," she said to Gloria out of the corner of her mouth, "that we wouldn't have allowed them to be near a power tool together."

Gloria cackled, and Kendra said, "What?"

"Nothing, sweetie." She lifted a hand as Cassie caught sight of her. "Hi."

"I heard you were coming to line us out," Cassie said, pulling off her gloves.

"I thought we'd finalize the decorating plans, since we only have a week to go, so I brought my decorating guru."

Gloria had an eye for design and the only difficulties the two had ever encountered were in choosing the colors for their house and shop. Gloria had wanted the deep jewel tones that were her go-to shades, and Rosalie had wanted more muted neutrals. It was a testimony to their friendship that they'd managed a compromise that they both loved.

"This isn't bad," Gloria said on a note of surprise, turning a full circle as she studied everything between the floor and the rafters. "Much better than I'd hoped for. We'll easily get the rented tables into that area." She pointed to the west side of the barn. "The floral archway can go there and the gift table here." She tapped her chin as she studied the interior. "I like those rustic…walls…you guys are making. We could put the buffet tables in front of them. Perhaps a quilt or two draped over the walls for a bit of color?"

"That's a good idea," Rosalie replied. "And quilts for the gift table?" Which she hoped would be empty, because she and Will had expressly stated on their invitations that they'd prefer donations be made to the local food bank.

"Butcher paper with burlap runners for the tables, and twig baskets with live petunias."

"Yes." Rosalie noted with some amusement that Travis and Cassie were standing side by side with identical looks on their faces as she and Gloria batted ideas back and forth.

"I'd like to drape the edge of the loft and those columns with some kind of floral garlands," Gloria said, and Rosalie immediately picked up her thread.

"And those could be switched out for evergreen garlands for Katie's wedding."

"Instead of quilts over the walls, we could mount wreaths for hers." Gloria tapped her chin again then glanced at Rosalie. "Would you like wreaths instead of quilts? We could do flowers or just greenery."

"Quilts," Rosalie said. "They'd be easier to deal with all in all. I don't want to go to a lot of trouble— Girls!"

Kendra and Bailey stopped in their tracks, Bailey's little leg frozen on the bottom step of the ladder leading to the loft. "Stay on the ground floor. No going into the loft."

There was nothing that even vaguely resembled a safety rail at the edge of the half floor above them.

"But, Grandma, we saw a kitty up there," Kendra said. "A little baby one."

"He might fall," Bailey added.

"Cats don't fall," Rosalie said. "Little girls do."

She waited until the girls were clear of the ladder before turning to Travis, who said, "I'll have that blocked off for the wedding. Otherwise the braver young souls will probably attempt to climb the ladder of death."

"What's that?" Kendra said on an awed breath.

And, being a rookie with children, Travis pointed to the ladder leading up the wall from the loft to a smaller crow's nest at the top of the barn. Rosalie's eyes went wide as she saw the long ropes draped up there. "Please tell me you didn't swing on those."

Travis gave a shrug and Rosalie quickly looked down to her granddaughters. "You are not to go up into the loft. Understand?"

They nodded in unison.

"Thank you." Rosalie gave them an approving smile, then turned her attention back to Gloria. "Now, where were we?"

"With our feet firmly planted on the earth," Gloria said with a mock shudder.

Rosalie firmly agreed. Thank goodness Travis was going to block off the loft, and she, for one, would check his work the next time she was there. The last thing she needed was for her little granddaughters to tackle the "ladder of death."

CHAPTER SIXTEEN

"GOING WITH THE FLOW sounds easy." When Darby had said she'd check in, Cassie had assumed it would be in a week, not the next day while she was driving home from the McGuire ranch. "It's not easy," she reiterated to her friend after pulling over.

"But you did it."

"With a few hiccups." Like facing off about the rules. Technically, there shouldn't have been any rules, but talking about the future seemed like the opposite of going with the flow.

"I think Travis is a great guy."

So did she, and therein lay the problem. The what-ifs were overwhelming. Her grandmother was a holiday person, and due to her poor track record, Cassie was determined to make it home for the biggies. But what if she and Travis were on the outs?

"Well, he's persuasive" was all Cassie would say on the matter.

Darby laughed, then after a few silent seconds passed, she said, "I'm thinking of moving home."

"Really?"

"I've always wanted to come home, but I also wanted to make big bucks. My job in recruitment was great in that regard, but the big bucks come at a price, and right now my job is so tenuous that I figured, why not come home, live where I want and get small bucks?"

"Can you do that?"

"I think. I'm still working out a plan."

"If you need to bounce ideas, I'm here. You know I excel at planning."

Darby laughed again. "I'll use your planning skills, and you can use my familiarity with the more laid-back approach to life."

"Deal."

After ending the call, Cassie pulled out onto the county road, making a conscious effort to relax.

She didn't know how. She wanted Travis; she was afraid of being with him.

Afraid of making those tough choices, aren't you?

Oh, yeah.

How would giving in to her need to be with him affect her professional life? What if she chose to give up everything and move home and then everything imploded? She'd be starting off from square one.

That was a scary thought.

You're getting ahead of yourself.

Totally. But how could she not? It was dishonest to pretend that she didn't want to be with Travis, that she didn't enjoy the way he could fire her up. That she didn't like looking at him, being close to him.

That she hadn't fallen for the guy.

You have. You're a goner in that regard.

So what now?

Play the game. See how it shakes out.

In other words, go with the flow like everyone is suggesting.

Cassie parked her car in her usual spot next to Nick's chore truck, and instead of going into the empty house, she walked to the garden to take a look at the weed-free rows. She wouldn't be taking out her frustrations there. And then she looked beyond the garden to the pasture where Nick's horses grazed. He'd brought them home from Alex's house, where they'd been eating down her small pasture—so much easier than mowing.

Huh.

Less than five minutes later, she was walking in from the pasture with Billy, Nick's go-to gelding for ranch work. She might not be able to pleasure ride on McHenry's Gold, but Billy was another matter, and she was glad he'd come home.

TRAVIS TOOK HIS TIME sweeping up the sawdust around the bench where the chop saw sat. After Rosalie and Gloria and the girls had arrived, they shut the power equipment off and he and Cassie had concentrated on putting together the last of the panels with some enthusiastic help from her little nieces.

Then, almost as quickly as they'd arrived, Rosalie and her entourage left for town, where they would start gathering materials, and Cassie, whom he thought might linger awhile longer, had taken off at the same time.

He was on his way back to the house to rustle up something so that Lester and Will could have dinner when they got in from the fields, when the landline rang from inside the kitchen.

He hurried his steps and caught it on the third ring. Reynaldo.

"Hey," Reynaldo said. "I'm not calling about a job."

That was a first. He and Reynaldo had roomed together in college and worked together as interns during the summer breaks. Then they'd both been hired by Agri-Tech, but Reynaldo had been the only one who'd shown up for the job.

Reynaldo had climbed the ranks quickly and whenever a job came open, he called Travis, just in case his circumstances had changed.

"What are you calling about?"

"To see if you have a job."

Travis sat down at the table. "You're kidding." He'd offered jobs as a joking counter to Rey's requests that he go to work for Agri-Tech, but Rey had always laughed it off.

"I'm not. My company got swallowed whole by a larger company, and now they're spitting out the pieces."

"You're one of them?"

"I will be as of the end of September. And if I don't get something nailed down by then, well, I'm preparing for the worst."

Travis and his grandfather had talked more than once about hiring full-time help, instead of relying on day hands when there was extra work or emergencies, but always tabled the matter. But now that Will would be spending more time in town, maybe it was time to reopen the matter. There was a lot of downtime, but when harvest was upon them, they needed help.

"I'll talk to my grandfather," Travis said. "Let you know."

"I'd appreciate it. I might not need a job—"

"But then again you might."

"Exactly."

Travis pulled open the fridge after ending the call. If he had taken one of the jobs Rey had asked him to interview for, then he would be in the same boat. But he had a ranch to come home to. Rey had next to nothing as far as a support system.

He pulled out a package of hamburgers and opened it on the counter, thinking sloppy joes, which could be kept warm until Will and Lester came in. And, once they'd eaten and headed to town, he was going to fire up the swather and cut more hay. They needed to make up for the time lost with the uncooperative tractor.

BILLY WAS SURPRISINGLY skittish when Cassie had first gotten on him, but he'd settled quickly and had an excellent ride over the bridge and along the edge of the Ambrose Mountain foothills— her favorite ride.

When she got back to the ranch, her mind was finally clear. Not that she had any better answers to any of her questions, but they were no longer crowding to the front of her thoughts.

She'd just started making a sandwich for supper when her phone rang. Anna Lee.

So much for serenity.

"What's going on?" Cassie asked after a quick hello.

"I don't know," Anna Lee confessed. "But

I'm beginning to think I cried wolf and I want to apologize for that."

"No problem." She'd rather be clued in that something might be going on than to be left in the dark.

"There was an air of tension at the last board meeting, but no one made reference to anything that couldn't be talked about. And now I notice that the only jumpy department is Accounting, which I don't understand because they are understaffed. Everyone is safe there."

"Maybe some entity has called for an audit."

"That's what I've been thinking. The board might be twitchy about that, but they wouldn't say anything until it was official. And they'd have to get their ducks in a row, so yes. I think that's it."

"Has, uh, Rhonda joked about not retiring?"

"Yesterday she almost pulled her hair out after meeting with the cadre of upper-elementary teachers who hate the new math program. If you'd offered her retirement papers then and there, I think she would have signed on the dotted line."

Cassie laughed, and it felt good.

"I'm sorry if I got you rattled for no reason. Like I said, there is an air of tension, but I don't think it has anything to do with personnel or big changes."

"Just an audit."

"That's my guess."

"I appreciate being kept in the know, Anna Lee, so please, call anytime. It'll help me do my job better when I get back."

"I'm looking forward to that. I like working for you best."

Cassie hung up smiling. Ninety-nine problems and her job wasn't one of them.

"I THINK I'VE done enough in the barn." Not that he didn't enjoy spending time with Cassie, but even with the hours he'd put in the previous evening, they were behind schedule knocking down the hay.

Will gave Travis a look. "Lester and I can handle it. And we have Adam lined up if we need more help." Yet another of Will's retired coffee klatch buddies.

"Adam can't see."

"He can see well enough to drive circles in a field. The ladies need some muscle in the barn, and who better than you?"

"You?" Travis asked pointedly.

"I'm the patriarch."

Who was about to move to town and wasn't getting any younger. Maybe this was his last hurrah as far as haying went.

"Fine. But next haying season, you're going to do the wedding decorating."

Will slowly lifted his gaze. "You think there might be another wedding next summer?"

Travis managed to refrain from rolling his eyes. His grandfather might be acting more normally, but he wasn't done with the idea of bringing Travis and Cassie together.

Neither was he, but he didn't need help. Not Will's help anyway. A little cooperation from Cassie would not go amiss.

"I'm thinking of getting extra cash by renting out the barn as a venue. I found a website where I can list it."

Will's eyes went wide, and then his eyebrows crashed together as he realized he'd been played. "Lester's waiting." He snatched his gloves up from the counter. "Have fun in the barn."

Travis gave a soft laugh. If Rey came on board, could he handle Will?

He'd yet to bring up the matter, but he would. When the time was right. With Will, you had to choose your moments.

A car drove over the cattle guard and Travis pushed aside the curtain to ascertain what he already knew. The Callahan women had arrived, and it was time to start tacking doodads around the barn.

He reached for his ball cap and headed out

the door as Will and Lester headed out into the fields.

Lucky.

And it was no surprise that when Rosalie outlined the plan for the day, he and Cassie were paired together.

"Would you two mind handling anything that requires a ladder?" Rosalie asked before she ended the meeting.

"You bet," Travis said. He exchanged a look with Cassie, who merely raised her eyebrows—probably because everyone was watching them. But it didn't seem to bother her one bit.

"You're in a good mood," he commented later as they lay on their stomachs on the loft floor, tacking garlands to the edge. They hadn't spoken much that morning, mainly because of watchful eyes, which in turn made him wish he was haying, like he should be doing.

Cassie's staple gun slipped, and she fired a shot into the air. She tried again and managed to tack the garland to the old floorboards. She swung around so that she was sitting with her legs crossed in front of her. "I got a call from my associate last night."

"Must have been a good one."

"It was. And I went riding. Nick brought his horses back from the Dunlop ranch and his gelding and I went for a ride along the foothills."

"What you guys doing up there?" Gloria called in a playful voice. "Working or gabbing?"

"Discussing garland placement," Cassie called back.

Travis gestured to the straw bales stacked against the wall and they scooted over to them, effectively out of sight from below as they sat side by side, leaning their backs against the bales. "If they want us, they can shout," he said.

"Like they won't. And Gloria isn't above climbing the ladder to see what's going on."

"We're taking a break."

This was their last day alone together before the families arrived. After that the wedding whirlwind would begin with a cocktail party, followed by a rehearsal dinner and then the wedding itself. One week after that, Cassie was leaving, heading to campus to start taking classes to earn her doctorate in education— and once she was off the ranch, focused again on her career, Travis suspected that despite good intentions, she would slide back into being the Cassie she'd been when she'd first arrived home, which was so different from the woman with her shoulder pressed against his as they leaned against the straw.

"Tell me about the ride."

"What's to tell?" she asked. "It felt good. Relaxing." She leaned closer to him and said in a conspiratorial voice, "It had the exact effect I'd hoped for and has convinced me that I need a kitten *and* a horse...just maybe not the horse I bought."

"What are you going to do about that?"

"I have a proposal for you."

Maybe the last thing he'd expected. "Do you?"

"What would you say to using McHenry's Gold as a brood mare?"

"I'd say I couldn't afford her because someone jacked up the price at the auction."

Cassie lifted her chin. "What if I was talking a trade?"

"What kind of trade?"

"I would trade the mare for her first foal... if you trained it for me. I'm talking more than thirty days. I'd like a finished, dependable horse."

"And I would get all future foals?"

Cassie nodded.

"I would definitely consider that. But what will you do for a horse in the meantime?"

She gave a shrug. "Make do with my kitten." They sat side by side watching the activity below. Gloria and Rosalie placing floral arrangements and decorating the old hay rake that they'd placed in the far corner. Katie was setting up folding tables while the little girls played hide-and-seek with the kittens, who were becoming friendlier by the minute.

"Have you ever taken a vacation?" Cassie asked.

Travis gave her a frowning look. "Where'd that come from?"

"I'm curious."

"My entire life is a vacation. I live on a ranch in Montana." Sweating in the sun, freezing in the winter. Work that never ended, because the forces of nature were constantly brewing up surprises to deal with.

"Stop hedging. You said you thought about places you'd like to see, things you'd like to do. Have you done more than *think*?"

"Cassie…"

"Oh, what? It's not so comfortable to be on the receiving end of helpful life advice? You know, like hearing, 'Hey, you look really stressed.'"

"I'm good with my life as it is, Cassie." Or he had been until she'd walked back into it. Now he didn't want her to leave, and he was thinking more and more about what he hadn't done.

She put a hand on his knee. "*Have* you taken a vacation? Done any of the things you've thought about?"

His mouth tightened as he gave his head a slow shake.

"That isn't healthy."

"Maybe I like my life as is." And maybe he felt as if he'd missed something along the way. Something that Cassie and most of the people he grew up with experienced.

"Do I have to challenge you to take a vacation?" she asked softly. "Do I have to issue a double-dog—"

His mouth came down on hers and Cassie's hand slid up around his neck as she answered his kiss. When he raised his head, she met his gaze in a no-nonsense way. "An excellent deflection, but time passes quickly, and you need to think about this, Travis."

He pressed his lips into a flat line. He knew about time passing quickly. It wasn't long until Cassie headed off to work on her degree, and he wanted things more settled than they were.

"I can't think of anything specific that I missed out on. And more than that, the company I was going to work for has been taken over by a conglomerate. My friend there is being let go in a couple of months. I'd probably be doing the same."

"Cassie!" Cassie jumped as her sister bellowed from below. "Are you playing hooky?"

"We're discussing important stuff."

Travis gave her a what-the-heck look, but she

merely shrugged as she rose to her feet. "Trust me. That will make them leave us alone."

Travis also stood. "No doubt." He shook his head as he looked down at her. "We make our choices, Cassie. I chose family, you chose work. Neither of us is totally right nor wrong."

"And that leaves us without much of a middle ground."

"I think—"

But he didn't get a chance to tell her what he thought because a crash, followed by a cry from one of the girls, had them on their feet, heading for the ladder. He headed down first, then caught Cassie by the waist as she missed a step on the way down. They'd secured the heavy panels with wire and there was no way they were coming loose, but there were other things that could fall...like a box filled with glassware and florist marbles that had been set on a low step stool. As near as Travis could tell, one of the little girls had hit it while chasing a kitten.

"It's okay," Rosalie crooned as she stroked the hair back from Bailey's forehead. "But please be more careful."

"Thank goodness these things are sturdy," Gloria said as she picked up a vase that had rolled close to her feet unharmed.

Yes, the thick glass vases were okay, but there

were pieces of rounded glass everywhere that were meant to hold flowers in place.

They'd barely gotten things cleared up when Lester came into the barn, holding his old-school flip phone in one hand. "Travis? I hate to do this, but I gotta head to town. Mavis's car broke down and she's blocking one of the entrances to Hardwick's."

"It's okay," Rosalie said to Travis, tucking an errant gray curl behind her ear. "We have this under control. Go cut hay."

Travis gave Cassie a quick look.

"Be right back," she said to her grandmother and walked with him and Lester to the door.

"I hate to abandon you guys," Lester said after unnecessarily pointing to the swather parked in the field.

"We'll be fine, and Hardwick's and Mavis will thank you," Travis said.

"Right. And I'll be back tomorrow."

After Lester started across the driveway to his car, Travis turned to Cassie. "We'll pick up this discussion of middle grounds later. I have some thoughts on the matter."

And since Cassie hated unfinished business, he could see that she'd like very much to hash it out then and there. "Later," he said softly before leaning in to give her a light kiss on the lips.

"Later it is." She smiled ruefully. "If we get a minute alone after the families arrive."

"We'll find the time."

CHAPTER SEVENTEEN

"THERE THEY ARE!" Kendra pointed toward the staircase that led from the security level of the Bozeman Yellowstone International Airport to the area near the baggage claim. Bailey gave a happy holler and both girls launched themselves at their grandparents almost before they'd stepped off the bottom stair.

"Come on, loves, let's step out of the way," Frances said in her delightful accent, while Pete leaned down to scoop a girl up in each arm.

"I'll get these guys to safety," he said, making Bailey giggle. He handed Bailey off to Frances, then held out his arm to Cassie, who stepped in for a hug.

"Long time, Dad. I'm sorry about that."

"Don't be. We're staying longer this time to make up for it."

"What about your vet practice?"

"We're training the couple who are going to buy it from us," Frances said. "We'll work together for a year, then Pete and I will start phasing ourselves into retirement." She looked around. "And then I guess I'll get used to living in Big Sky Country."

"We'll visit back home, honey," Pete said, and it struck Cassie that her dad thought of Australia as home. She'd never really thought of Wisconsin that way, despite living there for over a decade.

"Katie, get over here," Pete said as he set Kendra on her feet. "So good to see you, hon," he said as he enveloped her in a bear hug.

"You're going to sleep in Katie's bedroom," Kendra said. "You have to share with Tigger." Katie's big ginger cat.

"I'm sure we'll all enjoy that," Frances said with a laugh.

The baggage claim buzzer sounded and Frances set Bailey on the floor before they made their way closer.

"My bag always comes out last," she said, "so I don't get too excited." She smiled in the direction of her husband, who was toeing up to the carousel. "Pete has a different philosophy." She adjusted the strap of her travel bag. "Is the order of events the same as the email from last week?"

"It is," Katie confirmed. "We'll have the wedding rehearsal tomorrow, followed by drinks and hors d'oeuvres. The next day is the wedding, and then we're free to do some visiting and maybe see some sights if the rain lets up."

"Yes," Pete said from over his shoulder. "What is it with this rain? I came home to see some blue skies and mountains."

"Like we don't have those back home," Frances sniffed.

Cassie watched the interplay between Frances and her father with a smile. It was wonderful to see him so happy. When he'd had to make the hard choice five years ago as to whether or not to marry Frances and emigrate, he'd made the right one. Compromise in action.

"Oh—here one comes," Pete announced, shifting his feet at the edge of the conveyor like an athlete ready to spring into action.

He'd barely yanked the bag off the belt when Frances said, "There's the next one."

Once both bags were clear, Cassie took one and Katie the other, leaving Pete and Frances with free hands to offer granddaughters.

"Where's Mom?" Pete asked as they left the terminal.

"She's at the ranch. You'll see her soon. Dan and Marge McGuire are also getting in today. They're staying at Will's house in town, so you'll see them at the rehearsal tomorrow."

"Will's son has a disease and uses crutches," Kendra explained to Frances.

"Will's going to be our new grandpa," Bailey added.

"I know, sweetie. Isn't it exciting?" Frances replied.

"And how's Travis?" Pete asked Cassie. "I hear you guys are working together."

"We are," Cassie said mildly, ignoring the little jolt she'd felt at the mention of his name. "And Travis is…" *Attractive, challenging, thought provoking, hot.* "Travis is fine."

Her father lifted his eyebrows, making her suspicious as to what he already knew—or thought he knew.

"Have you heard otherwise?" she asked lightly.

Her father grinned at her. "No. I have not."

THE CALLAHAN RANCH HOUSE kitchen was filled to capacity. Frances and Pete sat at one side of the table and Cassie and Rosalie on the other. Katie and Brady perched on the island stools and, since all the chairs were taken, Alex and Nick stood side by side, leaning against the blue quartz countertop, their shoulders pressed close together. Every now and again their gazes met and held, making Cassie smile inwardly, glad that her brother had found happiness, while also stirring a touch of jealousy. Even though they came from different worlds, Nick and Alex had worked things out, but they'd had the necessary proximity to do that. There hadn't been a ticking clock involved.

She and Travis had a clock. There wasn't a lot of time before she left, and while going with the flow had sounded fine a few days ago, it didn't feel so fine now.

"My body is so confused about time right now," Frances said to Bailey, who was snuggled on her lap.

"It's bedtime," Bailey told her.

Kendra instantly started shaking her head from where she stood leaning on her grandfather's chair, but Pete laughed and said, "Your sister is right. Grandma and I are going to bed, too. We have to get our body clocks set to your time."

"Why?"

He reached out to touch Kendra's chin. "Because it's near lunchtime where we live."

Kendra put her hands on her hips, as if not quite certain whether to believe him or not.

"It's true, love," Frances said with a gentle smile. "And before we move here, we're going to have you and Bailey visit us and see the sights."

"I want to see where it's lunchtime at night," Bailey said as she slid off Frances's lap.

"I think you'd be surprised at how much it

looks like lunchtime here," Pete said with a laugh.

After Frances, Pete and Rosalie said their good-nights, Brady topped off wineglasses and the five of them took seats at the table, making Cassie, literally, the odd person out. Normally she wouldn't have minded, but tonight...tonight her thoughts were drifting to a guy who was doing night work in his fields. When would they find time to hammer things out during the hub-bub of the wedding activities? Or did they have anything to hammer out?

As the time to leave drew closer, Cassie realized that there were matters she wanted settled.

"Cassie?"

She jumped after her sister said her name, quite possibly for the second or third time, judging from the amused tone of her voice.

"Yes?"

Everyone laughed and she realized that she hadn't been called upon to answer a question—they'd simply noticed that she wasn't there mentally.

"Is everything okay?" Alex asked.

All eyes were on her when she put her hands on the table and pushed her chair back. "I...uh... think I'm going to..." When had she ever hesitated to express her intentions? "I'm going to see Travis. He should be getting close to done."

She got to her feet and when no one said a word, she made her way to the door, grabbing a hoodie off the coat hooks before stepping out into the warm night air.

THE LAST OF the hay was baled, and with the help of Will's co-op friends, it would be stacked tomorrow, before the predicted rains came. Travis rolled the kinks out of his shoulders as he turned the baler and headed toward the ranch, which was dark except for the yard lamps—and the headlights that appeared on the driveway.

The lights were too close together to be Will's truck, and besides that, Will was supposed to be picking up his son and daughter-in-law, whose flight came in at 11:00 p.m. It was after ten, so that left…Cassie?

His heartbeat ramped up as he got closer and recognized her car. She got out as he parked the big machine and then climbed down the steps from the cab. Had something happened? If so, wouldn't she have simply called?

He started toward her and she met him halfway, coming to a stop a few feet away from him.

"What are you doing here, Cassie?"

She cocked her head and said, "I needed to see you."

"That's a good start."

She gave a self-deprecating laugh. "Isn't it,

though?" She lifted her chin in the direction of the field. "Done?"

"I am."

She shifted her weight. "I'm not staying long."

"Just popped by to say good-night?" The knot in his gut was relaxing. He'd been half-afraid that a night visit meant that she didn't want anyone around to hear the fallout from whatever she was there to say.

She held out her hands and he took them, holding her smooth fingers in his. "Okay, I might be staying awhile, but the family is still sitting at the table and—"

"We wouldn't want talk," he said with a half smile.

"I don't know what to do here, Travis. Time is passing quickly and next thing you know I'll be deep in my classes and… Do we leave this thing hanging?"

"What do you want to do?"

"I…" She pulled her hands away and clasped them together, glancing down before raising her gaze again. "I'm thinking of staying here until my sabbatical is over."

Travis's heart knocked against his ribs. "Your doctorate?"

"I don't need it to qualify for the top job in my district. I'd like to have it, of course, but I can do without it for a while."

"I…didn't see this coming."

"I've changed."

"No argument there." The tenseness that had defined her after she first arrived was gone. Everything about her was more relaxed.

"Do you like me better like this?"

"I think you're happier."

"That wasn't the question."

"I like you *any* way you are, Cassie." One corner of his mouth lifted. "Some of your personas are more exhausting than others, but…I like them all." He settled his hands on her shoulders. "What happens after your sabbatical?"

"I have months to figure that out."

"More going with the flow?" he asked with a smile.

"I think the flow will be smoother without a ticking clock. I checked while the family was catching up, and I can get back eighty percent of my tuition if I cancel before next week."

"Not much time to make a decision."

"No," she said as she tilted her lips up to his. "My decision is made."

TRAVIS AND CASSIE didn't manage much alone time as families caught up and final touches were put on the wedding barn. Before the very short and rudimentary wedding run-through, he and Lester and Will had set up dozens of rented folding chairs that Gloria had brought out in a small U-Haul trailer, and then oversaw the setting up of the caterer's buffet tables.

He had to admit that the barn was perfect for a rainy event. It was roomy and dry and, thanks to Rosalie's and Gloria's expertise, really nice-looking. It was amazing what flowers and greenery and a thorough pressure washing could do for a hundred-year-old structure.

"There you are." Travis's older sister, Amanda, tucked her arm in his. "This looks good. Grandpa said you had a hand in it."

"I had no choice. They wouldn't let me hay."

"I heard that you cut hay at night."

"A little."

She let out a satisfied breath as she studied the barn. "I can't believe how much work you guys did in here." She smiled up at him. "And you didn't kill one another."

"We did not."

"Which Grandpa takes as a sign that you should be together forever."

"I wouldn't mind."

Amanda stilled. "Imagine that."

"There are obstacles." He wasn't foolish enough to think there weren't, but with a long stretch of time ahead of them, he was hopeful that they could work things out slowly, instead of under intense pressure.

"You always did love a challenge." She stepped back to look up into his face. "But from my perspective, there's a lot of things at play here."

"Uh-huh."

"Awkwardness if things go bad."

"Yes."

"All this stuff has crossed your mind."

He gave her a look and she bit her lip. "Okay. Well, best of luck." She stepped back and gestured toward the driveway. "People are getting ready to head to town for the dinner." Which Gloria was hosting at Will's town house.

"I guess I'll join them." Cassie had already left with Gloria and Katie after the practice run-through, and he was looking forward to seeing her, sitting with her and watching the families interact, and not feeling the pressure to come to some resolution. Now.

He was still amazed that Cassie was giving up her classes. Amazed and thankful. If things worked out between them, he'd see to it that she got that doctorate.

Although he was still a little iffy on how things would work out. Like he'd told his sister, there were obstacles, but at least they had time to deal with them.

CASSIE HAD NO PROBLEM making snap decisions when it came to things like whether or not to take on a bully or accept a challenge to ride a cow, but when it came to the bigger decisions in life, the career-affecting decisions, she *always* took time to weigh pros and cons, assess possible outcomes, consider consequences.

But she'd made the decision to drop her classes and stay in Montana while sitting in the kitchen with her family happily chatting away.

And it still felt like the right thing to do. If she'd needed any reinforcement as to the rightness of her decision, every time Travis looked her way during the dinner at Will's town house, she got it.

They had months to figure this thing out, so there was no need to move quickly. They had the luxury of time—and proximity, just as Nick and Alex had had—to figure things out.

It was possible that they may conclude it just wasn't working out between them...but as she watched Travis balancing a plate on his knee as he listened to Bailcy explain something possibly involving kittens, her heart squeezed. Honestly? She didn't see that happening.

If she needed more evidence that she was making the right choice, she got it when she and Travis walked to his truck to say goodbye for the evening. Will was spending the night at his ranch, along with Travis's parents and sister. A full house. Gloria had shooed away all offers of help cleaning up after the meal, explaining that she'd hired a couple of high school kids to take care of matters the next day, so Cassie and her family were about to head out to their own ranch. It was only seven o'clock, so they had plenty of time to enjoy one another's company before heading to bed prior to the big day.

"I guess I won't see you until you walk down the aisle tomorrow," he said as he ran a hand down her arm to capture her fingers in a light grip. He grinned then. "I didn't mean that like it sounded." His expression sobered. "I'm all about no pressure while we figure this out."

Meaning a compromise that would make it all work. Cassie didn't know what that would look like, but she had months to figure out her priorities.

"I believe you," she said simply, meeting his lips in a quick kiss. "See you," she said, stepping back as her nieces raced down the sidewalk to the car, followed by Frances and Rosalie. Rosalie held out her hand just as Cassie felt the first drops of rain hit her face and hair.

"And it begins," she said to Travis.

He smiled down at her.

"So it does."

CHAPTER EIGHTEEN

"HOW DOES FRANCES feel about leaving Australia?" Cassie asked, and Katie leaned forward from where she sat on the fireplace hearth to hear Pete's answer. Rosalie and Frances and Nick were putting the little girls to bed, which allowed Cassie to ask the question she'd been wondering about. Big life changes were on her radar.

"Surprisingly good with it. I think it helps that she has no real home there anymore. Her brother moved to the UK and her parents have been gone for years now." He leaned his head back against the same recliner he'd sat in when she and Katie were little girls. "She'll be homesick. I was, but life is all about give-and-take. I'm sure it'll work out. And we can vacation there."

"Good compromise," Katie said.

Cassie's phone rang from where she'd left it in the kitchen, but she ignored it and continued to talk to her father about his retirement plans. The second time her phone rang, just minutes after the first, she excused herself to answer it, passing Nick on the way to the kitchen.

"They're down?" she asked.

"All of them. Frances and Rosalie were more tired than the kids."

Cassie laughed as her phone rang again.

"Better get that," Nick said.

"I just need to see who it is." Because she didn't want to disturb her evening.

Anna Lee. Cassie pulled in a breath as she picked up the phone. She didn't have time to worry about district goings-on, and was about to say so when she noticed she had two other missed calls—all from Anna Lee.

"What's happening?" she asked after a quick hello.

"I'm so glad I caught you." Anna Lee sounded breathless, like she'd been running.

"What happened?" Cassie repeated. She barely got the words out before a second call came in. She lifted the phone from her ear and saw Rhonda's name on the screen. "I have a call from Rhonda."

"Take it," Anna Lee said. "Then call me."

The phone buzzed again, but Cassie didn't switch calls.

"What happened?" she asked Anna Lee, not wanting to go into a call with Rhonda without some details.

"While Doug was gone, there was an audit." Anna spoke so quickly that it was hard to understand her. "He's been skimming money."

Cassie's heart dropped. "You're kidding." The phone buzzed a third time and she said, "I'll talk to you later," before switching to Rhonda's call.

"Hi, Rhonda." Now *she* sounded like she'd been running. "What's up?" Exactly what she would have said had Anna Lee not warned her about what had just happened.

"Serious matters. Is there any chance you can cut your sabbatical short?"

Cassie swallowed. Could she? "What happened?"

"There is a serious issue with Doug. He's taking a paid leave now, but, frankly, I think he'll be stepping down."

"Can you give me details?"

"We're looking at an embezzlement charge. And it's not a small sum."

"How could he…?"

"With help from Marie Smits." The longtime bookkeeper.

"I don't know what to say."

"Cassie," Rhonda said earnestly, "you're the only one who can step into my shoes while I take over Doug's duties. School is starting in less than two weeks. I've already spoken to the board about returning you to active status. I need you. Now. Is that possible?"

Cassie shot a look through the dining room door to her family. Her father was in a deep discussion with Kendra. Her father, whom she'd barely seen.

"I need you," Rhonda repeated when Cassie didn't immediately answer. "The district needs you. We'll reimburse you for the money you'll be out for canceling classes at this late date. If there is any money left in the district accounts." She gave a small laugh that sounded as if it was close to slipping into hysterical territory. "Doug has done some damage to our bottom line. I mean *allegedly* done damage, of course."

"How soon would I have to be there?" she asked, her stomach tightening as she said the words. She'd put out some fires in her day, but this one was by far the most serious.

"How soon can you get here?"

"I can't come until after my grandmother's wedding."

"There is an emergency board meeting with the attorneys the day after tomorrow. I need you for that if possible."

Cassie swallowed. "Would it be possible to be there for the meeting, then take a few days? My father is here from Australia."

"We can evaluate after the meeting. There

are so many things going on. I need your experience and expertise. I need you."

"I'll be there." Cassie pressed her fingertips to her forehead, trying vainly to ease the building pressure.

"Good." For the first time since the conversation started, Rhonda's voice relaxed. "Thank you."

"Is he guilty?" Cassie asked, still having a hard time wrapping her mind around the fact that her mentor was an alleged criminal.

Rhonda hesitated, then said, "Yes. The evidence is overwhelming."

WHAT HAD SHE just agreed to?

After slipping out of the house into the damp night, Cassie started walking with no particular destination in mind, glad that the rain had stopped. More was coming, but at least she had a few minutes to herself without being drenched.

She couldn't face her family just yet and share the not-so-happy news that she was heading back to Wisconsin—just as she'd done the last time her father had visited.

But this time she was going back before his visit was over. She would leave her car, fly back to Wisconsin, find out exactly what she was up against, then return for at least a couple of days before her father left.

She got as far as the tractor, then turned and studied the house where she'd thought she'd be living for the next nine or ten months.

So much for plans.

Sighing deeply, she turned to lean against the big rear wheel, not caring what the damp black rubber did to her skirt, which was the same one she'd worn when she and Travis had gone to Tremaine's.

Things were a mess, but she knew from experience that when cleaning up a mess, she needed to focus on one task at a time, complete it and move on to the next.

Doug? An embezzler?

Well, wasn't she a great judge of character?

The district had to be in crisis mode, what with bond levees, orientations, insurance negotiations and classes about to start. And who knew how this was being presented to the parents. There was a huge need for damage control.

Her first responsibility was her job. She'd help Rhonda put the district back on track and then she'd figure out what to do about her feelings for Travis. If there was anything she could do. It was one thing to give up college classes to figure out her love life, another to give up the career she'd worked so hard for. The career she loved.

She tipped her head up to study the sliver

of moon that showed between the dark clouds, then squeezed her eyes shut. She'd always had strong feelings for the man, but she hadn't expected to fall in love with him.

What if they burned hot and bright for a short period of time, only to have the fire go out? Then where would she be? Was she ready to take that kind of a chance?

She needed more time to decide, and time was the one thing she didn't have. Rain started to spatter her bare arms and she pushed off the tractor and headed back to the house.

"What happened to your skirt?" Katie asked as she walked into the kitchen.

Cassie twisted to look at the back of the skirt and grimaced at the dark smear. "Tractor stain."

"What?"

Cassie pushed her hands through her hair, then fixed her protective younger sister with a look. "There's a crisis at the district."

"What?"

Katie did not have an understanding expression on her face. "You can't go back now."

"I'm leaving after the wedding, but then I will come back before Dad and Frances leave."

"Are you sure?"

"I could use a little moral support right now." She was serious.

Katie folded her arms over her chest. "Tell me."

So Cassie did, pouring out the story of the embezzlement and how at this critical point, she did need to step back into her old job.

"I see your point," Katie said. "But is this ever going to stop?"

"You have to admit," Cassie said in a low voice, "this is an honest emergency."

"Yes. It is." She let out a breath, then said, "Do you honestly think you'll be able to come back for a few days?"

Cassie considered, then, in the name of honesty, shook her head.

"Maybe Dad can visit you there."

Cassie raised her gaze. "Thank you for understanding."

"Not a problem." Katie jerked her head toward the living room. "You'd better go tell Dad."

TALKING TO HER father wasn't exactly easy, but it wasn't as difficult as she'd thought it would be.

"I understand," he said as they sat on the covered deck. The rain kept drizzling down, but it was not particularly cold outside, and the deck was the most private place in which she and her dad could talk.

"I wish I did," Cassie said in a sigh. "Doug was a great advocate for both teachers and students. He could walk the thin line. I learned so much from him."

"Not accounting, I hope."

Cassie gave a choked laugh. "I worked so hard for this, Dad."

"You don't have to convince me."

But as she sat staring out across the dark back lawn, she still felt the need to enumerate her reasons for returning to her job. And once tallied, she tallied them again, as if trying to convince herself she was doing the right thing.

"The district is depending on me. It would take a while to bring someone else up to speed. I'm stepping back into my old position."

"You have to go," her father said. "And I like your idea about Frances and me taking a few days to visit your area of Wisconsin. We can see the country and perhaps visit after you get off work in the evenings."

Cassie's heart swelled. "That would be so excellent. It's beautiful and there's a lot to see." She reached over to pat her dad's shoulder. "This means a lot to me."

"The visit or the job?"

"Both."

"What about Travis?"

Cassie expected the question since she and Travis hadn't tried to hide the fact that they were, well, friendly, but it was still hard to answer.

She cleared her throat. She had never in her

life discussed a personal relationship with her father, except for the occasional squabble with her siblings. Now she knew why. It was awkward.

"I will tell him after the wedding." She didn't think she needed to add to the tension of the day by telling him before. The ceremony was less than twenty-fours away. The ridiculously expensive flight she'd booked was thirty-six hours away.

"Will he understand?"

"I don't know." Her mouth flattened into an expression that felt almost hopeless. "I hope he does. It isn't like I can force him to."

But she'd like to. To her surprise, her dad laughed.

"The one thing on this planet that you've never been able to control in this life has been Travis."

"There are a lot of things I can't control."

He smiled at her. "I know that. But you still try, don't you?"

"That sounds like a sickness."

"It sounds like a child who lost control of her world when her mother died way too young."

Cassie closed her eyes as she pressed her lips together. She was aware of the effects of losing her mom young. She knew that she had anxiety issues because of it. But identifying the cause had helped her cope.

"Do you still want to talk?"

"Why wouldn't I?"

"Natural defenses would be my best guess."

She managed a wry look. "Ever the natural scientist."

"Pretty much," he said with a thoughtful nod. "When I fell for Frances at the vet clinic… What? Six years ago?"

"Maybe seven."

"Yes. When I fell for her, it was very inconvenient. She lived half a planet away and she had a thriving practice there. A state-of-the-art clinic she'd built from the ground up. If one of us was going to move, it had to be me."

"Not an easy choice," she stated for him. She knew it hadn't been easy. He'd agonized over it.

"You guys were grown, but I'd always been within a day's drive of you. And after losing your mom, you kids were even more important to me. And then there was *my* mom." He gave a little laugh. "I leave her alone and look what happens? She elopes with the guy next door."

"Not exactly an elopement." Cassie half turned in her chair, starting to relax for the first time since receiving the news about Doug.

"No. It was not an easy choice. It felt like an end-of-the-world choice. And it was. One of the worlds I loved was going to end—the one with Frances or the one in Montana."

"Did you make the right choice?"

"I did. But there were sacrifices." He gave a small shrug. "And ultimately a compromise." They'd agreed that Frances would sell the clinic ten years after their marriage and move to the States.

"So, in three years, one of Frances's worlds ends."

"Choices. Sacrifices."

They fell silent, then her dad smiled at her. "You probably expect a crescendo ending to this little talk, right? Something that will suddenly make the way clear?"

"Could you please do that?" Cassie asked in a small voice. He obviously knew, somehow, maybe some kind of dad radar, that she was still agonizing over the decision she'd made.

Her dad laughed and reached out to rub her shoulder. "I wish, kiddo. But I just thought I'd throw my story out there. And tell you that if you ever need to talk, I may not have all the answers…but I'm as close as a text or call."

"SADDLE UP BILLY and go for a ride." Katie spoke from behind Cassie as she stared out the kitchen window after the second call from Rhonda that morning—Rhonda, who didn't seem to understand that it was Saturday and that Cassie was in the middle of a family event. "There's nothing more to be done here, and you need to relax."

The rain had let up early that morning, and it wasn't supposed to rain again until that evening, so yes, it was a good time to slip away, sort through a few things.

"I don't know."

Katie put her hands on Cassie's shoulders and massaged.

"You are a tightly wound spring, and I don't want Grandma to start worrying about you."

The bridal party wouldn't be traveling to the McGuire ranch for several hours and at the moment Frances was playing with Bailey and Kendra, and Rosalie and Gloria were drinking tea and laughing about something.

Everyone seemed relaxed.

Except for her.

Katie glanced at the clock. "You have hours to burn before we start dressing."

"You're saying that I'm driving you crazy and you want me out of the house?" Cassie's attempt at dry humor came off flat.

"Maybe a little?" Katie looked past her to where Rosalie and Gloria sat. "I don't want Grandma to notice that you're pacing a trail in the dining room tiles."

"Sorry. And I'm sorry about the calls, too. I know they're disruptive." And in a way necessary. Rhonda needed to bring her up to speed quickly. She'd missed a lot in the past weeks.

Katie let go of Cassie's tense shoulders. "You'll figure this out. I know you will."

"You sound confident." And she wasn't telling her to not think about her job, which was a step forward.

Katie seemed to read her thoughts. "I understand more about your job now that you've been home. I know you love it in a way that I never loved my job."

"Thank you." She let out a breath, then looked past Katie out the window at the Ambrose Mountain foothills.

"Billy's pretty dry. I saw him hugging the barn when I fed Wendell and Lizzie Belle this morning."

"If I go now, I'll have plenty of time to shower and pretty up when I get back."

"And hopefully the wind in your hair will help you push a few things out of your mind," Katie added.

Cassie met her sister's gaze. "I'm not looking forward to telling Travis."

"I know," Katie said gently. "All the more reason to have some wind in your hair."

"SO HERE'S THE THING," Travis said, trying to ignore the fact that his grandfather was tapping his foot under the table. He had cause, after all. The wedding was only hours away, and Travis and his dad, Dan, were doing their best to keep him occupied. Talking ranch seemed like a good way to do it. "I'd like to offer Rey a job. For real."

Will's foot abruptly stopped tapping. He was careful with money. Generousness in some regards and tightwaddery in others. He gave a big scholarship because his mother had been a dedicated teacher, but he made do with day hands and working overly long hours, instead of hiring permanent help as the Callahan ranch had done decades ago.

"That might not be a bad idea," Dan said.

"Will he stay?" Will asked brusquely.

It was no secret that Will could be hard on help. His lack of patience in that regard was legendary. Yet the guy had been one of the best rodeo-team coaches around. Will McGuire was a walking contradiction.

"Why wouldn't he?" Dan asked. He used both hands to lift his coffee cup, his misshapen joints making it difficult for him to grip the mug. "Dad, now that you've got a wife, you should be spending more time with her and less time here. Travis needs help he can depend on."

"I'm not ready for a full retirement," Will grumbled, looking as if he was about to shoot the idea down.

"The ranch is in good shape," Dan said. "We can afford the extra pay. It makes sense."

Travis leaned back in his chair as his mother came into the room. "Is everyone okay?" she asked brightly, sending a pointed look in Will's direction.

"I'm not as nervous as you guys seem to think. I'm just not used to being cooped up for this long. Waiting."

"I see your point," Marge said with a gentle smile. She held up the coffeepot, which was filled with decaf, although Travis was the only one who knew it. He figured the last thing Will needed was something to twang on his taut nerves.

"We're good," Dan said. "We were just discussing hiring help."

"Great idea," Marge said. "Are you good with that, Will?"

Travis's mother was one of his grandfather's favorite people and it was all he could do not to roll his eyes as Will's expression shifted. Rosalie was the only other person he knew who could make his grandfather go soft.

"I'm coming around."

"It would be good for everyone," she said, running a hand over her husband's shoulders as she took a seat in the chair next to his.

"I don't know if he'll take the job," Travis said.

"Ask him," Dan said. "And if he won't, then I'm sure there are other decent guys out there looking for jobs."

CHAPTER NINETEEN

GREAT. JUST GREAT.

Cassie picked herself up off the ground and ran a hand over her mud-caked behind. In the distance, Billy disappeared over the rise, heading for home, reins flying. He'd be there before the wedding, but would anyone be at the home ranch to see her return? If the family kept the schedule they'd agreed upon, they should be leaving for the McGuire ranch within the hour. Cassie was to drive herself over after returning from her ride so that they had an extra vehicle if necessary.

Tears of frustration pricked at her eyes, but she wiped them away with her grimy sleeve. Crying wouldn't help. Walking would. She took one experimental step, then another. Okay. She was in one piece. The beauty of landing on rain-soaked earth was that it didn't hurt as much as a gravel road. She knew—she'd experienced both.

She pushed back her hair and looked around for her hat, which was lying ten feet away from where she'd fallen. After scooping it up, she slapped it on her head and started walking after her horse. Of all the horses to do her wrong—trustworthy Billy.

Cassie walked as fast as she could through the misting rain, but there was no getting around the fact that she was a long way from home. A couple of miles on a trotting horse was not the same as a couple of miles trudging on foot.

Would they delay the wedding for her?

Probably.

Would they be concerned when she didn't show up on time?

Definitely.

A choked laugh escaped her lips. Or maybe they'd assume she'd already left for Wisconsin. Rhonda had called three times that morning, and each time Cassie had hung up the phone feeling like she had to get there *now* to help shoulder the load.

And she resented it.

She let out a breath and kicked the tall wet grass in front of her as she walked. Her jeans were getting soaked, her thighs were going numb. The ride had been going so well—right up until good old trustworthy Billy had taken offense at a log jutting out of the tall grass, spun and dumped Cassie on her behind.

Her fault. She'd been daydreaming and the log did look fearsome at first glance.

She automatically patted her pocket for her phone, even though she'd purposely left it behind so that Rhonda wouldn't call and destroy the calm she was trying to develop before the wedding. No, she hadn't magically tucked it into her jacket at the last minute, as she'd been tempted to do.

Once again, the tears prickled as she studied the distance between her and…anything.

And what bugged her most was that she wasn't the kind who caused weddings to be delayed. She was responsible and punctual and currently miserable in ways she didn't want to think about.

But the one thing she didn't do was to give up. She was going to make it to the wedding… and then she'd finish off a fine day by telling Travis that she was not going to be staying in Montana as planned.

TRAVIS PULLED THE dry-cleaning plastic off his vest and freshly laundered white shirt. Outside, the catering van had just pulled up and the people from Tremaine's were setting up service. The day had seemed strangely empty without some time with Cassie, but once the wedding was over, they'd have more time together.

He laid the shirt on the bed when a knock sounded on the front door, the door no one ever used. When he opened it, Brenna Caldwell, who was overseeing the catering setup, stood on the step.

"There's a loose horse," she said. "It's wearing a saddle and talking to the other horses over the fence."

Travis's gaze jerked toward the pasture and, sure enough, a saddled bay horse was visiting over the pasture fence with its sisters, with the Callahan brand on its front shoulder. Even at a distance, he recognized Cassie's trophy saddle—the one she'd won in high school during her junior year.

"Thanks," he said automatically. "I'll take care of it."

He picked his phone up off the counter and dialed the Callahan ranch. Frances answered. "Hi, uh…is Cassie there?"

"She went riding. We're expecting her back at any moment. The phone calls have been driving her crazy this morning. Poor thing needed to blow off some steam."

Phone calls?

"Is Katie there?"

"One moment."

A few seconds later Katie came on the line. "Hey," Travis said. "I think Cassie's horse showed up here without her. I'm heading out to look for her."

"What!"

"Do you know where she likes to ride?"

"I do. She crosses the bridge and heads up the old hiking trail that winds around Ambrose Bluff. That puts her on your side of the river."

"I'll head out and keep you posted. Does she have her phone with her?"

"She went on her ride to escape her phone."

"Tell you what, why don't you grab whatever she needs to get ready for the wedding and I'll find her?"

"Sounds good. Do you think I can kind of downplay this with Grandma?"

Knowing Rosalie, no. "Do what you can. I'll phone when I find her."

And hopefully it wouldn't be on the way to the hospital.

"I might just have to do her bodily harm," Katie muttered. "If she's all right, that is."

"She'll be all right," Travis said before hanging up. She had to be all right, because he couldn't handle it if she wasn't.

THERE WAS NOTHING like a long, wet hike while delaying one's grandmother's wedding and probably terrifying the family to put one in a really bad mood. And to consider all the deep questions of life, like why had she worn socks that crept down into the toes of her boots when she walked? And how could she be fair to everyone in her life—her employer, her family, Travis?

No easy answers popped into her head, but she was one or two steps away from pulling off her boots and throwing away her socks.

Cassie tucked her chin, squinting against the light rain pelting her face. A faint sound caught her ear, and in the distance, she saw a fast-moving dot come over a hill, then disappear again.

A rescue? Cassie began to hurry her steps, but her slick-bottomed cowboy boots kept sliding on the mud and slippery grass. The roar of the ATV grew louder, and then it appeared over the brink of the hill in front of her, a rain-slickered Travis at the controls.

He jerked to a stop and jumped off the machine and a second later she was enveloped in a wet hug. And for one brief moment she allowed herself to hug him back, to cling to his hard frame and draw his warm scent into her lungs.

"Are you okay?" His gaze traveled over her muddy coat and pants as she pulled away, her hands sliding down the front of his wet coat.

She gave a jerky nod. "Have you seen Billy?" The horse hated crossing the bridge to her ranch, so there was a good chance he would detour to the McGuire place, where he would find his own equine kind.

"He's fine. Your reins not so much."

Of course the gelding had broken them on his dead run to the McGuire ranch. How could he have avoided stepping on them as they flapped loosely around him?

"What happened?" Travis asked, seeming perplexed by the fact she was keeping her distance. "Are you hurt?"

"I'm not hurt." But she was alone with Travis, miles from the family and wedding preparations. "I was going to talk to you after the wedding. Alone."

"Those are not good words."

"There's an emergency in my school district."

"Those are worse words." He cast his gaze skyward for a second. "You're going back."

"I have to. Rhonda is stepping into the superintendent position and I'm going back to my old job."

His mouth tightened. "When?"

"Tomorrow. Early."

"And then what?"

"I don't know, Travis. That's the thing. I. Don't. Know." She was wet and she was cold, and she really didn't know.

"We can work through this." He reached out for her again, but she took a slow step back.

"I hope we can, but things are too muddled right now—"

"For us to touch?" His hands dropped back to his sides and the look on his face made her swallow dryly. She was hurting him, which was the last thing she wanted to do, but a little pain now was better than dragging things out.

"If I touch you, it'll be harder to leave." She'd barely dragged herself out of his embrace a few seconds ago. "I don't know what's going to happen when I go back. I know I'm going to get sucked in. Immersed."

"Are you ending things before they start?"

"I'm not calling it an end. I'm trying very hard not to mess things up."

"Then why not say, 'I'm leaving. I don't know when I'll be back. Wait for me.'"

She shook her head. "I'm not ready to ask anyone—" she swallowed "—to ask *you* to wait for me. Not when I don't know…" Her throat started to close, and she dragged her gaze away from his. Everything was happening so fast.

Too fast.

"A new relationship needs time and care." She clasped her numb hands together so tightly that she began to have feeling in them. "We don't have the foundation—"

"How do you propose that we get a foundation if you walk away?" He took hold of her shoulders. "I'm in love with you."

And the truth was out. Now what was she

going to do with it? His heart beat against his ribs as he stared down at her.

"Oh, Travis." Her chest tightened as she fisted her hands by her sides.

"Too much?" he asked roughly. "Too honest?"

"Too soon." And she could only imagine what would happen if she told him she loved him, too. Loving didn't mean that there was an easy way to be together. "I need time."

An odd look crossed his face. "I'll give you time."

"I don't see myself moving home anytime soon." When it looked like they had months to be together, to explore and plan, it was different. Those months would have given them the foundation they'd spoken of, but now…now they'd have a good thousand miles separating them.

Travis wasn't having it. "Unlike you, the things in my life aren't carved in stone. I can do something different."

"Tell that to your grandfather." Because she was pretty certain his life had been set in stone when his father's condition debilitated to the point that he had to come home.

"I might."

"Don't." The word rang through the meadow. "I need time to figure out what I'm going to do. What's best for me. And fair to you."

"I see." He stuck the toe of his boot into the mud, then glanced in the direction he'd come from. "Right now we've wasted a lot of time. Your grandmother is getting married. We will talk later."

Talk later?

What was there to say?

Travis jerked his head toward the rear of the machine. "You better get on. Katie is bringing your dress and stuff. They should be at the ranch by the time we get there."

He gave her an impatient look when she still didn't move, and she climbed onto the ATV behind him. He was furious with her.

He loved her.

And she was afraid to tell him she loved him because complications and fear of loss scared the crap out of her.

She lightly grabbed the edges of his jacket, taking care not to hug into him, but when they hit the first bump she gave up and wrapped her arms around his waist and pressed her cheek against his back, breathing in the scent of damp canvas and Travis.

She closed her eyes and held on.

"I'M SO SORRY." Katie wasn't one to repeat herself, but she'd apologized three times as Cassie peeled out of her muddy clothing, then headed straight for the shower, and now she was apologizing again as Cassie finished drying her hair.

"It's not your fault." Cassie stepped into her pale pink dress and turned around for Katie to zip it. "Billy hates surprise stumps in the grass that look like bears."

"And what about Travis?" Katie asked as she ran the slide up Cassie's back.

"I don't want to talk about Travis." Who'd unceremoniously dropped her at the door, then drove away. They weren't done, but he had to get dressed, too.

Katie met her gaze in the mirror and for once took Cassie at her word. "I understand." She made a sympathetic face, then headed out of the bedroom to where Frances and Rosalie were taking care of last-minute details.

Cassie closed her eyes.

"We're leaving in five," Gloria called into the bedroom. "Make sure you have your shoes."

"Thanks," Cassie called back. Thankfully the rain had stopped, and the bridal party would wear their regular shoes to travel the fifty yards to the barn across the wet driveway, then change into easily stained wedding shoes. Shortly thereafter the ceremony would commence, and almost as quickly as it was over, Cassie would drive to Bozeman to catch the million-dollar, last-minute flight she'd managed to book.

The school district would pay her back, but given the reason that the superintendent was on paid leave, it seemed that it might be a while before she got her money reimbursed.

Cassie rubbed her sore jaw muscles, then turned back to the mirror. She hadn't clenched her teeth in days, despite the number of unknowns she was facing with Travis. Her jaw muscles had enjoyed a long vacation until Rhonda started calling. And calling. Now look at her. Tense and pale.

Cassie grabbed Katie's blush and dabbed a little more on her cheeks, looking up at the knock on the open door. Her grandmother poked her head in.

"You look beautiful," Cassie said, crossing the room to hug her. "I love you in champagne." The simple lace shift and jacket were perfect.

Rosalie hugged her back, ignoring the fact that her corsage was getting squished. When she leaned back, she kept hold of Cassie's shoulders. "Will and I understand why you have to go. Please do not let any worries about that cloud your mind."

"Maybe you and Will can come visit me?" Her voice wobbled a little. Now that she'd been around family for more than a couple of days, she felt like she needed family.

"Yes. I'll speak to him about it soon."

"Thank you for understanding. I think you guys are going to be so happy."

Rosalie smiled back at her. "Me, too, or I wouldn't be taking this step."

"Are you ready?" Katie called.

Cassie stepped out into the living room, then made a big show of being stunned at how beautiful her nieces were in their dark rose silk dresses. Bailey didn't have a "veal" as she'd wanted, and she'd been disappointed that her great-grandmother didn't have one either, but she seemed thrilled with the silk-flower wreath Gloria had made.

"Wibbons," she said, turning around to show off the long satin streamers, then quickly looking over her shoulder to catch sight of them.

For once her sister didn't correct her speech, but instead pushed her own ribbons back over her shoulder, then slipped her hand into her great-grandmother's.

"Is everyone ready?" Rosalie asked. She was honestly close to glowing. Why not? Her family was with her and she was marrying a man she loved.

Cassie's jaw muscles tightened again as she started fighting tears for no given reason.

TRAVIS ALMOST PUT his hand on his grandfather's shoulder to keep him from vibrating in place as he stood next to the fancy flower-covered arch where he would exchange vows with Rosalie. Dan, who was leaning on his crutches next to Travis, caught his son's gaze and rolled his eyes. Travis smiled, but it didn't feel real.

Since Will was a no-nonsense kind of man, Travis expected him to be pretty much oblivious to all the work that had gone into transforming a barn into a wedding venue, so he was surprised when Will leaned close and said, "This place looks really nice. I appreciate you helping Rosalie."

Travis cleared his throat and said, "You're welcome."

Will gave a nod and then turned toward the paper partitions where the bridal party was waiting. The music started and then Rosalie's granddaughters came out together, and darned if Bailey wasn't holding tightly on to a kitten. Frances came out from behind the screen and gently took the little animal, then Kendra and Bailey started down the aisle.

After the little girls came Katie and Cassie, tight-jawed and pale, looking nothing like her usual confident self. Tense or not, she was so beautiful that it made his chest tighten. The woman was going to be the death of him.

When Rosalie appeared, Will stood taller. Travis had a feeling that he could have lit the floral archway on fire and Will still wouldn't have torn his gaze away from Rosalie.

"You're a lucky man," Travis murmured.

Will gave Travis a small nod of acknowledgment, then stepped forward to take Rosalie's arm. And even though he told himself not to, Travis glanced at Cassie, who had one hand on each of her nieces' shoulders as they stood in front of her, as if needing to ground herself. She swallowed as the justice of the peace began to speak, but she didn't come close to looking his way.

And it wasn't because she didn't have feelings for him. Quite possibly it was the opposite.

That was the frustrating part.

IF SHE LOOKED at Travis, and then he looked through her, she would be lost. So Cassie focused on the ceremony, listening to the words the justice of the peace read and their explanation of how love transcended all obstacles and showed up in the most unusual places in the most unusual ways. For a civil ceremony, it was surprisingly beautiful and choked her up in ways she hadn't expected.

Will was a different type of man than her easygoing grandpa Carl, but Rosalie was a different woman after losing her husband of so many years.

This worked.

It was…perfect.

Katie had dabbed under her eyes, which gave Cassie the courage to give a small sniff. Then Bailey leaned her head back to look up at Cassie and whisper, "Why is Gloria crying?"

"She's happy," Cassie murmured back. When Bailey looked as if she was going to demand an immediate explanation, Cassie had put her fingers to her lips. Bailey took the hint and shuffled her feet as she waited for the short ceremony to end.

Just before it ended, Cassie heard the low buzz of a cell phone set on vibrate from behind the paper screen where the bridal party had gathered. If that was Rhonda again…

Travis must have heard it, too, because he raised his gaze and Cassie met it. His expression didn't change, but Cassie felt the impact of his disapproval.

The justice of the peace pronounced Rosalie and Will man and wife, and the small group of guests jumped to their feet, giving whoops and cheers. Then began the procession and Katie was paired with Travis, Cassie with Travis's father.

She smiled and laid her hand upon his as he maneuvered down the aisle with his forearm crutches.

"I hope the rest of your stay is enjoyable," she said as they reached the end of the aisle.

"I wish you could stay longer."

"Duty calls. But I'm done missing holidays, Dan. If you're here for Christmas, I'll see you." She didn't know Travis's father well, but she liked him.

"I'll hold you to that," he said.

For some reason his simple words brought a lump to her throat. "Do."

Then Cassie hugged her grandmother. Rosalie held on tight as Cassie murmured congratulations. "Keep me posted. Texts at every stop."

"I will." She eased back, still holding her grandmother's elbows. Will nodded and she let go of her grandmother to give him a hug. "You're a lucky man," she said fiercely.

"I keep hearing that," he said in a chuckle. But when Cassie stepped back his expression sobered. "You…you take care now."

Cassie nodded instead of speaking and then made her way through the small throng of people to find her parents. She'd see them within a week, so that goodbye was easier. After kissing her nieces and her brother, she changed her shoes, then headed for the door, her satin sandals dangling from one hand.

She stopped on the threshold of the door, and took a moment to search the small crowd. She didn't see Travis and even though she knew it would be hard to speak to him, her heart sank.

There would be no goodbye. No thank-you for the rescue.

Just a whole lot of stuff left unsaid.

She put her head down and stepped out into the darkness. The pole lamp near the house lit the way across the drive. Behind her a whoop of laughter made her shoulders tighten. She hated leaving.

The damp gravel was slippery and she focused on her steps, not wanting to hit the ground twice in one day, then nearly jumped out of her skin when she raised her gaze and saw Travis leaning against her car, his arms folded over his chest.

She stopped dead, and then, when he didn't move, she started forward again, her heart attempting to hammer its way out of her chest. When had she ever reacted to a man like this?

When had it ever mattered this much?

"All packed?" he asked, his low voice rolling over her, giving her a frisson of hope.

"Everything is in the car. I've just got to change into my travel clothes." Which were in the house. "I'm leaving the dress." As if that mattered.

"I wanted to say goodbye."

"Yes." And since it was the last time she

would see him for who knew how long, and not knowing how things might change, she rose up on her toes to kiss him. Travis took hold of her upper arms and met her halfway, meeting her lips with a kiss that had her taking hold of his shoulders to keep her knees from buckling. When he raised his head, she took a slow backward step, needing to put space between them before she gave in to temptation and kissed him again.

You're leaving this behind for a job.

Cassie shushed her small, shaken voice.

Travis brought a hand up to her cheek and, as he met her gaze, she caught a glimpse of something that made her heart twist. A split second later his expression shuttered, and she was left facing the same cool Travis who'd dropped her at the house.

"Are you sure about what you're doing?" he asked.

No. Not even close.

"I'm sure about the first step."

He tucked a strand of hair behind her ear, his fingertips gentle on her skin, and she had the craziest feeling that he was memorizing her face.

She didn't want him to have to memorize… She wanted to be there with him.

"This is getting hard," she said. "Really hard."

"Yes," he said softly. "I know."

He leaned in to give her one more soft kiss. "Text me when you get there?"

"Yes." She was barely holding on, and she needed to get a grip, step back into the old persona she would use to handle drama at the school district. The fact that she couldn't instantly do so was telling.

"Drive safe." He stepped back, gave her one last look, then turned and started for the barn where the reception was in full swing.

Cassie watched him go, her chest tightening to the point that she could barely breathe. He disappeared inside the warmly lit building and she forced her shoulders back.

One crisis at a time.

CHAPTER TWENTY

"I CAN'T BELIEVE it ends like this." Will took another turn around the living room, but Rosalie didn't point out that he was going to wear out his socks if he didn't stop. "They're both too stubborn for his own good."

"Where do they get it?" she asked mildly. But she was frustrated, too. She understood why Cassie had left four days ago. And she understood why her granddaughter didn't want to make promises and commitments that early in a new relationship. But still…

"Stubbornness is a virtue when used in the right situation."

"And they're not doing it right?"

"You know I'm not a romantic." Rosalie nodded patiently as Will shot her a look. Satisfied that she agreed, he continued pacing. "However, Travis isn't exactly a kid anymore. If he's going to settle down, he can't be holed up on the ranch all the time. It isn't like women are going to find him there."

That was a new take on the matter.

"Who will run the ranch?" She gave him a look that clearly said, *It better not be you, who are retired and living with your wife.*

"Travis mentioned some possibilities a couple of days ago. If that's what it takes to keep him happy, well, I guess it's what it takes."

"I don't think Travis wants to leave the ranch. I think he needs to not be the heart and soul of it."

"Agreed. He needs time to go see Cassie and work all this out."

Rosalie focused on her embroidering, pulling her mouth tight to keep from smiling. For not being a romantic, Will seemed determined to have everyone in his immediate sphere happily paired up.

"Maybe they're not right for one another," she ventured for the sake of argument.

Will turned. "Do you believe that?"

No, which made her almost as frustrated as Will. Cassie had had a glow about her that Rosalie hadn't seen in years. A glow she hadn't had when she'd arrived back on the ranch a month and a half ago.

"I believe they have to work this out themselves. Why don't we give them a few months before intervening?"

"Like I would intervene." Frustration colored

his voice as he added, "I can't figure out a way to intervene."

Rosalie put her embroidery aside and got to her feet, then crossed the room to put her arms around her husband, who was *not* a romantic.

"Set up a cage match?" she said.

"If only it was that easy, Rosalie. If only."

FIVE DAYS AFTER Cassie had said her goodbyes and flown back to Wisconsin to fight the good fight, Travis took a tour of the ranch with his dad in the side-by-side UTV. His parents were full partners in the operation and Dan wanted to see the changes Travis had made since his last visit more than a year ago. Travis was happy to oblige.

He was happy for anything that took his mind off Cassie for a spell. Not that he was wringing his hands and lamenting. No. He'd spent his time since her departure in the same way that she would have. Setting out a course of action and attending to detail.

"I sometimes forget how beautiful it is here," Dan said. The sun had finally come out and the rain-washed air was crystal clear. The grass seemed greener and the distant mountains bluer. "I haven't smelled wet pine and juniper in a long time."

"You probably haven't smelled anything wet

in a long time," Travis joked, even though he knew Arizona got the occasional torrential rain. "I'm hoping to get down your way in the fall, when it cools off."

"Are you sure it's Arizona you want to visit?"

"I'm going to make a couple of visits to different places," he said. "Cassie was right about getting off the ranch being healthy."

"Dad is stubborn. And frugal."

"And close to rich, but we won't go there."

"Have you minded your time on the ranch?" his father asked.

Travis gave his head a shake as he slowed the side-by-side at a gap in the trees, where they could look out over the Ambrose Valley. "Granted, I wanted to work somewhere else for a while after graduation. I didn't want to be one of those bubble people who never experience anything—however, I've found there are other ways of expanding horizons."

"But time off the ranch will still be welcome."

"Totally."

They sat in silence looking out over the valley. Gavin was just visible in the distance. His cultural hub. Travis smiled a little. He'd done a lot of thinking since Cassie left. Thinking and trying not to panic.

His dad seemed to read his thoughts. "What are you going to do about Cassie?"

"Continue to let her drive me nuts, I guess."

"I'm serious."

"Yeah." Travis rubbed his temple. Maybe sharing his deep thoughts on the matter wasn't a bad thing. He didn't do a lot of it; the Mc-Guire men tended to work through their difficulties alone.

"Cassie is afraid of not being able to balance a new relationship with her job demands." There it was in a nutshell. He kept the part about him wondering if she was going to use her job as an excuse to keep from taking a chance with him.

"What are you going to do?"

"Convince her otherwise."

"How?"

"I'm still working that out."

He couldn't just show up in Wisconsin. That would only add to her stress and make her feel cornered. When Cassie was pushed, she pushed back.

"She's not an easy woman," he added, and his dad gave a bark of laughter.

"That's an understatement. She used to get so far under your skin. There were a couple of times when she got you and it looked like smoke was about to roll out of your ears."

She was still under his skin. He couldn't imagine her not being there. Under his skin. In his life. Driving him nuts.

"Have you heard from her?"

"One text after she'd gotten home safely." He hadn't expected more. Good thing, or he would have been disappointed. "I imagine she's neck-deep in her crisis."

His father gave a slow nod. "I hope you work this out. And if Rey says yes to the job, then that'll free you up."

"The ranch needs two people most of the time," he pointed out.

Dan gave him a look. "But not all the time."

"That's what I'm banking on."

CASSIE'S PHONE RANG as she began putting away groceries after yet another long workday, and when she saw Darby's name on the screen rather than Rhonda's, she snatched it up from the counter.

"How are you?" she asked, awkwardly balancing the phone on her shoulder while she continued stashing cans in a cupboard. Canned soup, a quick and easy dinner. She was once again all about quick and easy with next to no time at home. It was a good thing she hadn't brought a kitten home. It would have perished from loneliness. She'd been back at work for two weeks and could count the waking hours she'd spent at home in the low double digits.

"You sound funny."

Cassie pushed the last can into place and adjusted the phone. "Better?"

"Yes. Guess what?"

"You tried out for the San Francisco Giants?" Darby's favorite baseball team.

"I'm going home to stay."

Cassie almost dropped the phone. "Home, home? Like Gavin home?"

"Yes." The sheer delight in Darby's voice made Cassie smile even as she felt a tiny stab of jealousy.

"Do you have a job?"

"No." She spoke the word in the same happy tone. "I'm moving in with my brother for now, and when I get a job, I'll get my own place. Please don't think I'm being irresponsible, but, Cassie, I haven't been able to find a job in my field, and then, a couple of nights ago I realized that I don't want a job in my field. I want to go home. I want to be happy."

Cassie rubbed her forehead as she took a couple of steps across her kitchen to the small dining room, where she sank down onto a chair. She'd been giving this happiness thing a lot of thought herself.

"I don't think you're being irresponsible." A few months ago, she might have tried to talk Darby out of such a move, but she was not the same woman now. "I think you have to go for it."

"It won't be easy, but I'll be closer to my family and… Yeah."

"You're my hero," Cassie said softly.

"Really?"

"Yes. What you're doing takes guts. Good for you."

"Thank you." A beat of awkward silence followed, as if Darby was waiting for Cassie to bring up Montana or Travis or any of the things that were eating away at her, but she wasn't ready. "So hey, I'll keep you posted," Darby continued. "I know it's late, but I wanted to share."

"I'm glad you did. I think you're doing the right thing."

"Thanks."

After Darby ended the call, Cassie set the phone on the dining room table and then glanced at the clock. It was late. Close to eleven, and tomorrow was a long day which would end in a special meeting of the school board meant to finalize all the many changes shc and Rhonda and their team had poured their lifeblood into over the past fourteen nonstop workdays.

But despite having next to no time to herself, she still managed to stew about her life choices.

The good. The bad. The misguided.

"CAN YOU BELIEVE Nelson tried to derail me?" Rhonda took another long drag on her cigarette while Cassie turned her head to avoid the smoke. They had a lot of informal meetings on the park bench across the street from the school since Rhonda had once again taken up the habit.

Joe Nelson, one of the board members, had questioned Rhonda's commitment to her new position as acting superintendent, asking if she planned to retire next summer. If so, he suggested that they start the search for a permanent superintendent now. He'd looked directly at Cassie as he spoke, and in response a wave of panic went through her.

She'd thought about that unexpected panic for the remainder of the meeting, until a motion had been made to officially move Rhonda into the top slot. The motion passed and Cassie all but slumped in her chair with relief. She wasn't ready for the top job.

She didn't even know if she wanted it.

Her time at home had had an unexpected effect on her. It had made her question not so much her career trajectory, but her priorities. The conclusion she was coming to, slowly but surely, was that a job might keep the electricity on, but a significant other kept you warm at night. Her professional life, which had once felt so rich, seemed rich no more. In other words, there was a big Travis-sized hole in her life.

A car drove by and the person behind the wheel waved. Lucky Sheila, the maintenance director, heading home after the emergency board meeting. Cassie and Rhonda still had work to do, and Cassie was struck by the fact that not that long ago, she patted herself on the back for staying longer than anyone else to tie up details and plan for the next day.

"I'm going home." She got to her feet.

Rhonda did a double take before putting out her cigarette and dropping the butt into a sand-filled bucket near the bench. "We have to put together the last details of the insurance negotiations."

"I've already put in a thirteen-hour day. I'm going home."

"This isn't like you."

"Yeah. I know." Cassie smoothed her chiffon skirt. She was dressing a bit freer than she used to. Somehow climbing into her suit didn't feel as empowering as it once had.

"Where is your head?"

"Montana." Cassie met Rhonda's gaze dead-on.

"You aren't thinking of…" Rhonda's mouth worked as her words trailed off, as if she was afraid to put an idea in Cassie's head.

"I'm thinking of figuring out a balance between life and work."

"You have a commitment here."

"I do. But I don't owe the place my soul."

Rhonda gaped at her, then gave her head a small shake as if to clear it. "I'm not asking for your soul," she snapped.

No. Just eighteen-hour days. Cassie didn't mind hard work. She didn't mind eighteen-hour days, but she did mind people expecting it of her as a matter of course. The school district was going through rocky times, but the worst of it was past, yet Rhonda still wanted to work until the evening hours and beyond. They'd done an amazing job of getting things back on track, but there was no need to continue working ridiculous hours.

"This is a job, Rhonda. It's not healthy to make it a lifestyle."

And truthfully? She couldn't stop thinking about Darby moving home. Darby had chosen what she wanted and was determined to make it work.

Cassie had changed what she wanted—she could see that now. Did she have the courage to make it work?

"I'll see you in the morning," she said as they crossed the street to the parking lot behind the district office.

"Do you want this job?" Rhonda asked when they reached her car.

"I'll do my best for the district." She wasn't yet ready to say she might walk.

"That's not an answer."

"It is, Rhonda. Just not the one you want to hear. And another thing…that long weekend coming up? I'm using it to go home."

"Cassie…" Rhonda took her boss voice, the one she used before putting forth a non-negotiable. "There are other people who could fill your position."

Cassie almost laughed. "If you can find someone willing to put in the hours, do it."

Rhonda's eyebrows slowly lifted. Cassie had just crossed a line. Not a wise move where Rhonda was concerned. So Cassie did what her gut was telling her to do to resolve the situation.

She doubled down.

"I'll resign my position if you find someone you think is more committed."

"Don't tempt me, Cassie."

Cassie smiled the same smile she'd worn when Travis had dared her to eat an onion in fifth grade.

"Consider yourself tempted, Rhonda."

TRAVIS STUDIED THE calendar on his phone as he finished his last cup of coffee.

Rey would start work in two weeks. Once he'd floated the job offer, things had moved rapidly. Rey drove to Gavin to meet with Will, had managed to come out of the interview unscathed and had then given notice on his apartment in Spokane. He wasn't going to make nearly the money he'd made at the Agri-Tech job, but he was getting a good severance package and like he'd told Travis, sometimes working at a job that allowed you to connect to the earth instead of to bureaucrats was worth a cut in pay.

It also made Travis think that perhaps he hadn't missed that much by coming back to the ranch after college.

But he did miss Cassie.

Almost three weeks without a word and the radio silence was getting to him. Had she forgotten him?

He didn't believe that for a minute, but Cassie was stubborn, and she was deeply into her job.

He pushed his chair back and grabbed his hat off the table before heading outside. Cassie's McHenry mare was grazing with the others. He'd thought about using her as an excuse to contact Cassie, then decided he didn't need an excuse. If he didn't hear from her in the next few days, he was initiating contact. The worst thing she could do was to shoot him down. The best thing would be to agree to his plan to fly to Wisconsin and see her.

The one thing he couldn't do was to ambush her—show up out of the blue—although he'd thought about it more than once. That wasn't fair.

But it might be effective.

He stopped at the front gate and pulled his phone out of his pocket. Enough was enough. He punched in Cassie's number, brought the phone to his ear and waited with a sense of grim foreboding.

She didn't answer.

Travis cursed to himself and shoved the phone into his pocket and started toward the barn where the four-wheeler was parked. It was impossible to walk into the place without thinking about Cassie. The wedding. The goodbye.

Crap.

He'd just swung onto the four-wheeler and was reaching for the ignition when he thought he heard a car pulling up on the soundproof side of the house. He got off the machine and started for the bay door when he definitely heard a car door slam shut.

He wasn't expecting visitors of any kind. Will and Rosalie were on their honeymoon cruise and it was a Saturday, so there was no package delivery. He was halfway across the drive when

Cassie walked around the corner of the house and he stopped dead in his tracks.

He glanced down at the phone in his pocket, then back up at her.

"I thought we could talk in person rather than over the phone," she said as she stopped a few yards away.

"Why are you here?" He didn't care about the why, but his brain needed time to come up to speed.

"Big life change."

"How so?"

She pulled in a breath, then exhaled as she tucked her thumbs into her front pockets. "I double dared my superintendent to find someone to fill my shoes and she did."

Travis had never in his entire life experienced the sensation of knees going weak, but at that moment, he was close.

"You're back. And you never thought to give me a heads-up?"

"Are you mad?"

He considered, then slowly shook his head, keeping his gaze locked on hers, as if she might disappear or something.

"I like to take care of one thing at a time," she explained.

"I kind of noticed that about you." He gave a shrug. "Recently, in fact."

"I chose wrong then."

"I understand your reasoning."

Cassie looked down at the toes of the boots she'd been wearing when he'd rescued her in the rain. The boots she'd worn when she'd come close to breaking him. "I still have to move my stuff from Wisconsin to Montana, but I'm coming back for good."

"No kidding." He cleared his throat, which was getting thick. "Want help moving?"

"I thought you'd never ask."

He didn't know who moved first. Maybe her, maybe him, but they met in the middle and suddenly he had his stubborn woman back in his arms where she belonged. He pressed his cheek against her hair, barely able to believe that she was there, in his arms, in Montana, and that she wasn't leaving.

She pulled back to meet his gaze. "Are you going to kiss me or what?"

He kissed her, and when he lifted his head, they were both breathless.

"I missed that," she said as she planted her palms on the front of his shirt. "I missed you."

"You could have called," he said gruffly.

"I needed the time to torture myself into the right decision."

"And that decision is?" He needed to hear it, to know for a fact where they stood.

"That decision is to put love first in my life. Because I love you, and I believe you when you say you love me."

He brought his forehead down to lightly touch hers. "I was afraid I was going to have to fly to Wisconsin for a throwdown before you came to that conclusion."

She gave a small laugh. "Our throwdown days aren't over, you know."

He folded her back into his arms. "I know."

He wouldn't have it any other way.

EPILOGUE

"You can't take full credit for this," Rosalie murmured to Will, whose chest was swelling to the point that his buttons were in danger as he watched Travis and Cassie playfully arguing over who was going to climb the ladder of death to secure the high end of the evergreen garlands that would spread over the loft to various points on the opposite wall.

The argument ended in a kiss and Will let out a gusty sigh.

"Not taking any credit at all. I'm just glad for the ending." He slanted a sideways look at her. "You should be glad, too. This barn is going to see a lot of weddings."

"That it is." They were preparing for Katie and Brady's Christmas wedding, and not long after that, Nick and Alex were going to be married at the end of February. They'd decided not to go with the obvious Valentine's Day wedding, but were anxious to officially start a life together.

Bailey and Kendra were over the moon at having Alex become part of the family, not to mention the heady prospect of having two weddings in a row.

"I'm thinking June," Will said thoughtfully, as he watched Cassie start up the ladder with the garlands in one hand. "Travis will propose in June."

"Travis is going to propose in December," Rosalie said on a note of certainty.

"You don't know that," Will said. A suspicious look crossed his face. "Do you?"

"Travis spoke to me this morning. He wanted my opinion on a ring."

Will's jaw dropped, then he quickly closed his mouth. "Well," he said gruffly, "that doesn't mean he won't propose in June."

"Do you think he'll wait that long?" From the way Travis was hovering beneath the ladder, waiting for his lady to get herself back to safety, it didn't seem likely.

"I hope not." Will rolled his shoulders. "No. I do not. And if he starts dithering—"

"You'll do nothing," Rosalie said in her no-nonsense voice. Then she smiled at him. "Okay, maybe a small nudge."

But as it turned out, no nudge was necessary. Rosalie had just turned to the half-grown kitten Bailey held, when Will said, "Look at that," in a low voice.

Sure enough, Cassie had barely stepped off

the ladder when Travis took her hands and went down on one knee.

"He said he wanted to surprise her," Rosalie said vaguely, her gaze glued on her granddaughter.

Seconds later Cassie gave a nod and then threw herself in Travis's arms. He swung her in a circle and Will, no longer able to contain himself, yelled, "Did she say yes?"

Travis and Cassie, apparently unaware of how visible they were, gave Will startled looks.

"What's going on?" Katie asked, coming to stand next to Rosalie. Alex abandoned the garlands she was draping around the uprights and joined them, all four of them, plus the little girls standing with their heads tilted back, as if they were watching a fireworks display.

"What's happening is that I'm getting married," Cassie called down to them.

A whoop went up and Kendra and Bailey joined hands. "Three weddings!" Kendra laughed.

"Three weddings," Will repeated. He cast a satisfied look around the interior of the barn. "Travis was right. We might just have to start renting out the place."

* * * * *